MOON STONE

MOON STONE

LAURA PURCELL

MAGPIE

Magpie Books
An imprint of HarperCollins*Publishers* Ltd
1 London Bridge Street
London SE1 9GF

www.harpercollins.co.uk

HarperCollins*Publishers*
Macken House,
39/40 Mayor Street Upper,
Dublin 1
D01 C9W8
Ireland

First published by HarperCollins*Publishers* Ltd 2024

2

ISBN: 978-0-00-856282-3 (HB)
ISBN: 978-0-00-856283-0 (TPB)

Typeset in Sabon LT Std by Palimpsest Book Production Limited, Falkirk, Stirlingshire

Printed and bound in the UK using 100% Renewable Electricity
by CPI Group (UK) Ltd

CHAPTER ONE

At night I dream I am deep in the Felwood, after dark. Twigs snap and bushes crackle where the hidden things creep. I am not afraid. This isn't the scene of horror I fled; it's one of enchantment, of stars shaken like grains of salt across an indigo sky. The moon curves in a scythe above the trees. Colours pale in its pearly light, but I have no need of them. I can smell the ferns dripping green from a shower of rain, the purple heather buds ready to burst. The air tastes richly of damp earth. I am at peace.

Then I awaken and the torment begins.

I never knew there could be pain like this. My own body has turned traitor against me. When I was little, I feared Napoleon invading or the Cock Lane Ghost; now I know real danger comes from within.

A thousand insects seem to scurry beneath my skin; the itch burrows deep, right down to my core, where it turns into hunger. A craving I cannot satisfy.

I twist and writhe in the sheets. When I lived at Felwood Lodge, I used to long for my own bed, these quilted coverlets, the pillows of soft eider down. The irony is, I was more comfortable on my narrow pallet there. The walls of Felwood Lodge used to bother me with their deep timber groans; here the creaking isn't wooden planks or dead ivy rustling in the breeze. It's me. My bones shifting, breaking of their own accord to re-set in a new and terrible shape.

How long can I keep it in? How long before the physician realizes mine is no ordinary malady?

I grope for the pendant hanging on a chain around my neck, the one object that soothes me. A moonstone presses cool and smooth against my burning palm. Since my illness began, I've seen the world around me in shades of grey, but I can always make out a blue gleam on the surface of this stone. It's like hope, flickering in the darkness. While the moon in the sky tugs me in one terrifying direction, the stone which bears its name pulls me gently, gently back.

But it's not strong enough. What's one small pendant against the power of a whole satellite? The moonstone might slow my decline, but it can't save me. It won't stop the pain.

A howl rips from my throat.

'Camille?' Someone's coming – footsteps along the boards. Marie enters the chamber, looking flustered. I used to recognize my elder sister by her mahogany hair and the dusting of freckles across her nose; now the first thing I notice is her scent. A waft of buttery milk and freshly baked bread. 'Camille, what's wrong?' Marie drifts towards me, a high chignon at the back of her head and a gown of figured muslin caught by a sash at her waist. 'Here, let me help.' She bends over the bed and loosens my fingers from their rictus around the moonstone. I'm ashamed of my nails, my roughening palms. 'There, now,' she coos. 'Mr Leiston will be here soon.'

Maybe the physician is adept at healing gout or setting a broken arm, but he can't help me.

'I'm so hungry,' I pant.

She hesitates. 'I'll fetch you some broth before he comes.'

Decades seem to pass before Marie returns with a tray.

Ravenous, I almost leap up from bed and snatch the food out of her hands, but I force myself to wait. She pulls over the chair, fills a spoon. Such a small, measly dribble. My sister grimaces as she feeds me. She's disgusted by the drool, the lap of my tongue, the sounds that I make.

'Camille,' Marie whispers. 'What happened to you? Can't you tell me?'

Only a whimper escapes my lips. Marie sighs and starts spooning again. She shouldn't have to degrade herself like this. She should be preparing for her wedding, not waiting hand and foot upon me.

The broth disappears with upsetting speed. I ate it so fast that I barely noticed the taste and I'm far from satisfied. All it's done is whet my appetite.

Marie stares at the empty bowl. A delicate willow pattern shows through the skin that the soup left behind. 'This is all my fault,' she says.

'No!' My voice comes out hoarse and she flinches. 'Why would you think that?'

'Because . . . I'm the reason you were sent away! If it weren't for me, Papa would never have taken you to Felwood Lodge and you wouldn't have fallen ill.'

I did agree to go to Felwood Lodge for Marie's sake, but it wasn't her idea. Our parents had hatched the plan, along with our brother Pierre. 'I never blamed you! Not for a minute. I might have resented you, envied you . . . but I didn't blame you for wanting me gone.'

She scrubs her tears away. 'You should have. Who else is there to blame? I'm the one who whined and pouted that you were causing a scandal.'

'But I *did* cause a scandal. That was my fault. My own behaviour brought this down upon me.'

'I wish none of it had ever happened,' Marie says wildly. 'I wish the King had never been crowned. I'd take it all back, even give up my engagement to Adam, if it meant things could return to how they used to be.'

I'm not sure I would. The memory of that night is precious now, an oasis shimmering on the horizon of my sick-bed, full of the music and colour to which I can never return.

I hadn't set foot inside Vauxhall Gardens before we attended the masquerade for George IV's coronation. I wore my new gown of royal purple silk and a white domino mask. It had been a thrill to hide my face and assume the character of someone else, finally breaking free of my own dull personality. All my life, my parents had compared me unfavourably to Marie. I understood why: she was the elder, prettier and more accomplished. She could dance a minuet and play the pianoforte without any of my clumsiness. But that night, as we bustled across Vauxhall Bridge towards the gardens, you could hardly tell the two of us apart.

'Hold on to me, girls,' Mama had hissed. 'Do not wander.'

I couldn't help going astray. The gates to the pleasure gardens opened and transported us into another world. Glass lanterns hung between the trees; it looked as though stars had dropped straight from the sky to nestle in their branches. I craned my neck back, the better to see them, and gasped at the sight of a tightrope-walker balancing above my head.

'Watch where you're walking!' Papa pulled me clear just in time. A juggler passed by, so close to us that my cheeks stung from the heat of his flaming torches.

'How does he catch them like that?' I marvelled.

'With great difficulty. Come, my dear, let us sit and watch the fantoccini puppets. We shall be out of harm's way there.'

Although the marionettes amused me for a while, it was impossible to concentrate on the show. Strains of 'God Save the King' floated from the octagonal bandstand where masked revellers waltzed. Every so often, a pop punctuated the music as fireworks lit up the sky.

We took supper in one of the finely painted boxes. Excitement filled my belly, leaving no space for food; I drank wine instead. Pierre droned on about his horses, the thinness of the ham. In pretending to listen to him, I scarcely noticed Adam Ibbotson's attentions towards Marie. My parents must have been sitting on smiles, nodding to each other across the table, certain that this would be the night he finally proposed marriage, but I saw none of it. Peering over my brother's shoulder, I watched a dowager sparkling in diamonds, a giggling hoyden, a gentleman wearing an old-fashioned periwig with footmen at his side.

After a brief consultation with the waiter, Papa turned to the table. 'This fellow tells me they are about to light a transparency of the King in his coronation robes! Twenty-four feet long!'

'Oh! We must see that!' Mama nursed no real affection for the new king; few people did. But as a family with its roots in France we had to appear more patriotic than everyone else, or we could be suspected of sympathizing with the nation that had fought against Britain for decades.

I left the supper box with my companions. Marie hung on Adam's elbow, Papa walked ahead with Mama, and Pierre escorted me. We fell a little behind. I was unsteady on my feet, and my brother kept looking at a gaggle of young men dressed as harlequins, who were skimming stones into one of the ornamental ponds.

'I know that chap,' he burst out at last, withdrawing his arm from mine. 'He owes me money for a bet. Wait there,' he commanded, before he strode off, hailing the man. 'Hey, Bradshaw!'

I wasn't sorry to see Pierre leave. He was too loud and he occupied too much space, forever obtruding on my reveries. But now I was free. A moth flitted past on the summer breeze. I followed it out of the dazzle into a dark, sweet-smelling walk.

The path down which it led me was perfectly secluded. Noise echoed far away; grottoes glinted in the distance. I was intoxicated, not only by wine, but by the feeling of finally being alive. I leant my aching back against a tree and stood for a while, well contented. Languor spread through my limbs. As the alcohol began to take effect, I thought I could quite happily spend the rest of my years just here, watching the lights from afar.

That was when he took my hand. His touch jolted, yet I wasn't afraid. I sensed his warmth, the heat of him, welcome as a fire on a cold night.

'At last, the chance to speak alone.'

I turned to the right. Shadows rippled over a half-mask and the lower part of a young man's face. He was tall, athletically built, dressed for the ball as a soldier in a red military coat.

'Sir?' My tongue seemed too large in my mouth. 'Do I . . . know you?' Surely I did, if only from a dream. I'd seen this vision before. Hadn't I once spent my nights conjuring up an admirer with the same ink-spill of black curls?

'Don't say you have forgotten me.'

Brown eyes implored mine from behind the sockets of the mask. Chocolate irises, flecked with sparks of gold. Familiar, somehow, as was the sound of his voice.

'Mr Randall,' I whispered, his name rising to mind along with my blush. 'Is that really you?'

I could hardly believe it. He'd grown since I last saw him. Truly become a man, and not the student who once attended the same college at Oxford with Pierre. After their quarrel, I hadn't dared to hope I'd ever meet the fascinating Mr Randall again. I never really knew what happened to sour their friendship; something to do with a horse race and then Pierre was rusticated for a term, vowing he'd never speak to Colin Randall as long as he lived. But Pierre's disapproval held no weight with me. Whatever had occurred between the young men, I was certain it must have been my brother's offence. He could never hold his temper in check and Mr Randall had always been so amiable.

He offered a slow, crooked smile, showing me a row of pearly teeth. 'Yes! I knew you were too kind to banish me from your memory entirely. You cannot imagine how you have haunted mine, Miss Garnier. That blessed week I spent at Martingale Hall feels so long ago now. But I recall every detail.'

My heart gave a kick. Pierre's friends usually remembered Marie, the elder, eligible daughter, her age closer to their own. When Mr Randall had visited, he'd scarcely seemed to notice my existence at all, although I spent my time hiding around corners spying on him. But there could be no doubt that tonight his gaze was trained solely on me.

'You must come and join our party,' I urged him. 'Everyone will be so pleased to see you.'

He reached up and twirled one of my curls around his index finger. My breath seemed to stop. 'I wish that I could. How often I've longed to travel down and visit you all again!'

'You have? Why didn't you?'

I'd wept when he left – silly, girlish tears Marie had chided me for. But seeing Mr Randall here, I couldn't blame myself. Who *wouldn't* cry to have such a man snatched away from them?

'I'm afraid your brother holds me in utter contempt these days.' He frowned. 'He must have told you of our disagreement? He wouldn't let me within a hundred yards of his home now; if he knew I was talking to his sister, he'd be furious.'

A thrill ran through me. The thought of Pierre's rage only made Mr Randall more exciting. I longed to ask why they'd fallen out, to discover where Mr Randall lived, what kind of people his family were. Instead I stared dumbly, caught by his delicious smell of sandalwood.

'We have only this moment, Miss Garnier. Who knows if we'll meet again?' Epaulettes winked faintly from his shoulders as he moved closer. 'I've already missed so much of your life. Look at you! You have blossomed into the perfect young lady.

Gentlemen will soon be clamouring for your hand, and you'll spare no more thoughts for me.'

'That's not true!' I protested. Mama always complained that I was too gauche to attract a suitor. But maybe she was wrong, maybe tonight I could be everything Mr Randall saw in me with those beautiful eyes. A woman grown. Desirable.

He sighed, toying with my hair again. The intimacy of it made me shiver. Only Marie or the ladies' maid ever touched my hair and their hands felt nothing like his. 'If only there were a way to stretch time, Miss Garnier. Make this brief encounter last an eternity.' His eyes met mine. 'But we cannot. So how shall we spend it – our one precious moment together?'

My chin lifted, almost of its own accord. I couldn't help myself; enchanted by the night, bewitched by the wine, emboldened by the mask he wore. Everything carried a dreamlike air and it was the deep, unconscious part of me which dared to offer up my lips.

The mouth that pressed, insistent, against my own was rich as a fine wine. I had never been kissed before. My body responded without question. A chamber unlocked, deep within, spilling secrets I had always known.

I wished we could have done as he said: frozen that moment and kept its sweetness. But I was startled by the sound of Mama shrieking my name. Her voice broke the spell. All at once I remembered what my parents had said about the notorious dark walks of Vauxhall Gardens, where no respectable lady should venture alone. I opened my eyes, suddenly and dreadfully sober. Mr Randall swore before he fled, disappearing into the shadows as quickly as he'd materialized.

My mother stood at a distance, frozen in horror. Her cry had brought others to her side. Mr Ibbotson let go of Marie's arm. Strangers tutted at me, raised their quizzing glasses and chuckled lewdly. An old, heavy-set man said, 'If she were my daughter, I'd horsewhip her.'

My brother stepped forward from his group of friends, his back rigid as a poker. He seized my arm so hard that I cried out in pain. 'I told you to wait for me!' he barked. 'What the devil have you done?'

I wasn't sure. But as I peered up at him, his countenance stark and frightful in the lamplight, all the magic of the evening turned to ashes in my mouth.

CHAPTER TWO

Overnight, I'd transformed from an ordinary young lady into a pariah. People changed towards me, too – everyone except my baby brother, Jean. That one slip of decorum had been enough to brand me wanton and out of control. I'd displayed appetites no well-bred girl should possess.

Despite my parents' interrogations, I didn't dare tell that it was Mr Randall who'd kissed me. No one had recognized him in the mask, and I judged it best not to whip Pierre into an absolute frenzy. His pride had suffered enough as it was.

'You humiliated me in front of my acquaintance!' he stormed, back at home. 'Besmirched the family honour!'

My disgrace couldn't have come at a worse time. Mr Adam Ibbotson had been on the point of proposing to Marie at Vauxhall Gardens, but my actions had made him think twice about allying himself with our family. So often we'd hear the sound of hooves clopping by and Marie would run to the top of the stairs to look out. 'It's him!' she'd cry. 'That's his horse.' But Mr Ibbotson would carry on past Martingale Hall, snubbing us. Marie would return to her sewing crestfallen, tears shimmering in her eyes. All I could do was hug baby Jean tighter, knowing he would still reach for me without judgement.

Something in his wise expression told me things would improve.

Yet they didn't improve quickly enough for the rest of my family. Less than two months later, I found myself rumbling down toll-roads in our family chaise, my belongings packed into trunks and lashed to the roof. The world slipped past my window: striped fields, ricks of wheat and straw, men in country smocks tanned brown from a summer spent working the land. Normally I'd delight in any new sight, but now the view was bittersweet. I wasn't passing through; I was being taken away.

My parents had arranged for me to spend a year out in the depths of Yorkshire with a godmother I'd never met. A whole twelve months of exile felt a high price to pay for one moment of indulgence – like eating a bonbon and being sent to prison for gluttony. But leave I must, at least until the neighbourhood gossips forgot about me and Marie's suitor came to his senses. If he ever did. I'd either be returning home to play bridesmaid for my sister, or coming back to the crushing knowledge that I'd ruined her happiness forever.

Papa sat on the squabs opposite. He'd scarcely breathed a word since we'd left our home just outside Stamford, the day before. For the first time, I felt he was ashamed of me. My lack of elegance might have embarrassed him in the past, but this was something different. A thickness in the air between us. An inability to meet my eye.

Sighing, I leant my head against the window. The scenery outside was changing, becoming more rugged. At home I was used to flat expanses and huge bowls of sky, but further north the hills rolled. Trees formed wild thickets, twisted into odd shapes by the wind.

'Are you sure I'll be welcome to stay with Rowena, Papa?' I asked at last. 'She doesn't seem to value me as her goddaughter. She's never once visited us.'

My father shifted uncomfortably in his seat. 'It has not been within Rowena's power to return to Lincolnshire since her marriage.'

'Why? Is she so very poor that she cannot travel, even to see her friends?'

'Money is one consideration,' he admitted. 'Another is the indifferent health of her daughter, Lucy.'

His words drew a dismal picture of my destination. A household of poverty. A sickly companion. It would be no adventure, no taste of the unknown. Once more, I'd be left with only my books for escape.

Pulling out Ovid's *Metamorphoses,* I watched the pages fall open upon the story of Daphne. A printed engraving showed the woman who transformed herself into a laurel tree to escape the lustful god Apollo. Bark closed over her breast; leaves blossomed from her fingertips. Was that how I should have behaved in Vauxhall Gardens? Stopped being a woman and turned instead to unfeeling wood? The circulating library might lend out stories of romance that began in glens and forest glades, but in real life there was a strict code to the way a young lady could be courted. Respectfully, at a distance. The way Mr Adam Ibbotson had been courting Marie.

Shaking my head, I turned the pages to another story. I was no Daphne. When I remembered Mr Randall's kiss, the surge of energy inside, I knew that I'd lived more fully in that moment than any other in my sixteen years. I didn't truly regret my indiscretion; only that it had caused my family pain.

I read until my head began to ache, then I dozed lightly, aware of the carriage wheels muttering on like a distant storm.

Suddenly Papa was touching my arm. We'd stopped. I opened my eyes to a world drained of light and warmth. Mist gathered outside. The windows were running with damp.

'Where are we? Is it another stage to change horses?'

'No. We have arrived.'

Our footman opened the door and unfolded the steps. We

climbed out beside an inn of dreary grey stone, set back from the road and spanning three sides of a cobbled courtyard. Candles burned behind its mullioned windows, but the dirty glass diluted their light. The sign that creaked above the door read *The Grey Lady*. A few men milled around the courtyard, smoking pipes. The colours of their plain clothing bled into their surroundings; hues of sage, mud and rust.

'What time is it?' I asked.

'A little after six of the clock. Rowena will not meet us for a while yet, but I sent ahead to order refreshments.'

Our team of horses stood with their heads bowed, foam dripping from their lips, as the servants unloaded my luggage in the failing light. A vast forest crowded right up to the edge of the road. The trees were packed so thickly that I could see nothing beyond them, only the mist that teased eerily between their trunks. Most of the leaves were still green, but a few had crisped to bronze and came spiralling down as I watched.

'Come along. I'm sure you must be thirsty by now.' Papa offered me the crook of his arm to lean on and I took it, suddenly apprehensive. The idea of being left without him in this deserted place made my stomach clench.

We ducked to enter the low-ceilinged inn. It was a mass of wooden beams inside. The landlady emerged at once, her face rosy and bright. 'Ah! Mr Garnier, I take it.'

'Yes.'

'Good evening, sir. Come right through.' She ran her eyes over me. 'The young lady looks awfully pale. I'll have some tea fetched for her at once.'

A great brick fireplace dominated the parlour. Toby jugs leered down from the mantelpiece, their lips spread in grotesque grins, while horse brasses glimmered from the wall. We sat on a threadbare sofa that creaked beneath us.

A waiter hurried over, bearing a tray of the promised tea, alongside a well-thumbed copy of the local newspaper. My hands shook as I poured my father a cup. The china sounded like rattling teeth.

Papa's face softened in the firelight. 'You must not be afraid, Camille. Rowena is a very old friend of ours. You will be safe staying with her.'

Harm was not exactly what I feared. My dread was of loneliness, of boredom; of returning after a year to find I'd become a stranger among my own family. I'd often yearned to escape the routine of Martingale Hall, but not like this.

'Are you sure, Papa? Will she really be kind to me? I've never received so much as a letter from her.'

He moistened his lips. 'There is a reason we asked Rowena to care for you at this time. She has a certain . . . sympathy with your predicament. Your godmother understands what it is to have her reputation . . . called into question.'

My eyes flew up to his. 'What do you mean?' I whispered. 'What social *faux pas* did my godmother make?'

My father leaned forward and sipped at his tea. 'You must understand, it was not Rowena's fault. What befell your godmother was a misfortune, a circumstance best concealed, and we *have* concealed it from you. We always said that your godmother was a widow, but . . .' another sip '. . . that is not precisely true.'

'It isn't?'

He shook his head gravely. 'No. I am afraid to say that Rowena's husband is living still.'

I nearly dropped my cup. This was a scandal even worse than mine. 'Rowena is separated from her husband? So *that* is why Mama never goes to visit her? She's afraid of tarnishing her own reputation?'

'No, no, it is more complicated than that.' He motioned for me to lower my voice, glancing furtively around the parlour in case we were overheard. 'The man your godmother married is . . . dangerous. Given to great violence. She fled from him just before Lucy was born. We were able to hide her for a while at Martingale Hall; she was confined in childbed there.'

My eyes widened. I had to remind myself that this wasn't the thrilling plot of a story but something tragic that had befallen a real person. 'Rowena's own husband hurt her? That's dreadful!'

'Indeed it is. He left her grievously injured . . .' Papa cleared his throat. Anger simmered beneath his calm exterior. He'd lived in France until the age of fourteen, and when something enraged him his accent became more pronounced. 'What cowardly blackguard attacks a lady, I ask you? A lady carrying his own offspring? No gentleman would ever behave thus. Poor Rowena and Lucy have been in hiding from him for sixteen years now.'

'Why?' I breathed. 'What would he do if he found them?'

'Well, for a start, he would have the legal right to take Lucy away with him.'

I gasped. 'Would the courts really rule in his favour, Papa? Even though he is such a vicious man?'

Papa shrugged. 'He is a baronet. His family have money and influence. There's nothing – except Rowena's word – to prove that he attacked her. So you see, this is the reason we keep our distance: not because we are ashamed of Rowena, but because we wish to protect her. The fewer visits, the less attention called to her situation, the better.'

'It's dreadful,' I repeated. Already I was out of my depth. I gulped down some tea, wondering what I'd say to this woman. How foolish I would look in her eyes. She had known true hardship and I . . . I was just some silly girl whose head had been turned by a red-coat.

After taking tea, we moved to wing-chairs by the parlour window and watched the darkness deepen outside, spreading across the sky like an inkblot across paper. A bone-white moon emerged to frost the tops of the trees and illuminate the mist that lingered below. The mail coach to London left, taking the other occupants of the inn and leaving us quite alone. A carriage clock struck nine.

'Why is Rowena so late?'

'She will be here soon,' Papa said from behind the newspaper. 'As I told you, she leads a secretive life. We arranged to meet here at a quiet hour on purpose. Rowena's every thought is to evade the notice of others.'

I couldn't imagine living like that, hidden from sight, viewing the world forever through a narrow casement. How tiresome it must be. Were there not times when my godmother felt she'd simply ceased to exist? I was only obliged to spend one year in exile, while Rowena had to live her whole life in hiding like a rat. And for what? She'd done nothing wrong.

Papa read on. Presently, a light bobbed in the forest opposite, parting the veils of mist. I watched it, curious who could be gallivanting about the woods at this hour. Perhaps a poacher? But as the figure drew closer it revealed its true shape: that of a woman holding a lantern aloft, her shawl wrapped over her head. The lamp caught the mist and made a jaundiced aureole around her.

'Whoever can that be?'

Papa put down his newspaper and rose from his chair. 'It's Rowena. She has arrived on foot.'

I'd expected to see her on the road, not bursting forth from the trees. For a lady to walk alone by night was practically unheard of. But Rowena was clearly a woman of determination. Rather than waiting for any staff at the inn to greet her by the door, she set her lantern down outside and came straight through into the parlour, as if she were mistress there.

I bobbed a curtsey, in awe of her. Papa bowed.

Rowena merely nodded. 'Emmanuel. Camille. How delightful to see you. I am glad you arrived safely.'

Her regal manner sat at odds with her attire: a gown of dull woollen material. She unwound her shawl, exposing a tight braid of iron-grey hair beneath. She must have been around the same age as my own mother, but I struggled to believe it. Sorrow had bleached her complexion. Four deep grooves raked over the socket of her right eye and into the cheek. Was this the injury Papa had mentioned, inflicted by her own husband? Whatever had scraped her had left her half-blind; her pupil rolled cloudy and opaque between the scars.

I averted my gaze, afraid to be caught staring. 'May I offer you a cup of tea, Godmother?'

'No, thank you. We cannot tarry here for long. I have put Lucy to bed but I don't like to leave her.'

Poor Lucy, abed already! She must truly be unwell.

Papa nodded his understanding. 'The unfortunate child. Please send Lucy my regards. Do you know, I still think of her as that downy premature baby with her eyes fused shut . . . I wish that I could see her fully grown.'

'It is perhaps best that you do not meet again. Lucy's nerves may not withstand it. Too many new faces at once would over-whelm her.'

'Is your daughter so very ill, Godmother?'

Rowena fixed me with her blue, working eye. I almost took a step backwards. She was impressive, formidable, and so tall. 'I have much to explain to you about Lucy's condition. As I wrote to your parents, you must take care to follow my instruc-tions. It is a matter of life and death.' I stiffened, petrified, and her expression mellowed. 'But enough of that later,' she went on in a gentler tone. 'First . . . a gift.'

I blinked at her. 'For me?'

Nodding, she reached into her pocket and drew out a little shagreen box. 'Yes. A present is well overdue, is it not? I have missed your entire life. A great many birthdays and Twelfth Nights are rolled into this.'

A needle of guilt pricked beneath my ribs as I reached out to take the box. Rowena was too poor to travel, too poor even to dress like a gentlewoman, and yet she'd spent money on me. 'Thank you.'

I cracked the lid open to see a curious round pendant set on a silver chain. *Moonstone from India*, a tiny card announced. I'd never heard of it. A dull, milky gem . . . Yet as I moved my hand, the stone caught the firelight and a blue-white cloud billowed up from its depths. The brilliance of diamonds and the warm glow of rubies paled in comparison. This was a shimmer like magic.

'You approve of it,' Rowena smiled, watching me.

I loved it. This moonstone gave me the same feeling as the lanterns at Vauxhall Gardens had: enchantment. 'It's beautiful!'

'Wear it now,' she urged.

A strange request, but I was prepared to indulge her. Papa helped me to fasten the chain at the back of my neck. I felt instantly brighter, as if I'd tied a talisman around my throat.

My godmother watched on, benign now. 'How Camille has grown,' she observed to Papa. 'I was certain she would reach maturity. Didn't I tell you so at her christening? She was born under a lucky star.'

Papa returned her smile unwillingly as he moved out from behind my back. 'I would not say Camille has experienced much *luck* of late. These past few weeks have been trying for us all. Susannah is beside herself.'

Rowena gave a little scoff. 'Susannah ought to be more charitable about her daughter's indiscretion. She forgets that I knew her, long before your marriage, and she was quite the coquette back in our day, I can tell you.'

Papa flushed. I bit back laughter. My mother, a flirt! I couldn't believe it. What other stories would my godmother have to tell me? Perhaps this exile wouldn't be dull after all.

'You left my dear friend well, I hope?' Rowena continued. 'She was delivered of little Jean in . . . May, I think? Does he thrive?'

My father hesitated before he responded. My last two siblings had arrived early and died during their infancy. Although Jean was plumper and lustier than they'd ever been, we all nursed a secret fear he would meet the same fate. 'Susannah is in perfect health, thank you. And, so far, Jean appears to prosper.'

Rowena watched the fire play. 'I am glad to hear it. May God bless him always and keep him well. There is nothing worse for a parent than seeing their child suffer.' Something shifted in her face; she clasped her hands together, businesslike. 'Now, Camille, why don't you gather your belongings? It is time we were getting back to Lucy.'

I thought I'd packed lightly, considering I would be away from home for an entire year, but when I assembled my various trunks, hat boxes and portmanteau Rowena raised her eyebrows.

'Goodness. I doubt we can carry all of that, child, unless you are much stronger than you look.'

'Why should we carry them?'

Her mouth quirked. There was no malice in her expression, yet it made me feel about two feet tall; as though I were indeed a child who had asked an ignorant question.

'I keep no servant at Felwood Lodge, nor do I have a carriage of my own. We must return as I came – on foot.'

'We're *walking* back to Felwood Lodge? In the dark?'

Rowena nodded. 'Have no fear. I'll keep you safe. It's a full moon tonight; we shall see our way well enough.'

I stood dismayed.

Papa cleared his throat, searched his pockets. He presented me with a small, foldable penknife, prettily worked in silver. 'Take this with you, my dear. It's not much, I know, but I should feel better if you carried it. Something to defend yourself with. But of course it is unnecessary, an anxious father's whim. I know Rowena will take excellent care of you.'

'I shall guard Camille faithfully, but it is a wise precaution for any woman to keep a weapon about her person.' A look passed between her and Papa. 'A blade like that once saved my life.'

Swallowing, I tucked the folded knife, still warm from my father's hand, into my pocket. Again I felt how unequal I was to this new place, how utterly unprepared. 'All of my trunks . . .'

'You must leave what you cannot carry and I'll convey them home again,' Papa said.

Leave my belongings behind? Wasn't it enough that I'd had to abandon my home, my family? I glanced from case to case, trying to remember what was in each.

Papa must have seen my eyes filling, for he pulled me into an awkward embrace. 'All shall be well. You always wanted to travel, didn't you? See this as an opportunity. Now, behave for your godmother. Do exactly as she tells you. I will write to you soon.'

He was right: I'd hungered for adventure. Now I rather liked the idea of spending the rest of my evening by the fire with Papa. But there was nothing to be done; I had made my own bed by kissing Mr Randall and now I must lie in it. I hugged a hat box in one arm and dragged a portmanteau behind me with the other; I could manage nothing else.

Rowena lifted my heaviest trunk as though it weighed no more than feathers. 'Ready?'

I wasn't, yet still I found myself struggling over the threshold of the inn, into the clutches of the night.

All lay cool, quiet and dark outside. The breeze carried moisture, slick as a dog's tongue. Rowena strode ahead of me with her lamp flashing over the forest opposite. How dense it was, how packed with shadows. I caught glimpses of moss crawling over stumps, ivy strangling the remains of an oak; a spiteful parody of the beautiful grottoes at Vauxhall Gardens.

'At least we'll build up your muscles this year,' Rowena said by way of encouragement. 'You'll return to Martingale Hall as strong as an ox.'

I thought it more likely that I'd dislocate a shoulder. Hadn't I been sent here to rehabilitate my ways, not grow wilder still? This wasn't how ladies behaved at all. They weren't *supposed* to have muscles or go gadding about after the sun had set . . . I couldn't imagine what my mother would say if she could see me now.

Hooves clopped in the distance as we crossed the road. I turned my head to see the lanterns of a carriage glowing on the misty horizon – someone was out travelling even later than us.

'Camille! Make haste!' Rowena's lamp glided down a track heading into the forest. 'Come, hide yourself from view of the road.'

But I hung back, wary of the thick canopy of branches that threatened to choke out the moonlight. 'Why are you going down there? Is your home in the *woods*?'

'It was a hunting lodge, originally,' Rowena told me, without turning around. 'It belonged to my mother's family. Come now, don't dawdle.'

Yet I did. I watched the carriage and its pair of matched black horses slow, turning into the courtyard of The Grey Lady inn. I'd never seen an equipage so fine, so well-sprung, brocade curtains hanging at the windows and a crest emblazoned on the side. It carried an aura of such wealth, such decadent style, that I yearned to glimpse its owner. Who would climb out of a vehicle like that? I peered intently, caught a gleam of something through the window . . . Was that a pair of eyes shining back from the dark interior?

I never found out. Rowena returned to seize my arm and drag me into the bowels of the forest. 'What did I tell you? You must listen and follow my instructions. This way.'

Rain must have fallen earlier that day, for the earth was soft and gripped at my boots as I stumbled onwards. Rowena moved as sure-footed as a cat, but the woods didn't want me to pass. Holly snagged at my skirts, pulling me back. A root protruded into the path of my case and stopped it dead. Every piece of foliage proclaimed that I wasn't welcome.

'Come here, Camille. Give me your hat box; I can hold it by the string. Is that better?'

Even carrying less weight, the walk seemed interminable, a nightmare through which I ran but made no progress. I focused doggedly on my steps. I didn't notice the woodland swell around us and then thin once more, nor did I see the turret rearing out of the darkness to catch the glow of the moon. Only when I paused to gather my breath did I lift my head, and there before me stood Felwood Lodge, still and soundless, shrouded by oaks from the view of men.

Ivy stretched a web across its two storeys of granite stone. The camouflage would have been complete, were it not for the parapets that lined the roof, and the turret, pointing up towards the stars. Had Rowena called this a hunting lodge? It was more like a gentleman's ornamental folly.

'This is your home?' I whispered, incredulous. 'You are living inside one of Mrs Radcliffe's Gothic novels.'

Rowena made a grumbling noise in the depths of her throat. 'In more ways than you shall ever know.'

Reaching under her shawl, she produced a ring of keys. I followed her apprehensively to the front door. It whined open, revealing a small, smoky kitchen. Barrels occupied the corners and herbs hung in bunches from the ceiling. A middle-aged, coarse-featured woman was in the process of hooking a kettle over the fireplace.

Rowena nodded at her. 'That's Bridget. She'll make you tea, if you would like some. Sit yourself down, child, you look fit to drop.'

There was a rough-hewn table with stools grouped around.

I heaved my luggage inside and sat gratefully. Rowena shut the door fast behind us, locking it with her chatelaine of keys.

I hadn't known such a person as Bridget existed. Was she the maid here? My godmother had said she kept no servants, but I could think of no other function for this woman who set down two steaming mugs upon the table.

'There you are, young miss,' she said. 'Nice to meet you.'

I thanked her, taking a mug in my hands. The tea she served smelt green and herbal, not like the black Bohea tea at home. I didn't want to drink it, so I blew a dimple on to the surface instead.

Rowena sat beside me. 'So,' she said, reaching for her cup. 'You have kissed a soldier and thrown your family into disgrace.'

I spluttered. 'Yes, but – I did not mean – I didn't know—'

I saw then that she was grinning at me. 'Calm yourself, child. You will find no judgement here. God knows, both Bridget and I have been led down some sorry paths for the love of men. Trust me when I say they're not worth the pain.' She swallowed a mouthful, and when she finished there was no trace of merriment left on her lips. 'Your parents have explained my situation?'

I scarcely knew how to reply. 'My father said that you are . . . estranged from your husband? That he is seeking you.'

She exchanged a glance with Bridget, who stood unobtrusively by the sink. 'Yes. We lead a very different existence out here. This will not be like the life you are accustomed to, Camille. There will be chores for you to attend to. Rules to obey.'

Misgiving wallowed in my stomach. 'What kind of rules?'

'Most of them relate to managing Lucy's illness. As I said, my daughter is most unwell. We are risking her health by letting you come here at all. Do not repay my kindness by misbehaving.'

'I won't! I don't. I'm generally quite good,' I assured her and it was true, for the main part. My misdemeanours largely took place inside my mind, where they could hurt no one but me.

'I'm glad to hear that,' she said seriously. 'Now, see here. This is your first lesson.' Setting down her cup, she drew out a small book from her pockets and opened it to show me a page that listed every date in the month – September – and the estimated length of the days. At the top were four circles, shaded to different degrees. *New Moon, First Quarter, Full Moon, Last Quarter.*

'It's an almanac,' I said.

'Yes, and it's a useful tool to me, for it predicts quite accurately when the moon will rise. Perhaps you've read, Camille, of exceptional medical cases where people cannot bear the light of the sun? It hurts their skin, makes them ill. In rare instances it can kill them.'

I shook my head. 'I didn't know that could happen! Goodness, is *that* the ailment your daughter suffers from?'

'No. Lucy is even more unusual still. She does not fear the day, but the night. Moonlight aggravates her condition.'

'That's . . . the strangest thing I ever heard. A medical phenomenon.'

'Indeed. My daughter is certainly that.'

Bridget stole to Rowena's side and placed a hand upon her shoulder. 'We always send Lucy to bed early,' she cut in. 'It's more difficult to manage her symptoms at night. Especially when the moon is full. That's why we asked your father to bring you here tonight, when the worst is past. Tomorrow night, the moon will start to wane again.'

'So . . . Lucy will be better?'

'A little better. She can take a turn at any hour, any time of the month, but we find that by the time we get to here . . .' she ran her finger across the page to *New Moon* '. . . she is generally in a tolerable state of health. Provided we keep her from too much excitement. So you must do exactly as Rowena said. Don't misbehave and agitate Lucy. Don't go letting moonlight into the house or wandering around at night when she's feeling poorly. Just . . . stay in your room and stay quiet after dark.'

I could scarcely credit what I was hearing. I had no idea such sicknesses were even possible. 'I don't mean to pry but . . . what *is* Lucy's disease?'

Rowena drew a breath. I couldn't make out her expression in the shadows. 'She was born with it. A hereditary illness, running in the blood. Her father and every member of his family suffered. As far as I know, there is no absolute cure. But you see, I cannot consult a physician. Word might travel back to my husband. The Alaunts are as influential as they are violent; they have many spies.'

I shuddered. 'How awful for you.'

'All I can do is keep Lucy away from the factors that inflamed Sir Marcus's symptoms.'

'Are you sure there are no . . . specialists, for Lucy's condition? No learned men from London you might consult in great secrecy?'

Rowena snapped the almanac shut. 'No,' she said firmly. 'I have told you. There is no physician who can help.'

I held my tongue, afraid to push any further. This was clearly a sensitive subject. Nervously, I fiddled with the pendant around my neck. Moonstone. Was it not strange, that Rowena should choose this particular gem for me, when it carried the name of her daughter's nemesis?

'You must keep that on you always,' my godmother said, startling me.

'Must I?'

She reached beneath the high neck of her gown and drew out an identical pendant to my own. Glancing at Bridget, I saw that she wore one too. Gooseflesh skittered over my skin. Something strange was afoot here, something I couldn't put into words. The three gems winked at one another in the firelight, communing in some mystical and silent language. 'Yes. Don't take it off.'

'But . . . why?'

'Moonstone is considered holy in India. It restores tranquillity to a soul in turmoil.' That didn't answer my question at all. But Rowena was rising to her feet, signalling our conversation was at an end. 'Now, should you like to retire to your room?'

I thought that I would. The long journey was catching up with me, and her manner had turned so odd. Talking of Lucy's illness had changed her, moved a cloud across the sun of her disposition.

'Yes, please, I confess I am fatigued. Would you help me with my luggage?'

Bridget fetched a candlestick and lit the wick in the fire. She illuminated our path as Rowena took my belongings from the kitchen into a narrow hallway, towards a case of stairs. A creak accompanied us up the steps and across the landing. There were no pictures, no paper hangings, no sign of decoration at all. Ash timber panelled the walls up to waist height before giving way to plain, colourless plaster. The same wood formed the floorboards and the stairs. It was drab, but at least it was clean.

'There is our room.' Rowena gestured down the corridor to the left-hand side. 'Lucy sleeps in the turret. That door at the end of the hall leads to the steps upwards.'

A bedchamber in the turret and a girl who must not gaze upon the moon. It made Lucy sound like a princess in a book. I itched to meet her, to explore the lodge further, but Bridget pushed open the door to my room and held her candle inside. 'Here is the space we've prepared for you. I hope you'll be comfortable.'

Dismay dropped through me like a stone. I tried not to let it show on my face. When I'd dreamed of adventures, I'd imagined environments more beautiful than that which surrounded me at Martingale Hall, but it hadn't occurred to me how pampered my regular life was. The chamber at Felwood Lodge was without ornament, carpet or even a fireplace. A narrow crib of a bed took up most of the space. Beside it sat a chamber pot and a threadbare rug, the accoutrements of a monastic cell.

'Oh. Thank you,' I said, unconvincingly.

We could barely fit my luggage inside. For lack of room, I sat myself down upon the bed. It whined ominously. Bridget handed me the candlestick. 'There you go, this one can be yours.'

'Sleep well.' My godmother smiled. 'Be warned; we are early risers here. I shall call for you first thing in the morning with some hot water.'

'Goodnight, Miss Garnier.'

Despondent, I said not a word as they closed the door and retreated back down the stairs. It felt as though they had sealed me inside a tomb. My spare hand toyed with the sheets underneath me; they were scratchy, spiced with a vague must.

I wanted to go home. I wanted my sister, sleeping beside me as she always did, and our lovely room with its lemon paper. A room I would be allowed to leave during the night.

Below the candle, I could see my own tired face stretched and reflected back at me in the silver holder. As I turned it around, I realized it was more expensive than any stick in my own home. The candle too was fine-quality beeswax, not cheap tallow. It sat at odds with everything else I'd seen. Rowena wore plain wool, drank nettle tea; she didn't even have a pier table or a vase of flowers. Yet here was a luxury.

I was too tired to puzzle it through. Puffing out the light, I flopped backwards on the bed and closed my aching eyes. Perhaps when I opened them some miracle would place me back at Martingale Hall, packing my trunks for London and the Coronation Ball, and all of this interlude would prove to be a terrible dream.

CHAPTER THREE

Light washed across my face as the birds chorused outside. Consciousness returned slowly, along with the memory of where I was. But my recollections couldn't be right. I'd fallen asleep in a dark little cell of a room with a bristling, hostile forest outside. Now, with shades of gold playing upon my closed eyelids and a dawn symphony in my ears, I might be in the Garden of Eden.

I sat up, rubbing my stiff neck. I'd fallen asleep on top of the covers. My mouth was dry and stale, I felt as though I'd been wearing the same travelling dress for weeks. But the room looked better than it had last night, bathed in the morning's sepia tones. Still cramped, to be sure, but more homelike.

Kneeling on the bed, I threw back the curtain. My window did not have a view so much as a peephole into the life of the treetops. Oak boughs danced before my eyes, their green leaves all in motion as twigs beat a gentle melody across the glass. I could make out every whorl, every inch of rough bark. The acorns were tanning, readying themselves to drop. If I pushed open the casement, I'd be close enough to reach out and pick some. Suddenly, a wood pigeon fluttered into the topmost branches and began to coo. I craned my neck to see him. The bird regarded me with a black, liquid gaze, unafraid.

I climbed down from the bed and opened my trunk. Mama always said matters looked better by daylight, and perhaps she was right. I could grow used to the confinement of a tight chamber after dark if I had the freedom of the land outside while the sun stayed up. Although last night the woods had worn a grim and solemn mask, today they smiled. I would smile with them.

Rowena had promised to bring me hot water to wash, but I couldn't bear to wait. Stripping off my sweaty travelling dress, I threw it any which way upon the bed and picked out a gown of sage checked fabric. The cut was low; I usually added a fichu for modesty but the moonstone pendant nestled prettily in the hollow of my neck and I didn't want to cover it up. There was no looking glass to consult, no maid to help me arrange my hair. At least there were also no gentlemen to impress; the only opinion to care for was Lucy's, when we met for the first time today.

What would she be like? My imagination painted an angelic invalid, pale as alabaster with glittering eyes. Perhaps she would keep to her bed; perhaps I'd be called upon to read to her and play endless games of whist.

Footsteps approached my door. I was just tying my sash as it opened and Rowena's tall frame filled the gap. 'Good morning, Camille. I thought I heard you moving about. Did you sleep—' She stopped, catching sight of my gown. 'Oh.'

Why did she stare at me like that? 'Is something the matter?'

'Your dress. Have you anything a little more . . . sober?'

I brushed down the skirts, nonplussed. This was one of the plainest garments I owned. 'No. What's wrong with it?'

'Nothing. Nothing is *wrong*. It is the outfit of a gentleman's daughter, that's all. It won't survive a country life. How will you work on the farm?'

'Farm?' I repeated. No one had mentioned anything to me about a farm.

She shook her head as if in despair. 'Yes. How do you suppose we obtain our food? Never mind. We make our own clothes here, and I'm sure that with a bit of time we can rustle you up something more suitable. I've a spare cloak that may serve you meanwhile. Now, are you hungry?'

I was famished. 'Is breakfast ready?'

I started forward but she put a hand across the door to block my path.

'Just a moment. Lucy will be joining us at table. You must be forbearing with her. She is not accustomed to company.'

'Oh. No, I expect she is not.'

'She won't chatter and rattle away like other girls.'

'No, of course not. I won't upset her, Godmother. Remember that I have a baby brother at home. I know how to be gentle.'

She let down her arm. 'Come along, then.'

I stumbled on the uneven floorboards in the hallway as we left the room. A thick oaten scent was wafting its way up the stairs, warming the otherwise dull interior. My observations last night had been correct: there was no decorative detail that I'd missed. I expected to find at least a sketch hanging somewhere, or one of Lucy's childhood samplers, but there was nothing.

The steps whined under us once more, as though it pained them to be of service. I saw now that the hallway downstairs had three doors: one to the left, which led into the kitchen and the front entrance, one to the right, and another to the rear of the staircase.

I could hear Bridget clattering around in the kitchen. My stomach rumbled at the thought of food. When had I last eaten? I'd give any money for a cup of hot chocolate . . .

'Through here,' Rowena said, opening the door to the right.

The dining room she ushered me into was dim as a badger's den. No fire burned in the hearth. Although outside the day was bright, foliage smothered the two windows and cast a queer, green, underwater hue.

A dark figure hunched at one end of the table. Her forehead was pressed to the cloth, her hands laced around the back of her neck as though she would make herself as small and tight as possible.

'Lucy.' How forced and jovial Rowena's voice sounded, how utterly out of place. 'This is Camille Garnier, about whom I have told you so much.'

Lucy remained frozen. I was not certain she'd heard; I had a terrible misgiving that she might actually be dead.

But Rowena made a *tssk* of frustration. 'Lucy! Say hello.'

'Hello,' Lucy echoed, sullen, her voice muffled by the table.

Rowena gave me a look that announced this was the best we could hope for, and pulled out a chair for me on Lucy's left-hand side. Awkwardly, I sat. My place was laid with elaborate silverware, a bowl and spoon engraved with a family crest, every bit as fine as the candlestick last night.

'What a lovely service,' I observed, for something to say.

Rowena nodded. 'One of the few heirlooms I inherited from my mother's family, the Talbots. They owned this hunting lodge. They must have thrown fine dinners for their guests here, once upon a time. Now, let us have some light. I'll be back in a moment.'

I didn't want her to leave me alone with Lucy. What was I to say? Or was I supposed simply to ignore the girl and leave her slumped there in that extraordinary fashion? I'd expected a delicate creature of wan smiles, not . . . whatever this was.

A moment of silence stretched out after Rowena swept from the room. Then, slowly, Lucy began to uncurl. She lifted her head, spilling mousy hair from beneath her mob cap. She was tall, like her mother, and rangy with it. There was something noble in her aspect, more handsome than pretty: she had high cheekbones, strong features and a Roman nose.

I hoisted up a foolish smile. 'Good morning.'

She did not smile back. She stared at me with amber eyes that refused to blink.

My pulse faltered. 'It's nice to meet—'

Quick as a dart, her hand moved to seize my own. Cutlery rattled as I cried out. Lucy gripped me so tightly that I felt my bones shifting underneath the skin.

'You should not be here,' she said in a low voice. 'Go home.'

I gaped at her. Branches waved outside the window, moving the light across Lucy like water. She was a mermaid, a siren, beautiful and cruel. 'But . . .' I bleated.

'Go home!' she growled again.

'Here we are!'

Lucy released me at the first note of her mother's voice. Her hands whipped back beneath the tablecloth and she was the picture of innocence, but the red crescents on my hand spoke against her, vivid, painful reminders of where her nails had been.

Rowena placed a candlestick upon the table and Bridget followed, carrying a tureen. I was too shocked to speak a word to them. What on earth had just happened? Everyone had been so concerned about me upsetting Lucy; I never expected she'd upset *me*. What did she mean, that I shouldn't be here? I had imagined my visit would be a welcome jubilee to an invalid, but clearly not.

I kept my eyes trained on my cutlery as Bridget ladled thin gruel into the bowls. 'Bow your heads in prayer, girls.'

As soon as the grace finished, I grabbed my spoon and nervously scraped my bowl clean. I'd thought it a first course. But Lucy was still stirring hers, letting the gruel dribble in plops from her spoon, while Rowena ate in careful, delicate nibbles.

Was this sorry fare all I was to receive? At home there would be hot rolls, butter and coffee to come. Papa had warned me that Rowena was poor, but if I were her I'd pawn the fancy silverware in favour of more food. What use were gorgeous dishes if they held nothing of substance?

The gruel left a bland film inside of my mouth. I tried to remove it by drinking a glass of milk. That, at least, was pleasantly creamy and thick.

Bridget sat opposite me. I watched her as I sipped, trying to estimate her age. It was difficult, with the white threads in her hair and a face ravaged by exposure to the weather, but I thought she might be a little younger than my godmother, maybe two score years.

She noticed me looking. 'Do you want more?' she asked through a mouthful.

More of that sludge? I hesitated. Perhaps it was best to take the offer, in case there really was nothing else to be had. 'Yes, please.'

'You may help yourself.'

'Oh. Thank you.' I sat forward on the edge of my seat and reached uncertainly for the ladle. I'd never served my own food before. I made a dreadful clanging, slopping gruel on to the tablecloth as I filled my bowl.

'Dear me.' Rowena frowned at my mess. 'You will have to scrub that out, come laundry day.'

My shame burned so intensely that I felt a little sick. At Martingale Hall there was always a servant to plate my food, and, as for laundry, I'd never washed a garment in my life.

Maybe Lucy was right. Maybe I didn't belong here. But I had no choice.

I ate my second bowl in silence, fretting over what Rowena had meant earlier by working on a farm. My parents never warned me that I'd be expected to earn my keep! I'd be more of a hindrance than a help; I was useless at practical matters. Mama had even been obliged to help me pack my trunks before I came away.

No second course appeared and no hot drink was offered,

save for more of that herbal brew from last night. I took a mouthful. It tasted like metal.

Lucy dropped her spoon with a clatter that made me jump. 'I'm going to the barn,' she said, rising from her chair.

Of all things, I'd least expected that. Was she even well enough for manual labour? I supposed she must be; she'd seemed pretty strong when she crushed my hand. For all her thinness, her appearance didn't strike me as that of someone suffering under a great affliction. She was dressed plainly in wool like Rowena and Bridget, but instead of a moonstone, a thick silver choker looped around her neck.

Rowena dabbed her mouth with a napkin. 'Wait a moment. Camille and Bridget will be coming with you.'

Lucy tossed her head, releasing another shock of hair from her cap. 'They'll have to catch me up.' With that she left the room, sure of step and undaunted.

Rowena pursed her lips. 'I apologize for my daughter's lack of manners, Camille. Much preys upon Lucy's mind. She's best left to her own devices.'

Bolts slid on the kitchen door. In another instant, I heard it slam shut. Somehow it was easier to breathe now that Lucy had gone. What a peculiar girl! She wasn't at all what I expected, and I rather mourned for the vision I'd had of an easy, grateful companion. The agitation Bridget had warned me about wasn't palpitations, but a mood as prickly as thorns.

'I don't think Lucy likes me,' I blurted out. 'She told me to go home.'

Rowena sighed, swapping a look with Bridget. 'I am sorry for that. She will come around. It is not that she dislikes you. In fact, I suspect she is afraid of you.' I nearly laughed. That couldn't possibly be true. 'Just . . . leave her be for the present.'

'Now,' said Bridget, standing and starting to clear away the bowls, 'there is something we must discuss about the food here, Miss Garnier.'

'Please, call me Camille.'

'Very well. Your diet at Felwood Lodge will be rather different from what you are used to, Camille. Here we are what they call "Cowherdites" – or vegetarians.'

'What does that mean?'

'We do not consume meat,' Rowena explained. 'Much has been written in favour of the lifestyle. We have some pamphlets I can share with you, even an essay by the poet Shelley. You enjoy reading, do you not?'

I wiped my mouth to hide my perturbation. Must I really spend an entire year on what the doctors would call 'a lowering diet'? 'Yes . . . I'll certainly read them. But Lucy is ill. I thought she'd need red wine and beef tea, for her weak constitution?'

Now it was Rowena who almost laughed. 'There may be much disorder in Lucy's state of health, but I can assure you of one thing: she is seldom weak.'

Wind rushed in as Bridget opened the door, sending a ripple through the kitchen fire. I inhaled. Felwood air was pure, clean as a crystal stream.

Rowena wrapped me in her own cloak, which was miles too long. 'That will have to suffice. Don't blame me if you stain your dress at the farm.'

I followed Bridget across the threshold and raised my face to the sun.

'I expect you're used to strolling in fine shrubberies,' Bridget observed with dry humour. 'You'll find our land a little rough on your delicate feet.'

There were no rigid pathways to follow, only a beaten track winding beneath a tree-veined sky. By daylight, I could see all the obstacles that had tripped me last night: twigs, crisp leaves, and acorns that cracked like a gunshot underfoot. My spirits lifted. What did Lucy's strangeness matter, really? What did it signify if Marie was still angry about Vauxhall? Nothing could truly be bad while the birds twittered, hopping from branch to branch, and the rocks wore vivid cloaks of emerald moss.

Bridget stooped to collect nuts as we went. I paused and inspected a shelf of fungus sprouting from the side of a dead beech.

'Don't eat anything without asking me first,' she cautioned. 'These woods can feed you or they can kill you, and they don't mind which.'

At last we emerged into a clearing surrounded by a dark belt of trees, a wooded amphitheatre with a barn centre stage. Rough fences marked out paddocks, and, just beyond, I caught the gleam of a river tumbling fast.

As we approached the barn, there came the clang of a sheep bell and an inquisitive *pock, pock, pock*. A wheelbarrow and pitchfork lay discarded outside, but the door remained barred. No one had been in there today.

'Where is that girl?' Bridget murmured, placing her hands upon her broad hips. 'Rowena shouldn't let her go wandering off alone.'

For my own part, I was relieved to find Lucy absent. It would be easier for me to enjoy the sweetness of the day without her baleful stare. Manure leavened the breeze, but I resisted the urge to draw out my handkerchief and cover my nose; I would have to grow accustomed to the stink, along with the insipid food.

'Maybe she went for a walk instead?'

Following the curve of the river with my eyes, I saw a rickety footbridge that led across to the other side. Patches of earth had been furrowed there, presumably to plant crops, and beyond them, near the line where the forest began once more, rose a hillock with a door set into its side. It looked like the icehouse at Martingale Hall. But would they really need ice in such a small residence, where they didn't even preserve meat?

Bridget's vision was keener than mine. She started, spotting something that I had not. 'God's blood! If I've told her once, I've told her a thousand times!'

As she strode off towards the river, I raised a hand and shielded my eyes from the sun. There, by the water, crouched Lucy, her cap removed and her hair flowing unbound. When Bridget's feet clopped upon the bridge, she reared up to her full height, showing an apron peppered with soil and a smear of dirt across one cheek.

'Stop digging!' Bridget's order carried to me on the wind. 'Your mother shall hear of this!'

'I didn't touch your precious crops!' Lucy shot back, waving the trowel in her left hand. It was still claggy with mud.

'That doesn't matter. We have been over and over this! You are not to work the land any more. You are to tend to the animals with Camille.'

My heart plunged. Lucy clearly wanted nothing to do with me. Forcing us together would only annoy her. Hadn't Bridget said last night that we mustn't provoke Lucy or cause her to become agitated? She was certainly upset now.

'Look, I'm excavating on the riverbank, far away from everything.' A plaintive note crept into Lucy's voice. 'What harm can I do here?'

I couldn't see the problem myself, other than the stains on her clothes. She'd simply made a small divot in the mud, exposing clay and shale. It was a child's game. Amateur mudlarking, innocent as the dragonflies skimming the water.

But Bridget was adamant, her fury out of proportion. 'I won't have you digging like a dog.' She flung an arm in my direction. 'You get to the barn at once, young lady.'

Lucy dropped her trowel with a clang. It slid down the bank and vanished beneath the frothing surface of the river. 'To the barn,' she repeated, sardonic. 'With the livestock, where I belong. That's what you mean, isn't it?'

Although Bridget held her ground, I saw her arm waver in

the breeze, as if she'd experienced a sudden misgiving. 'Your words,' she said tightly, 'not mine.'

Huffing, Lucy pushed past her and thumped across the bridge. I swallowed through a narrow throat. Her anger quickened something inside me. I yearned for the courage, the self-assurance, to fight for myself like that. How would I have answered Pierre's tirades about Vauxhall if my tongue were loosed from the ties of decorum? If there were no need to respect the authority of an elder brother?

Lucy swept into the yard, tugging at her silver choker with one hand, refusing to glance in my direction. Shouldering the pitchfork, she swiftly unbarred the door to the barn and slipped noiselessly inside.

Was I supposed to follow her? I looked across the river for help, but Bridget had already turned her back to me and was inspecting her vegetable beds.

There must be some way to make myself useful here. With reluctance, I took up the handles of the wheelbarrow and drove it unsteadily towards the barn. The door remained ajar; inside was warm, and sweet with the scent of hay. Around a dozen sheep stood in metal pens – rams with curling horns, mothers nursing gangly lambs – and Lucy moved among them, murmuring softly. I hadn't expected to see her so gentle, stroking a fleece here and there. The sheep bleated their welcome; they even wagged their tails at her, as a dog might do. To them, she was kind.

'Good morning, Duchess. How did you sleep? Hasn't your baby grown?' When she smiled at the ewe, her face was remade. It didn't matter that her dress was soiled and her hair hadn't seen a brush for many weeks.

Passing through the pens with a greeting to each sheep, Lucy opened a broad side door on to the field and then unlatched the metal gates. At a click of her tongue, the flock filed slowly out into their paddock. She watched them fondly, real tenderness in her eyes.

Perhaps her anger had dissolved as swiftly as it appeared? If Lucy was nice to the sheep, might she find it within herself to be civil to me as well?

Taking courage, I set my barrow down and pushed open the door. Out of nowhere, a legion of chickens swarmed, moving like fluid to encompass me. 'Oh!' I gasped, trying to back away, but already they had tangled themselves in my skirts. I hit the wheelbarrow with a clang. Their clucks were more like squeals, painfully high-pitched. All I could see were flapping wings, scratching talons.

'What are you doing?' Lucy cried from somewhere beyond the chaos.

I couldn't answer her. Pain pricked at my calf as a black hen attacked my skirts. My foot caught the rooster behind me and he squawked indignantly.

'Mind Firetail! For heaven's sake.' Lucy strode over, parting the flock like Moses crossing the Red Sea. Taking up a bucket from beside the door, she rattled it, and the tide flooded in her direction. The chickens followed her all the way to the other side of the barn, where she emptied her bucket on to the floor. I was left with nothing but drifting feathers and a sense of humiliation.

'They won't harm you,' Lucy said. She didn't turn her head to speak to me, only watched the rooster she had called Firetail questing around for seed. 'They're just hungry.'

'I think they were trying to eat *me*.'

My jest fell flat at my feet. Lucy glowered. 'Chickens don't eat people. Didn't your fancy governess teach you that?'

I crept fully into the barn, now that it appeared to be safe. 'I'm . . . not used to animals. Only my father's dogs, and they frighten me a little. I've never even learnt to ride a horse. Mama says I'd be sure to fall off and break my neck.'

My humility didn't soften her any more than my humour. Lucy moved towards a ladder leading up into a hayloft and placed both hands upon the rails. 'You're not afraid of muck, are you?' she tossed over her shoulder.

'No.'

'Then fork out the stalls while I climb to the loft for fresh bedding.'

Warily, I lifted the pitchfork. It felt unwieldy; I was sure I was gripping it wrong. 'How do I . . . ?'

Lucy was already halfway up the ladder. 'You just scoop out the dung and wet straw and put it in the wheelbarrow. It's easy. A baby could do it.'

Mortified, I nodded. What had I been reduced to? At home, I didn't even empty my own chamber pot.

I began the miserable, smelly work. Wisps of straw plastered themselves to the hem of my skirt. I dropped a lump of excrement on my foot. Meanwhile, Lucy made her way up and down the ladder with easy grace. Wasn't she supposed to be sickly? So far as I could tell, her only disease was bad manners.

I stopped for a moment to wipe the sweat from my brow. Rowena had been right: despite her cloak, my gown was ruined underneath.

'That's what you get when you wear a ballgown to a farm,' Lucy observed. 'What did you expect? Orangeries and hot-houses, and a manservant to do all the labour? You'd better get back on the stagecoach to York if you're looking for luxury.'

My patience snapped. I threw my pitchfork down. 'What is your dispute with me?' I demanded. 'I've done nothing to you. Why don't you want me here?'

Her mouth opened, ever so slightly. There was a second that she was naked, vulnerable, before the shutters came over her golden eyes again.

'It's not safe,' she said gruffly.

'For whom?'

'For anyone.' She stooped to pick up the pitchfork. 'I'm ill, and your presence will make me sicker. Then there's the matter of my father.'

That part, at least, was a valid objection. 'Nobody knows I'm here,' I assured her. 'Your father won't find you just because I came to stay awhile.'

'It's not safe,' she repeated with more force, holding the fork between us. 'It's stupid. Foolhardy. I *told* Mama, but she insists on helping her *dear friend* Susannah and taking you in.'

Something in her sneer rang false. No doubt she meant to sound contemptuous, but I saw a chink in her armour. Living out here, in hiding, it was unlikely that Lucy understood how close friendships could grow. Did she really despise her mother's childhood intimacy with mine – or was she jealous of it?

I regarded her with a touch of pity now. 'Haven't you ever known a friend whom you'd help, no matter what?'

Her eyes slipped away. 'These animals are my friends. I don't need any others. Now go and collect the eggs while I finish your woeful attempt here. Do you think you can manage *that*, my lady?'

Blast her eyes, I'd tried my best to be nice, but I wasn't going to abase myself any longer. Who did she think she was? She might be a baronet's daughter by birth but she lived like a cottager. Incensed, I flung away from her and made for the nesting boxes. A wicker basket hung from a nail in the wall, so I yanked it down and began to root around for eggs to fill it.

The harvest was plentiful. Hopefully that meant we'd have something more substantial for dinner – fritters or omelettes. But I had to slow down. Move gently. If I kept grabbing eggs in anger I might crack the shells, and I'd be hanged before I gave Lucy another reason to despise me.

Gradually, my pulse slowed. The repetitive movement was soothing. Some eggs emerged from the straw warm and smooth in my palm; others were crusted with dung. I placed them side by side in the basket, flesh-toned, chalk-white, softly freckled like my sister Marie. How ardently I'd beg for her forgiveness when I wrote home! Even when she was sobbing angrily and calling me a strumpet, she was an angel compared to Lucy.

One of the rooster's long tail-feathers lay tangled in a nest. I picked it up by the quill, twisting it this way and that, watching green chase along the black. Sighing, I remembered the tall ostrich feathers the ladies had worn in their hair at Vauxhall Gardens. How had one night changed everything so utterly? Wasn't a kiss supposed to break a curse: turn a frog into a prince, or wake a maiden from her sleep? Mine had worked a different metamorphosis. Now I had rooster quills in place of plumes and skirts trimmed not with ribbon but with mud.

A single egg remained. I'd just placed my fingertips upon it when a throaty cry rent the air, raising gooseflesh on my skin. 'What was that?'

No response. It had not been the chickens, nor yet the sheep; it sounded further away. I turned to see Lucy in the sheep-pen. She was oddly frozen in place, pitchfork outstretched.

'Lucy? I said what—'

'A fox,' she replied mechanically. Still she didn't move a muscle. Straw fell through the tines of her trembling fork.

'It wasn't!' I'd heard foxes at Martingale Hall. They *could* make a fearful racket – in mating season, the vixens screamed bloody murder – but this noise had struck my ear differently.

Suddenly it came again, painfully raw. The sound of a creature whose sorrow was too great to bear alone.

The pitchfork dropped to the floor. Over the other side of the barn, chickens scattered.

'Lucy?'

She spun around and her face was . . . seething. I could think of no other word to describe it. Her mouth worked, her eyes seemed to pop from their sockets. Every inch of her slender frame quaked. 'I . . . I . . .' she gasped.

Frightened, I took a step back. 'What's wrong?'

She braced an arm against the wall for support. Illness had struck her like a thunderbolt; I wasn't certain she could breathe.

'Go!' she ground out. 'Fetch – help.' Then she plunged to her knees with a hacking cough.

I dropped my basket, caring nothing for the broken eggs, and fled the barn screaming for Bridget.

We hauled Lucy towards the lodge, one of us on either side, our shoulders propped into her armpits. For one so slender she was surprisingly heavy. The lean body that thrashed between us was corded with muscle. Lucy's own peculiar scent overpowered me: wool, hay and a hint of civet. I found my mind travelling back to the last time I'd held someone close like this: Vauxhall Gardens.

Rowena opened the front door and came speeding out just as we shambled in view of the house. 'What happened?' Her gaze flew to me. 'Camille, what did you do?'

'*Me?*' I cried.

'It wasn't her fault. Lucy was digging,' Bridget panted. 'She got herself worked up. And then we heard . . .' She bit her tongue, started again. 'The *foxes* were calling.'

Another coughing fit seized Lucy. Rowena shouldered me out of the way and scooped her daughter up into her arms, carrying her like a princess in a tale.

'Make tea, Bridget, quickly. There's still some water left.'

Bridget ran to the kitchen at once. Rowena trailed her, bearing Lucy, and I fell behind, terror weighting my steps. This panic reminded me of those awful days when my younger siblings had sickened. Gabriel first, then Emilie. I closed my eyes against an image of their little corpses, still and waxen as dolls.

Rowena manoeuvred her patient through the kitchen and back to the dining room where she propped her into a chair. The table was cleared, apart from the silver candlestick at the centre.

43

'Here. Watch this.' Rowena snatched the moonstone from her neck so fiercely that the ribbon snapped. She held it before Lucy as a pendulum, swinging gently back and forth. 'Focus.'

Lucy blinked, attempting to do as her mother bid her. She was wheezing for breath. A band of skin beneath her silver choker had chafed red.

'Find the light.'

The moonstone gleamed, opalescent before the flame.

'What does that do—' I began.

But before I could finish asking, Bridget rushed in with a cup of tea, a far darker drink than she'd brewed for me, something that smelt woody and nutty. At its scent, Lucy twisted away, disgust puckering her face.

'You must drink it!' Rowena commanded. She slapped the moonstone on to the table. 'Bridget, are you ready?'

She gave a tight nod. In a flash, Rowena lurched forward and pinched Lucy's nose, using the other to pull her jaw open. Bridget poured the tisane down her throat. Liquid bubbled horribly.

'Swallow it!'

I flattened myself against the wall, horrified to see the three of them struggling as though Lucy were a lunatic in a strait waistcoat. She had no choice but to drink whatever noxious concoction they'd given her with a rhythmic gulp.

'That's it. Good girl.'

Rowena and Bridget stood back, sweating and panting for breath.

Colour had fled from Lucy's cheeks. Her features had fallen strangely slack. Even her lips appeared pale and bloodless, save for the purple trickle of herbal tea at the side of her mouth. Her eyes, dull pennies now, swept over me. Worry extinguished all my earlier resentment.

'Do you feel . . . better?' I ventured.

'I feel—' she started, and then her eyes rolled back to the

whites. She dropped; Rowena caught her just before she hit the floor.

I gasped.

'It's all right,' my godmother said. 'Just a swoon. She will be well now.'

'I could run to the inn,' I offered. 'I could fetch help.'

Rowena tried to smile, but it looked more like a grimace. 'There is no one in this world who can help us.'

CHAPTER FOUR

Rowena's words come back to me now. I believe she spoke the truth. Our physician, Mr Leiston, can offer no useful treatment for what ails me, yet he's far from admitting defeat. Why would he, so long as my anguished parents continue to pay his fee?

The moment he arrived, he made the servants shutter the windows, seal the door tight and pile quilts upon my bed. Flames caper gleefully in the fireplace, goading me. I'm sweltering, basting in my own juices. Mr Leiston seems determined to put me through not just figurative but literal Hell.

'Water,' I gasp. 'Give me a little water. I'm so thirsty.'

Mama moves for the jug, but the physician stops her with a hand. 'No, madam. Nothing to cool her. We must raise perspiration. You see her skin remains quite dry.'

His does not. Beneath his periwig, Mr Leiston's forehead is awash with moisture, its odour mingling with Mama's cleaner scent.

'We can scarcely make it any hotter in here,' she objects, working her fan. 'My maids are on the point of fainting themselves.'

Mr Leiston blots his brow with a handkerchief and goes to

fetch his leather bag. 'If Miss Camille cannot sweat the illness out, we must draw it from her with her blood.'

My mother swallows. She hates blood. 'Is that really necessary?'

'She must be purged somehow.' He opens his case, produces a jar of squirming leeches. 'Bare Miss Camille's arm, please.'

Mama folds her fan and approaches my bed. I can hear the thump of her heart. 'Try to stay calm,' she murmurs, more to herself than to me, as she rolls back the sleeve of my nightgown. 'There's a good girl.'

My skin has lost its peachy ripeness. I look matt and grey, like a street urchin suffering from malnutrition, and I can't imagine a leech would relish my taste. But they're wriggling in their jar, thick, black commas, toppling over one another in their eagerness to feed.

Mr Leiston extracts one with a pair of tweezers, releasing a tang of blood. Not fresh blood – this is old and rusty, consumed long ago. Mama hides her face in her fan as he places the creature in the crook of my elbow. The leech fixes on, a needle prick against my skin, and begins to gorge itself, shimmering and pulsating as it swells.

I can't tear my eyes away. I want to . . . eat it. Feel it burst upon my tongue, let its hot juice dribble down my chin. There's just enough of my old self left to acknowledge how disgusting this is – yet I yearn for it, all the same.

Finally, the leech detaches and Mr Leiston returns it to the jar with his tweezers. A small, three-point wound weeps on my arm. I lick it clean.

'Camille! What are you doing? Stop that. Here.' Mama presses a wad of lint bandages to the mark. My blood blooms in a flower. She looks as though she might be sick.

But something stranger is happening in the jar, something that draws my attention away from her. There are tiny splashes as the occupants writhe within.

'What the deuce . . .' Mr Leiston mutters, tapping on the glass.

My leech quivers, then vomits up its meal. The water turns dark as sin. One by one, the leeches grow turgid and sink to the bottom of the jar.

'What is it?' Mama gasps.

Despite the heat, Mr Leiston pales with horror. 'The creatures are . . . dead, madam. Whatever runs through Miss Camille's veins has . . . poisoned them outright.'

I don't want to see the look on Mama's face.

Poison. How that word has followed me, across the moorland, over the crags, twisting through the beech trees and the bracken. Believe me, I know all about poison. But this is not that. If it were, I'd be dead. No. My infection is something worse: a taint without antidote, without cure – without even the mercy to kill me and end my suffering.

The morning following Lucy's collapse dawned damp; no rain, only a fine vapour in the air that speckled the window in my closet. Behind the glass every leaf, every twig stood curiously still. The wood pigeon didn't come to visit me as before. Perhaps he too heard the moans, the restless pacing that came from the turret room.

Whatever ailed Lucy seemed to require vast quantities of tea. My muscles were tender, not just from mucking out the barn but from an afternoon spent ferrying endless buckets of water from the river at Bridget's behest. Nonetheless, I washed and dressed eagerly, for I knew there'd be no toil for me today. Bridget and I were to take the handcart into the village of Deepbeck for supplies.

I donned my bonnet with the cornflower trims and a Clarence-blue pelisse. Rowena heaved a great sigh from the kitchen doorway as I creaked down the staircase.

'We do *try* to appear inconspicuous, Camille.' Dark smudges sat beneath her eyes; I had heard her, during the night, going up and down the turret stairs to Lucy. 'There is no need to be fashionable in Deepbeck.'

'I know, but I'm afraid I have only fashionable clothes to wear.'

'I don't suppose it matters what she puts on,' said Bridget, fastening her cloak. 'The lass is bonny. People will look at *her* however she is dressed.'

The comment came out a little sour, but it inclined me to forgive Bridget's strange show of temper the day before.

We set out slowly, Bridget pulling the cart behind us with a steady *click, click, click*. There was a fresh, earthen smell of damp grass and dew-beaded leaves. Now that the sky had clouded over, it became more obvious that autumn had laid its hand upon the trees. I saw touches of scarlet, ginger, mustard yellow.

'It really is quite beautiful here,' I observed to Bridget.

'For the moment. Do you see those sloe berries?' She nodded to the right. 'The blue ones.'

'Yes.'

'There are many about this year, and that heralds a harsh winter to come.'

We left the pocket of woodland, winding out on to a hedged pathway. A squirrel loped across our path. I smiled to see nature coming into its own, roaming free without fear of Martingale Hall's groundsmen or over-zealous gardeners. But I couldn't help remembering we'd left a house of sickness behind us; my glee was a little heartless, in light of Lucy's suffering.

Why had Bridget not wanted her to dig yesterday? Could it really have been that exertion which had made her so ill? Maybe Bridget would have time to explain it to me now.

'Will Lucy recover from her bad spell?' I asked. 'What could have caused that terrible paroxysm?'

Bridget pursed her lips, steering the cart around a pothole. 'Many factors aggravate her illness. It's always there, like a tune in the back of her mind, but generally she's been able to drown it out. As she's grown older, it's become more difficult. But don't you fret. We have ways of managing her condition.'

'Like the tea you brew for her.'

'Yes, that is one way.'

'How do you know what ingredients to put in it?'

Bridget brightened then, on safer ground. 'I'm an apothecary's daughter. Tinctures and medicinal herbs are my passion. I suppose that sounds contemptible, to a modish young lady like yourself.'

That explained her presence at Felwood Lodge, perhaps: Bridget was the closest thing Rowena could get to a nurse.

'I am not half as fine as you seem to think me. And why would I despise your talent? Everyone falls ill.'

'Yes, they do. I've always been rather proud of my healing knowledge. But I must admit that Lucy's disease has . . . tested my ability. And, as I said, it's taking a stronger hold. I've needed new ingredients this past year. We'll go to the apothecary today and restock our medicine for her.'

A little further on, the landscape opened up into rolling fields, seamed by dry-stone walls. Beyond them loomed the fells from which the forest took its name; wild and uncultivated, barren in their beauty. Only the occasional flare of heather or gorse lightened their frown.

We passed a milestone. The dirt path sloping downwards became more regular and then led on to cobbles that slowed the cart. 'How much further?' I asked.

'Not far now. Can't you hear the river running closer?'

I closed my eyes, listening for its boisterous tumble and splash beneath the trundling cart. There. I always loved that sound: a murmur that promised to bring excitement in the current. If we returned to the same spot tomorrow, this river water would be long gone and a fresh flow would have taken its place. There was no time for it to grow turgid and dull.

When I opened my eyes, I could see the river rushing gaily before us in a ribbon of silver; a stone bridge spanned its breadth and led into the village. My expectations had been low and I couldn't say they were exceeded; Deepbeck was nothing compared to Stamford's honeyed limestone. But there was a quaint charm in the shops that formed a square around the village well, and the street that rose higgledy-piggledy behind up to the churchyard. Every window bore a painted sign. The chimneys steamed with the fragrance of bread. My stomach rumbled. Maybe here I could find a meat pie, a vol-au-vent, a currant bun – anything to supplement the meagre rations at Felwood Lodge.

'Where to first?' I asked as we strode over the water.

'To the post office? Maybe there will be a letter waiting for you.'

I doubted Papa's carriage had even made it home yet but I nodded, distracted. The square seemed full of farmers and field hands, grizzled men in smocks and gaiters who stared at our approach. A pimpled youth standing in line for the well whispered something to the man in front as we passed by. They both guffawed and I felt my cheeks glow. How familiar they must all be with one another here: the same close-knit families, generation after generation. Most visitors probably stayed at the coaching inn, miles off. Rowena was right: it had been a mistake to wear my fine pelisse and draw attention to myself.

'Never mind them,' Bridget hissed. 'I'm not what you would call "popular" here.'

Leaving the cart outside, we hurried into the small post office. Eyes turned upon me as we joined the queue, a prickling, uncomfortable sensation I remembered all too well. Looks of scornful judgement, like those at Vauxhall Gardens. These villagers censured me for my finery as surely as I'd be snubbed for the lack of it back home.

The postmistress was a plump, watery-eyed woman who peered at us through her spectacles. 'Ah, Mrs Talbot,' she said, pressing on the name like a bruise. 'It is that time of the week already? How are your sisters faring?'

I frowned, confused, but Bridget answered readily. 'Tolerable, I thank you. Have we any letters?'

'None, I'm afraid, not after your little *flurry* recently.'

She wasn't exactly rude, but there was something in her manner, something artificial and condescending, that spoke of her dislike. Bridget didn't let it bother her.

'You see the result of that correspondence before you. My goddaughter, Camille Garnier, here to assist with my nursing. Has anything come for *her*?'

The postmistress lowered her spectacles and regarded me like a bug on her shoe. 'Ah, that accounts for it. We received something just this morning, and I was sure the direction must be a mistake. Too foreign for these parts.' She pushed an envelope across the counter. I thrilled to see Marie's handwriting. 'What is it, miss? A French name?'

The way she said it, as though I were Bonaparte himself. I snatched the letter and returned her false smile. '*Oui, madame. Mon père est français et vous* êtes *très moche.*'

'Heavens, how exotic.'

Bridget steered me out of the door. 'Whatever did you say to her?' she asked as she collected her cart.

I grinned. 'I called her ugly. I dare say she didn't understand me. Why was she so vile? Why did she call you—'

Bridget cut me off. 'I am "the widow Mrs Talbot" here. The name is well known in these parts; the Talbot family used to own much of the land towards Felwood. I buy items for my invalid sisters at home but they never come to the village, and no one has ever seen them.' Her look was pointed. 'Do you understand what I'm telling you?'

I nodded and followed her across the square in silence. I'd

known Rowena and Lucy were in hiding, but I hadn't expected them to take their concealment so seriously as to weave a misleading narrative among the locals. Would the dreadful baronet really seek them in a place so remote? He must be determined indeed; or else even more fearsome than my father had let on.

The distinctive marks on my godmother's face rose before my mind's eye, and I remembered how she'd come to meet us under the cover of darkness, wrapped in a shawl. Lucy's words returned to me. *It's not safe.* But surely my parents wouldn't have sent me here if there was any true danger? Marie's marriage was not more important to them than my wellbeing. At least, I didn't think it was . . .

We drew to a halt before a shop close by the river, displaying jars and bottles in the leaded windows. A customer with a package tucked under his arm came out of the door and down the steps. A rich herbal fug clung to him. Bridget sniffed appreciatively. 'Smells like home. Now, you stand here and mind the cart. I won't be long.'

She tripped lightly up the steps to the entrance. A bell tinkled as she opened the door and left me waiting like a servant for her outside. Why couldn't I go in? I found it hard to believe someone would want to steal this rickety old cart, and Bridget had left it by the post office happily enough.

Standing on tiptoe, I pressed my nose to the window and peered through. It was much like any other apothecary shop: mahogany cabinets lined with vials of every shape and size, neatly labelled drawers, a pair of brass weighing-scales on the counter and a door behind that led to the distillery. A large ceramic jar obscured my view, but I could just about see the back of Bridget's head as she approached the apothecary himself. His face was clearer to me, and I noted it wore a guarded expression.

A boy emerged from the distillery, bearing a sack of something that Bridget must have ordered in. She took it, gesturing to some dark bottles that sat behind the counter. The apothecary shook his head.

'Miss Garnier.' The voice came hot beside my ear. I started back, nearly cried out, but, as I caught sight of the young man who addressed me, my throat went dry. Mr Randall stood there, wearing the clothes of a prosperous farmer: kerseymere, boots and gaiters, his black hair curling playfully beneath a flat cap. Dear God, what were the chances? Of all the villages, in all of England, how did he happen to be here?

'What—' I started, overcome. 'How—' I tried to retract, become smaller, as if that could make my feelings shrink too.

'Don't be alarmed. I'm staying at The Grey Lady inn. To be frank, I followed you here.' His voice dropped a notch, he took a step closer. 'I would follow you to the ends of the earth, Miss Garnier. Ever since Providence drew us together again at the ball, I cannot drive you from my mind. You have bewitched me utterly.'

Heat crept up my neck. I'd always dreamed of hearing a speech like that. All at once I remembered his mouth upon mine, the press of his body, and I shivered. But I had to get a hold of myself. That moment of pleasure had nearly destroyed everything. What would Marie think if she knew of this meeting? My parents would be apoplectic if they realized they'd sent me a hundred miles away, straight into the arms of the very same bounder who had ruined my reputation . . .

'You – you used me very ill,' I gasped. 'It was – wrong – ungentlemanly of you to – to – take advantage of me at Vauxhall.'

He nodded, sheepish. 'Indeed it was. I am a scoundrel, a rogue, a blackguard, whatever you wish to call me. I cannot deny it. But that reproach in your face will inspire me to better things. Please accept my apologies, Miss Garnier.'

He gazed soulfully into my eyes. I saw again the scatter of

golden stars in those dark irises and my head went light. It felt absurd, making him apologize for such a sweet moment. I'd cherished that kiss, asked for it without words. But I must remember the respect that was due to my station, to my family.

'You just ran away and left me to deal with the consequences! I've been banished from my family, sent all the way out here, while you may go about your business as usual.'

He winced. 'Yes, upbraid me. I deserve it. My actions were detestable. But I am in earnest, madam. I have no intention of trifling with you.' His voice was tender, his look hot with intensity. I found my chin lowering, afraid to meet his gaze, fearful of what I might do. 'Come, say you forgive me. Say we may start anew. There need be no mention of what occurred before.'

Even if we didn't speak of it, the ghost of the kiss lingered in the air, on my lips. I took a breath.

Suddenly the bell over the shop door tinkled. I started, turning my head to see a disgruntled Bridget emerge, sack in one arm and an array of packages tied with string in the other. 'Camille,' she said, stomping down the steps. 'Camille, bring the cart here.'

I glanced back to the window, ready to apologize, to make my excuses and tell him that I must leave. But the air beside me held only a whiff of sandalwood cologne, and Mr Colin Randall had disappeared once more.

I went upstairs to my tiny room on the pretext of removing my outdoor things. Instead, I pitched straight upon the bed, never minding how I crushed my bonnet. Why had he fled? Bridget wouldn't have recognized Mr Randall; she wouldn't have suspected who he really was. But he'd vanished like a phantom once more, leaving me burning with desire.

My feelings pushed against the wooden walls, too large to be contained in a narrow space. He'd *followed* me. Followed me the way Valancourt followed Emily to Toulouse in *The Mysteries of Udolpho*. But to what end? I had to talk to him again. I had to know what he meant when he said he had no intention of trifling with me. Was he alluding to courtship? Was it possible he meant to speak to my father and straighten out all this mess? Maybe my girlhood fantasy would finally come true and he'd propose, as he had in my daydreams.

Though I knew little of Mr Randall's circumstances, he'd been prosperous enough to study at Oxford. He was the son of a gentleman, exactly the kind of man my parents would want me to marry. And what could Pierre really hold against him, other than an IOU from a bet or something of that nature? There were possibilities here . . . How vexing that my grand romance should be unfurling at Felwood Lodge, squashed in with the rag-rug and the chipped chamber pot, and not in the boudoir of a grand château up in the mountains. But it *was* a romance, nonetheless, and with the very man I'd nursed a tendresse for all these years.

I opened my reticule. Marie's letter was squashed inside. I could almost hear the familiar writing, speaking my name in a tone of reproach, judging me. But why should Marie's love affair take precedence over mine? It wasn't my fault she'd set her sights on a squeamish man like Adam Ibbotson who couldn't abide the merest hint of scandal. She'd never once stopped to ask me if I knew the man at Vauxhall or why I'd let him kiss me. All she cared about was her own heartbreak.

Still wearing my gloves, I tore the letter open. It was kinder than I expected. Marie regretted that we'd parted in anger and promised to write me an account of the ball at our neighbours' house in the coming weeks. She would be dancing and dressing up while I shovelled manure out here! But as I imagined her sneaking glances at Mr Ibbotson across a crowded room, never quite daring to approach him, my jealousy withered. *I* was the lucky one. Marie didn't have a gentleman who valued her as

Mr Randall valued me. *Her* suitor wouldn't travel a hundred miles for the chance of seeing her. His love was so weak that he withdrew at the first sign of trouble.

The wood pigeon began to coo outside. He'd returned to the dripping branches of the oak tree after all. I sat up and watched him fluff his feathers, feeling more optimistic by the minute. Mr Randall would find me again, I was sure of it. This might not be a year of banishment after all, but the year that secured my future match.

I reshaped my bonnet, took off my pelisse and folded it away. Once everything was safely stowed, I straightened my gown and went out on to the landing. The door at the far end of the corridor whined open. Lucy emerged, soberly dressed in her white cap with a grey wool skirt and bodice. 'Oh,' she said dully. 'It's you.'

The sight of her took me by surprise. I hadn't expected to see her up and about again already.

'Yes. I just got back from Deepbeck. How are you feeling?'

Lucy turned and shut the door to the turret behind her. 'I'm fine.'

She didn't look it. Her eyes narrowed against the light and she wore the blank, vaguely nauseous expression of someone who'd drunk too much alcohol the night before.

'We were all so worried about you! What caused that awful fit?'

'*You* did,' she announced. 'I told you you'd make me ill.' With that, she shouldered past me and headed for the stairs.

I scuttled after her, brimming with a sense of injustice. 'That's not true! Why would you say that? I didn't do anything to harm you.'

'It wasn't *just* you,' Lucy admitted, placing a hand upon the banisters and descending slowly, her footing insecure. 'It was too much, all at once. Bridget scolding me, your arriving here, and the howling . . . But that's over now.'

'I hope so.'

She looked up sharply to where I stood at the top of the staircase. 'Why? What did you see, what did I do?'

Her gaze made me feel like a rabbit in a net. For the second time that day I found myself fumbling my words. 'Nothing – nothing, you just . . . fitted. Don't you remember?'

The sound of our voices brought Rowena and Bridget out of the kitchen, their cheeks rosy from the warmth of the fire.

'There she is.' Rowena hastened up the few remaining steps to help Lucy down. 'Are you feeling better, my dear?'

Lucy brushed her mother's caresses away like a cobweb. 'I'm tired. More tired than usual. And no, Camille,' glancing back at me, 'I don't remember much about it at all. Were my convulsions particularly bad this time?'

Bridget wiped her hands on her apron as I made my way downstairs towards them. 'Well . . . there was something a little stronger in your tea,' she confessed. 'The ingredient we spoke of using, should it be required.'

Lucy stiffened. 'And *was* it required?' she demanded. 'Or were you just angry at me for digging?'

Bridget pursed her lips. There were cracks in the skin around her mouth, marks from all the words she'd withheld. 'I didn't want to take any risks,' she said. Her gaze flicked to me then back again. 'Now more than ever.'

Whatever that meant, Lucy seemed to accept it. The fight died in her eyes; she withdrew inside herself.

'What—' I began, but, as with many of my questions, Rowena chose that moment to interrupt.

'Go and sit in the parlour, girls,' she said, chivvying us gently towards the door behind the staircase. 'Have a little rest while we finish preparing your supper. It won't be long now.'

'What do we eat tonight?' I asked.

'Pease pottage and baked eggs with chives.'

Hardly a feast, but it was better than gruel.

The parlour was more interesting than the other chambers in Felwood Lodge; the window pointed at a gap between the oaks, giving greater light, and there was more furniture: a sofa that had once been velvet with patches worn away, a shelf of second-hand books and, on the other side of the room, a hand loom and spinning wheel.

Lucy deposited herself on the sofa by the window and picked up a drop spindle. It was already drafted with a length of wool. She used no distaff but let the spare fibre trail over her shoulder in a wild mane as her fingers played. Her concentration was acute. I watched her nimble hands, the nails pared almost to the quick. Mama would call them servant's hands, but I doubted even she could deny the elegance of Lucy's motions.

'I've never spun wool into yarn,' I said, seating myself beside her. She shuffled further away. 'How do you do it?'

'With much practice. I'm too tired to show you now.'

'Oh.' An awkward pause followed. 'I didn't bring any of my own sewing to occupy me . . .'

Lucy said nothing, just kept on twirling and twirling. I thought of my book *Metamorphoses* and the princesses who sat spinning. Lucy might look like a princess herself if her voluminous hair were not pinned up and tucked away from sight. It would be so pretty set in fat ringlets, woven through with ribbon, and she might cut a fine figure in satin or gossamer muslin. Not that any of it would matter while her face remained so dour.

'Must you stare at me like that?' she snapped.

'Sorry. I don't know what to do with myself . . .' My roving eyes fell upon the books, reliable friends. 'Maybe I'll read. Would you like me to read to you, while you spin?'

She shrugged, my kind offer falling straight from her shoulders. 'You may.'

She was so odd, so contrary to everything I'd been taught. A hostess's task was to make a guest comfortable, to bend to their needs and secure their entertainment at all costs. Lucy didn't seem to care whether I thought well of her or despised her utterly. How must it feel, to have that kind of security in your own skin?

Rising, I went to the bookshelves and tilted my head to read the spines. Many of them were cracked and some of the pages bulged with age and with damp. William Emerson's *The Elements of Optics. Astronomy Explained* by James Ferguson. Treaties on the discovery of Uranus, on the ichthyosaurus found in Lyme Regis. *A Lapidary, or the History of Precious Stones* by Thomas Nichols.

'It's all about astronomy or archaeology. Where are your novels?'

Lucy made a harrumph of derision. 'I don't read novels. I've no wish to fill my head with air.'

I bit my lip. 'Oh. You're a bluestocking, then?'

'I like learning, if that's what you mean.'

I liked to discover facts too, but there were times when only a story would suit my mood. Today in particular I yearned for a romance. A hero I could picture to resemble Mr Colin Randall . . .

'I think you *can* learn from stories,' I told her. 'I certainly have. *Waverley* taught me more about the Jacobites than any lecture, and I recall more geography from the plots of Gothic novels than from our maps. An attack of bandits or a haunted castle is sure to make a place memorable to me.'

'I daresay,' Lucy said drily. She didn't look up from the whirling spindle, but perhaps she sensed that her response was too tart, for she went on, 'Those books would only give me bad dreams. I've enough to contend with in my own life, without imaginary cares too. But I suppose you have the luxury of pretending and playing make-believe.'

The contrast between the pair of us did seem stark: me in my patterned muslin gown, standing leisurely by the row of books while Lucy toiled, dressed as a servant. I thought of her in the barn, saying the animals were her only friends. Yet there was still this envy, this burn behind my ribs. Even with all her disadvantages, I felt she was . . . *better* than me. Rather than sensing my good fortune, I only longed to be more like her. But that was ridiculous.

'There must be *one* story you enjoy,' I protested. 'Your mother must have read you *The History of Little Goody Two-Shoes* as a child, at least?'

With a sound of exasperation, Lucy stopped the spindle. 'You ask so many questions!' She began to wind her finished yarn around the shaft. 'It's not that I *dislike* stories. But something as descriptive as a novel . . . You must know that if you read a novel sometimes you go . . . beyond yourself. Travel out of your body, as it were.'

Of course I did; that was why I loved them. I could be anyone, do anything.

'I can't let my guard down in that way,' Lucy went on, putting her spinning safely aside. 'My illness would . . . pounce. As it did in the barn.'

What an odd way to describe her sickness: a creature lurking in the shadows, awaiting an opportunity. 'Your illness—' I began, but Lucy held up her hand.

'Enough! Stop prodding at me. I told you I was tired.' She shook her head, releasing the smallest curl from the base of her cap. 'Some of us were not born chatterboxes,' she added under her breath.

That was an understatement. I had so much more in common with the girls of neighbouring estates in Lincolnshire, who used to call upon Marie and me in the mornings. We'd sit for hours, talking over our tea and cake. But none of them would speak to me just now. Lucy was the only company I could hope for. And, to be honest, I was intrigued. You'd never find a girl like Lucy in Stamford. In society at all.

Abruptly, she rose from the sofa. 'Supper is ready. They're serving it up.'

Before I could ask how she knew, Bridget's voice summoned us to the table.

CHAPTER FIVE

'Do not slouch, Camille. You'll ruck up the fabric and the measurements will be wrong.'

I raised my chin and pulled back my shoulders, as my godmother bade me. My mind was elsewhere, not in the parlour where I stood, pinned into the rough calico mock-up of farm-yard clothes.

'We'll add a larger hem,' Rowena continued, extending a tape measure down my outstretched arm. 'If you're anything like Lucy you'll have grown by the time it's finished. I am forever letting down skirts and lengthening sleeves for her.'

I nodded, not really listening. I didn't want to think of dull cloaks and dresses without trains, but of gowns that would catch the eye across a ballroom, diaphanous muslins that clung. Wedding trousseaux. How could I summon enthusiasm for this ghost of an outfit?

'I must get under way quickly, or all the lovely clothes you brought with you will soon be reduced to rags. I doubt we'll wash that dung stain out of your striped cotton no matter how hard we try.' Relinquishing the tape measure, Rowena began to unpin me. 'All right. That will do for the moment.'

I frowned down at the rough-cut shapes as she removed

them. It was like being freed from some kind of chrysalis, the cocoon of what Rowena needed me to become while I stayed here.

'I don't think the cut of this new dress will show my figure to any advantage,' I said.

She smirked. 'It will be *serviceable*. I am no *modiste*, I'm afraid, and I cannot afford the rates of the one in Deepbeck.'

I tried not to pout. Imagine how mortifying it would be if Mr Randall saw me again, dressed as an absolute fright! 'You could probably buy yourself some nice expensive gowns, Godmother,' I ventured, 'if you sold your silverware.'

'Well, that's true. But my dinner service belonged to my mother's family.' She jabbed the pins she held back in their cushion and reached for another piece of fabric. 'Besides, I value silver over silk.'

'Why?'

'Because silver is pure. Forged and refined in a crucible. That makes it a useful aid for fighting against infections.' She pronounced her opinion calmly, without any hesitation or consciousness of how fanciful it sounded.

'You think silver has . . . magical powers?'

Rowena laid another panel of calico aside. 'I do not say *magical*. There may well be a science to it. But you must know yourself that many old tales show silver warding off evil. They can't all be without foundation.'

'I suppose not . . .'

More pins slid into the cushion. 'You think me whimsical. It's true that modern physicians discount the healing properties of metals, crystals and gems. But my experience has led me to different conclusions. I told you about the moonstone, didn't I? You saw for yourself how it countered the negative lunar influence upon Lucy.'

I'd seen nothing of the sort, only a wild tussle over the tea. But as I touched the pendant at my throat it did feel a little magical, and I let myself be swept along by her idea. 'So that's why you all wear moonstone necklaces? To help Lucy?'

'Moonstone gives Lucy focus when her illness tries to take control.' Again, Rowena was personifying Lucy's disease, talking as if it had malicious intent. 'She follows the moving light and it calms her. Now, some people in the East believe that very light is a good spirit, dwelling within the stone. It helps to remind a person of everything sacred.' She gave a little shrug. 'Who am I to say if they're right? All I know is that the moonstone helps my daughter.'

It was a pretty story, without doubt. 'Where on earth did you read about all of this, Godmother? I should like to see the book.'

Rowena smiled, removing the last piece of gown and setting me at liberty. 'You cannot. The story was told to me at my cradle. You don't know, perhaps, that I was born in India? My father worked for the Company.'

I shook my head. 'I'd no idea. What was India like?'

'Well, I wasn't there for long. All that lives in my memory is a swirl of heat and colour. My mother died in childbed and Father caught the malaria a few years afterwards. I was sent back to his only surviving relative in England, with nothing but my ayah and my mother's moonstone necklace for company.'

'Ayah?' I repeated the unfamiliar word.

'Yes, that was what I called her. A nursemaid, you'd say. She told me all about the moonstone, and many other stories besides. But after a while my guardian replaced her with an English governess and sent her back to Calcutta.' A sigh escaped her. 'I don't think I ever forgave him for that.'

My poor godmother didn't seem to have much luck. Orphaned at a young age with no siblings, married to a brute of a man, and now mother to a troubled daughter. Her ayah would have been the only person she could have loved simply, without complication, but even she was wrenched away from her. No wonder Rowena valued Mama's friendship so highly. It was one constant in a shifting quicksand of a life.

As she folded away her work, I went over to the bookshelves again, hoping something different would catch my eye. Surely Rowena would have *one* book on the country of her birth that I might read and find out more? But instead I saw a title written in my father's native language: *La Bête du Gévaudan*. A beast, in the South of France? It sounded like a horrid novel.

'What's this, Godmother?' I reached up, but before I could grab the volume my hand flinched back. 'Ouch!' A sting on the thin flesh at the crook of my arm. Rowena had missed a pin; it winked out maliciously from the hem of my half-length sleeve.

'What's the matter?' she cried. 'Are you hurt?' Dropping the mock-up dress she hurried over and seized my arm.

'Not really,' I said, and I wasn't, the pain had simply taken me by surprise. There was no need for her sudden panic. 'Sorry, I didn't mean to frighten you!' My wound was a mere thread. A single bead of blood welled up as Rowena pulled the pin away. Clenching her jaw, she turned back to her sewing materials and snatched a length of calico from the pile, tying it tight around the bend of my elbow; an excessive precaution for the size of the injury. 'Honestly, you don't need to—'

'I do,' she said. 'And you must take more care. You must not injure yourself here.' Dumbly, I nodded, wondering what had happened to the kindly godmother measuring me a moment ago. 'It's important, Camille. Stay alert. If you get a scratch working in the barn, anything that draws blood, you must leave Lucy at once and bind it up. Do you understand?'

'Yes,' I croaked out. Why had she not told me that before? Another strange rule . . .

'Lucy never was able to abide the sight of blood,' my godmother went on. 'It is the very worst irritant to her condition. There was an incident once, with the lambing—' She paused, seemed to decide the story was not for my ears. 'Now, each spring, I have to keep her away from the barn until all the ewes are safely delivered.'

I cleared my throat to dispel the tightness there. 'Oh! I see. My mother hates blood too. It makes her swoon or vomit.'

'Yes, well, that would be a mercy in comparison. Lucy's reactions can be more . . . severe.'

Something heavy thumped upstairs. It sounded like furniture falling over.

Rowena went rigid. 'Camille, I need you to go outside now and help Bridget on the farm. Can you do that for me?'

I could – I wanted to. Her tension seemed to be filling the room.

'Good girl. Quickly, now.'

Seizing my shoulders, Rowena spun me around and walked behind me to the door. It was only when we were crossing the hallway, *en route* to the kitchen, that I noticed Lucy. She crouched on the middle step of the staircase with her legs curled under her skirts. Her hands gripped the balustrade so tightly that her knuckles were turning white.

'Lucy?' My voice lilted up, turning her name into a question, because Lucy herself seemed strangely absent. Behind her intense focus there was . . . no one.

Rowena's fingertips dug into my shoulders. 'Never mind her.'

Lucy inhaled deeply, nostrils flaring and dilating like an artery.

Rowena yanked the kitchen door open and pushed me through. 'Off to Bridget.'

Lucy stared on unabashed, inspecting every inch of me. Even as Rowena snapped the door shut, I was conscious of her eyes moving across my body, brazen as the touch of hands.

What was the matter with that girl?

I hastened outside. A chill had crept into the breeze. Autumn verdure fluttered like a spill of coins at my feet. I took the path that wound beneath a canopy of beech and sycamore towards the meadow. The ferns glowed hunter-green. However hastily

I'd been thrust from the house, I was glad to be out here where I could breathe and roam. All I needed to make the scene perfect was for my young beau to materialize from the trees and kiss me, as he had done once before . . . It wasn't impossible. He was close by, achingly close, sleeping in the very inn where Papa and I had taken tea.

My daydreams followed me into the meadow, and across the grass studded with daisies. A knot of sparrows chirruped to me from the eaves of the barn as I passed. Wandering away from their song, I took the bridge to where Bridget knelt among the vegetable beds, her hands burrowed deep into the soil and releasing a mineral fragrance.

'What are you doing?' I asked, observing the row of yellow, wilting vines beside her. 'These crops look half-dead.'

'I'm harvesting potatoes,' she told me, falling back on her haunches. 'When the leaves die, it means they're ready.'

'Rowena said I should come and help you.'

'Well, come and help me, then.'

Arranging my skirts, I squatted next to her. 'Don't I need a spade?'

'No, it can puncture the tubers.' Seeing my grimace, she raised an eyebrow. 'Are you too fine a lady to get your hands mucky?'

In truth the prospect of broken, dirt-rimmed fingernails didn't appeal, but the idea of Bridget continuing to goad me for squeamishness was worse. My mettle must rise, or the year to come would be one of endless teasing.

'I'm not "too fine". I'm just imagining what my mother would think.'

Bridget laughed as I took a breath and plunged my fingers into the claggy mire. We worked in silence for a while, listening to a robin's crisp, melancholic song. I found satisfaction in the rhythmic sift and tug. Each potato unearthed shone gold as pirate's bullion. Why should this simple chore be forbidden to

Lucy? I burned to ask Bridget, yet somehow the subject felt taboo.

I pulled out a potato the size of a cricket ball, trailing stringy roots behind. As I placed it into the bucket with its companions, a flower growing in the bed behind caught my eye. The colour was unusual, somewhere between purple and blue, growing as a column of little weeping bells.

'What's that?' I asked. 'I've never seen that pretty bloom before.'

Bridget glanced up from her work. 'That is something you must never touch. My physic patch is strictly off limits to you.'

Yet another forbidden fruit. 'But why?'

'Because it's for medicine, not food. There are plants there that should only be handled with gloves, by those of us who know what we are doing.'

A piercing howl rose from the forest, startling the robin from its branch. My hands stilled. Bridget jabbed her fingers back into the soil as if she'd heard nothing.

'Bridget! What was that?'

'Foxes,' she said gruffly. 'Noisy beasts, always caterwauling. Didn't you hear them the other day?'

She was right in one respect; it was the same animal I'd heard in the barn, when Lucy had fallen ill. But I couldn't believe it was a fox during broad daylight.

'It's chilling! Doesn't it frighten you?'

'It'll take more than that to scare me,' she announced, defiant. I wondered why she raised her voice, whom she was trying to impress.

I shook another tuber free, removing its vine with a snap. Whatever the noise was, it had stopped now. I tossed my potato in the bucket, trying to remember what we'd been talking about before.

'You said your father was an apothecary? That's where you learnt about herbal medicine.'

'Yes.'

'Then tell me, Bridget, how is it you come to be at Felwood Lodge?'

She paused. Her hands were gloved up to the wrists with dirt. 'I was here before Rowena. Squatting. The place belonged to her mother's family, originally, but it had lain vacant for years. I never expected anyone to show up. Imagine my surprise when she arrived with a baby in tow!'

I thought Rowena's shock would be near equal. 'She agreed to let you stay, though?'

Bridget shrugged. 'I proved I could be useful to her. Now we're friends.'

I'd learned a little about my godmother today. I wanted to know more about Bridget too. 'But . . . why were you here in the first place?'

Her weathered face remained closed. Bridget wasn't about to reminisce at length like Rowena; her secrets were her own. 'I suppose my story is like yours. I ended up here because of a man. Another soldier.'

I smiled to myself. 'It was a masquerade ball. I do not believe the man at Vauxhall truly *was* a soldier—'

'Mine was. But it was a long time ago. Better left in the past.' Something in her brusqueness suggested that the wound was still raw.

'You never met Lucy's father, then?'

Suddenly, there came another wail, deep and steeped in melancholy. I craned my neck over my shoulder, searching the edge of the forest. 'That was *not* a fox!' I said. But there was no sign of any creature, vulpine or otherwise.

'Maybe it's deer rutting, then,' Bridget conceded. 'Nothing to concern you.'

It *did* concern me. The cry carried such human pain, like a soul in torment, like something I'd read of in a Gothic novel years ago. 'You're *sure* it's an animal?'

She set another potato down in the bucket, refusing to meet my eye. 'Of course. What else could it possibly be, you daft girl?'

I didn't want to say 'a ghost'. Even I realized that was pushing the bounds of possibility. But I continued to stare. Again I saw the rise of land that reminded me of the icehouse at Martingale Hall; we were closer to it on this side of the river. Such a strange, still place. A deadfall of moss and dry vines half-covered the door.

'Bridget, what is that little hillock?'

'Bless me, you're like an Inquisition! Never mind the root-cellar over there. We don't need it.' She gestured to our bucket. 'We'll eat all these before they start sprouting again; there's never much left over.'

So it was for storage. Could it be that a creature had stumbled inside and got trapped in there? Maybe it was hurt. 'Do you keep the door locked?'

'Always,' she said emphatically. 'Don't you go poking around there, young miss. The whole place is infested with vermin. Besides, it's old and the structure's weakening now. Near to collapse.'

I heard it again: a dirge, a lament. Foxes, my eye. 'We ought to check nothing has fallen in there and—'

'It hasn't,' Bridget snapped, dusting off her hands and climbing to her feet. 'And I don't even have the key to open it. The cellar is going to rack and ruin – let it alone.' Her eyes searched the treeline, where the robin had been. In his place were two crows. 'But something's afoot in the woods today. Mating, or a fight over territory, or young pilfered from a nest. It happens.' She turned back to me, frowned. 'Come on. We've got enough potatoes for dinner now.'

That night the wind lost its temper, weary of waiting for summer to perish. I lay awake on my hard bed, listening to it snarl around the corners of the lodge. Ivy crackled on the walls outside. Twigs tapped against the casement with skeletal fingers. Although I thrust my head beneath the pillow, the storm was only muffled, not muted.

How I missed Marie's movement beside me in the bed. I wanted her quiet breath, the comfortable sounds of servants snuffing out candles or locking up for the evening. But here there was only the voice of the gale to keep me company through the watches of the night. Something in its mournful note reminded me of digging with Bridget by the root-cellar. Restless animals in the woods and now a tempest. In one of my novels, today's events would herald trouble to come.

A book rested just beside my bed. Sleep was impossible amid this racket, but perhaps reading would tire my eyes. Emerging from underneath the pillow, I propped it against the headboard and sat up instead. It only took me a moment to light a candle. Air breathed through the gaps in the window frame, making it flutter. Ovid's words quivered ominously on the page beneath.

Frightened out of his wits, Lycaön fled to the country where all was quiet. He tried to speak, but his voice broke into an echoing howl. His ravening soul infected his jaws; his murderous longings were turned on the cattle; he still was possessed by blood lust.

Wood squealed and popped outside. Perhaps Ovid was a bad idea. It wasn't a night for tales of cursed kings, or gods disguised as animals. Much as I hated to admit that Lucy was right, this book would probably give me terrible dreams. There must be another; I remembered packing at least one volume of *Persuasion*.

Wriggling out of bed, I placed my feet on the rag-rug. The mattress creaked on its ropes, answered by a louder groan outside; something that sounded like the mast of a ship. As I rose, there came an almighty smash from behind. My candle expired in a blast of cold wind.

I jumped, falling forward painfully on to my luggage. I could see nothing through the darkness which throbbed with each heartbeat, hear nothing but the blood rushing in my ears.

'Godmother!' I cried.

At home, servants would have heard the bang and come running to help me by now. But even when my pulse slowed and sound returned, there was no answer. All lay quiet inside the lodge, a strange contrast to the windy chaos outdoors.

Air teased at the hem of my nightgown. Cautiously, one hand still holding the solidity of my trunk, I turned around to peer into the gloom.

Moonlight winked upon lizard scales and long, arachnid legs . . . No. That was my foolish imagination. These were twigs, ripping at the bedclothes. Twigs and glimmering fragments of glass. The bough of an oak had snapped and broken through my window, tearing the curtains to let the night in.

'Good God.' If I hadn't moved to get a new book, I might have been skewered. 'Godmother?' I called again.

Nothing. Carefully, I tottered towards the door, afraid I might step on broken glass. I just managed to squeeze out of my chamber before the wind snatched the door from my grasp and slammed it closed behind me.

A thicker darkness filled the hallway outside. Thudding along the corridor to Rowena and Bridget's room, I knocked for admittance. They might be angry with me for breaking the rules and leaving my room at night, but what else could I do? 'Godmother. It's Camille. I need your help.' No sound from within, no movement at all. 'Bridget?'

I worked the handle. The door creaked back on its hinges, showing a small room with the curtains still open and the trees swaying manically outside. A pair of shadowy twin beds sat either side of the window. They were flat and shapeless, the covers undisturbed.

I had too much pride to go crying to Lucy in the turret.

Blindly I groped my way towards the head of the staircase instead. Faint light flickered below; the kitchen door stood open. They must still be in there, lingering by the warmth of the fire. I headed down, the steps creaking like old bones.

'Godmother, I—'

My sentence hung suspended, for the kitchen was also deserted. What was more, it had been left in a mess. Vials and stoppered glass bottles were strewn upon the table, while the counters showed pestles and mortars scabbed with green. Herbs had fallen from the hanging bunches to crunch underfoot.

Yet no one had doused the fire. Flames turned pirouettes beneath the wind that barrelled down the chimney. All I could think was that Rowena and Bridget were in the turret ministering to Lucy; that would explain the signs of hastily prepared herbs. But Lucy had seemed well enough when I'd returned from the farm. She'd stopped staring at me like a lifeless doll.

Numb with shock, I pulled a stool close to the hearth and sat shivering in my thin nightgown. My fingers played with the bandage Rowena had insisted on tying around my scratched elbow. I might have come to far worse harm tonight. Imagine if I'd been asleep when that branch fell! Cuts on my face, or a twig driven into my eye. I could've been crushed to death and there was no one around to care. Where *were* Rowena and Bridget? They were breaking their own rule; they were out after dark.

The kitchen didn't have windows; the only way to watch the progress of the storm was through the flames. They twisted and spat, casting a hectic light over me. Although most of the kindling was wood from the forest, scraps of paper sizzled at the edge of the blaze. I made out the names of plants, written and now charring to ash. Were these failed ingredients for Bridget's medicines?

Just then there came a thump. A clunk. The branches gnashed and moaned. Suddenly, the front door flew open with a rush of cold air that made the fire swoop. I shrieked as it thudded back against the wall.

Rowena stood on the threshold with a lantern in hand, her steely hair falling loose, her shawl torn. She started at the sight of me, but said not a word.

'Godmother?'

Staggering inside, she subsided on to a stool. She looked like a feral woman who'd wandered in off the moors. Oversized gloves covered her hands, rising nearly to the elbow, rough suede gauntlets such as a falconer might use.

Bridget followed fast at her heels, in no better condition. A jagged rip ran up her skirt, a bruise flowered on her cheek – but I scarcely noted these details. My eyes were drawn to the cavalry sabre in her right hand.

'What are you doing down here?' she exclaimed as though *I* were the one acting peculiarly. 'Is it Lucy? Did she—'

'Lucy is fine!' I cried. 'What in heaven's name has happened to *you*?'

Bridget turned and shut the door. The sword trembled lightly in her grasp. It was a blade that might belong to a soldier, such as the one she'd mentioned earlier today.

'Were you attacked?' I pressed, thinking of the noises we'd heard in the woods. 'Did some kind of fox or badger set upon you?'

My godmother gathered her breath. 'No. Of course not. We were simply out walking when—'

'You were walking at *night*?'

'I often walk by night, Camille. I always have. Bad dreams plague me. I do not sleep well.'

'But you said I must never—'

She set the lantern aside with a clang, cutting me off. 'What brings *you* down to the kitchen? Why did you disobey me? Did you have a nightmare too?'

Her self-possessed manner sat at odds with her appearance.

I felt as if I must be seeing things, taking leave of my senses. 'No! It was the gale. A tree broke my window and sent glass everywhere . . .' I realized what she was doing, trying to evade the question by focusing on me. 'But that hardly matters now! What happened? Were you robbed?'

Slowly, Rowena removed her gloves. 'Nothing dramatic has occurred. We always take a weapon out with us at night, as a precaution. As for the bruises . . . I simply missed my footing in the dark and I fell.'

She was lying. I knew that she was lying, yet what could I possibly say? I raised my brows. 'And Bridget fell too?'

'Our arms were linked,' Bridget said, training her eyes on the floor as she passed us. She set aside her sword and picked up the kettle instead. 'I tumbled straight after Rowena.'

I sat in silence, utterly confounded. Did they think me a fool? No one in their right mind would go for a stroll in this weather, carrying a sword. It made no sense.

But Bridget was bustling around as usual, making tea. 'Chamomile and lavender for sleep,' she said with false cheer. 'We've all had nasty surprises tonight. A cup of this will settle us down.'

Flickering shadows played across Rowena's scars. They seemed to lengthen before my eyes. She was watching me, even as I watched her, each of us trying to read something hidden inside the other. But she was a deeper study than I. What did I have to conceal, aside from seeing Mr Randall in Deepbeck?

'Lucy did not wake when the window shattered?' she asked at last.

'How should I know? She didn't come out of the turret to help me, at any rate.' My grievances bubbled up, irrepressible. 'I knocked on your door, then I came down here. There was no one anywhere. I was so afraid! And where am I supposed to sleep? My room's covered in broken glass and the wind's blowing everything about . . .'

'Calm yourself, Camille, we are here now. You may use my bed tonight.' Rowena added, almost to herself, 'Sleep has gone to the devil for me.'

Bridget handed me a steaming mug. Scratches cross-hatched her knuckles. 'I expect I'll stay up late too; there's all this mess to clear before breakfast . . . You can have our room to yourself.'

I didn't want a room to myself. I wanted an explanation for their extraordinary antics. Why wouldn't they tell me what was going on?

'You should go up now, and take your drink with you,' Rowena suggested, kindly enough. 'You look pale. You've had quite a fright. Where's your candle? Never mind, I'll fetch another to light your way. You can enjoy your tea in bed.'

I might have appreciated her concern if it weren't a blatant attempt to get me out of the kitchen. But there was little use in arguing. I had no way of compelling them to tell me their secrets.

Rising stiffly, Rowena opened a cupboard and handed me a brand new candle, pristine in its whiteness. 'There are no more sticks, I'm afraid, you'll have to hold it at the bottom.'

I dipped the wick into the boisterous fire, snatching my hand back as the flames changed direction and made a grab for me. There was danger everywhere tonight.

Bridget held the door ajar and I shuffled out, managing to keep neither the tea nor the candle stable. I'd barely crossed the threshold when she said, 'Goodnight,' and shut me out.

'She's not stupid,' I heard her hiss. 'She knows there's something amiss.'

But Rowena made a hushing sound and I realized they were waiting to hear my feet on the stairs before they spoke. Any plan I had of eavesdropping outside the door evaporated.

Frustrated, I turned away. I'd only taken a few steps when a new sight arrested me; or rather, an old one. Nearly a repeat of the image I'd seen that very morning: Lucy sat on the middle of the stairs. This time, she wasn't clutching at the banisters. She pressed her index finger to her lips.

I knew she couldn't have slept through the crash against my window! But why hadn't she come to my aid? I frowned at her, demanding an answer with my expression, but she wasn't perturbed. She rose to her full height. The cap she wore by day had been removed and her thick hair drawn sternly back. A nightgown covered nearly every inch of her skin, the neck fastened just below her silver choker. Slowly, with deliberation, she stomped down the final stairs. They sang for her.

Still holding her finger to her lips, she stole noiselessly to my side. Her ruse had worked: Rowena thought the sound was me going up. I heard her exhale heavily behind the kitchen door. 'I know, I know, that was badly done. I ought to have prepared an excuse in case Camille awoke.'

'We should never have left her alone here . . . You'd better come up with another plan before the next time,' Bridget answered. 'She's an inquisitive chit. Did you think she'd just take everything we told her at face value?'

'No, of course not! I just didn't imagine we'd be making another visit so soon. It was quiet, before Camille arrived . . . I knew bringing her here was risky. But I thought we would manage.'

Lucy tilted her head, listening. In the low light her pupils were enormous, reflecting the candle flame. Only a breath parted us. A narrow strip of air charged with secrets we should not hear.

Bridget huffed. 'Well, I didn't expect *this* either. The danger period is growing longer. Each time, we lose a few days of safety.'

'But after tonight . . . that should keep everything at bay for a good while. There will be no further changes, will there?'

Bridget paused before responding. The tip of Lucy's tooth

appeared, worrying at the skin on her lower lip. Did the words make any sense to her, or was she as clueless as I?

'With such a large quantity, any alteration should be impossible. But there must be a tolerance, a resistance building. I'm pushing it as far as I dare.'

'And if you go further?'

'All my work could be lost. I don't suppose anyone would mourn, but . . .'

'But it would end our hopes for the future,' Rowena finished heavily. 'No more experiments. Lucy's fate would be sealed.'

Lucy's brows drew together. I couldn't read her expression, whether she was angry or afraid. We stood tête-à-tête, the candle wavering beneath our shallow breaths, but for once Lucy's focus was slack. She stared not at me but beyond, into the mystery her mother and Bridget were weaving.

'It was only ever a slim chance . . .' Bridget reasoned.

'A chance, nonetheless. We must keep trying for her.'

'I'm doing everything I can!'

Lucy hung her head. I felt the urge to reach out, to comfort her, though for what precisely I had no idea. But before I had the chance, she turned from me and slowly retraced her path up the stairs. There was no creaking this time. She was so graceful, so light of foot, that her feet made no sound.

CHAPTER SIX

I'd hoped that moment might serve as a connection with Lucy, something to finally break the ice that remained between us. I envisaged a day filled with gossip and speculation about what Rowena and Bridget were up to. But the next morning saw her withdrawn as usual. She sat on her milking stool behind one of the ewes, quiet and intent, her slender fingers curling and compressing the udders as if she were kneading bread.

Two sheep stood on the platform with their heads secured in halters. I was supposed to deal with the second. In all honesty I hadn't even known you *could* milk a sheep. At home, one of Papa's tenant farmers managed the cattle, the dairy and the cheese-making too. I had nothing to do with the process.

I moved reluctantly to the ewe's rear end, where the fleece was tangled with straw. 'Good girl, Queenie.'

'That's Duchess.' Without seeing her, I could tell Lucy was rolling her eyes.

I pushed the udders to gather milk, as Lucy had. The sheep bleated. 'Sorry.' It felt indecorous, even crude, to manhandle poor Duchess in this way. Her teat was unpleasantly hot to the touch. I managed to produce the merest trickle. She shifted on the platform.

'No,' said Lucy. 'Squeeze, don't tug. Make a circle with your index finger and thumb.'

'Like . . . this?'

Lucy exhaled and pushed back her stool. Striding over, she placed her warm hand upon mine and applied the correct amount of pressure. Milk hissed into the bucket. 'See?'

'Oh!' I looked up into her face, rewarded her with my friend-liest smile. 'Thank you.'

She cleared her throat and moved abruptly back to her own milking stool, as if she didn't want to be near me.

I watched in silence as she squirted rhythmic jets from her ewe – was *that* one Queenie? – and steam curled into the cool air. She made it look so simple. What I'd give to possess Lucy's dexterity, her clean, swift motions. It seemed cruel that this girl in particular should suffer from fits which took her control and poise away.

The hens squabbled softly in the background. Firetail, the rooster, came to inspect my work, or lack of it. I pushed him from the bucket. 'Shoo! There's nothing in there for you.'

'There's nothing much in there at all,' Lucy remarked.

I tried milking again, but I was fumbling as ever. Duchess bleated in protest.

'Just leave it. I'll milk Duchess when I'm finished here.'

'But what should I do instead?'

Lucy bit the inside of her cheek, as if resisting a very pert answer. 'You must be able to do something. What is it your governess taught you, in place of practical matters?'

Very little, in truth. I'd failed at dancing, singing, piano and needlework with equal aplomb. 'To be pleasant and make conversation?'

Again that little rictus of the face, holding something back. 'Try and amuse me while I work, then. Use those *conversational skills* and tell me about your family.'

'My family? Why?'

She kept her eyes on the milking. 'Because I don't have one. Not a family I'd own, anyway.'

I felt like a brute. Of course she was interested in my family, in how people lived away from this place. 'You have your mother,' I said, trying to cheer her. 'She was friends with my mama when they were both about our age. I expect she's told you that?'

'Oh, yes.' She cast her eyes to heaven. 'Mama never stops going on about how she played with *dear Susannah* as a child. But that's because she had no one else. There are no grandparents, no cousins, no connections on Mama's side at all. Even her guardian died before her marriage.'

I hadn't considered that. It hadn't struck me that, in fleeing from her father, Lucy had forfeited a relationship with other family members on that side – people who might be a good deal nicer than the baronet.

I moved my stool a little so I could face her. 'Well, my father's family come from France. I think that's the most interesting thing about them. They fled to England during the Revolution.'

'Why?'

Her question surprised me. Everyone knew about the bloodshed, the guillotine; in fact many of the stories circulating in England were far worse than what had actually happened. 'Because at first the changes in France were good. Needed. But sometimes changes can go . . . too far.'

Her eyes raised at this. 'That's very true. What happened in France?'

'After they killed the King, it all got very bloody. Papa said the true light of revolution went out and . . . people lost their way.'

Lucy muttered something under her breath that I didn't catch. Her bucket was full. She scraped back her stool, picked it up and moved around to Duchess. 'Haven't you anything nicer to tell me? Or is it all horrid novels and gory revolutions with you?'

'I can tell you about my siblings. I'm closest to my sister, Marie. She's very pretty, very accomplished.'

'Prettier than you?'

I glanced at Lucy. Her face was inscrutable, I couldn't tell if she was paying me a compliment or making a dig. 'Yes, much prettier than me. And she's good at doing things, as you are.'

'Can Marie milk a sheep?' Lucy asked, deadpan.

I smiled uncertainly – was this a jest or not? 'She can play the pianoforte.'

'I suppose that's something. Do you have any brothers too?'

'My older brother is called Pierre. He's a bit pompous. I like my baby brother better. Jean.' The memory of him made my eyes prick. There was no one for me to hug out here, no kindly touch, and I longed for Jean's wriggling warmth against my chest. 'He's only four months old. But if I'm here for a whole year . . . he won't even recognize me when I return!'

Lucy shifted slightly on her stool. 'I've . . . never seen a baby,' she admitted. 'Not out here. Only lambs and chicks. Tell me, are babies really everything that is pure and sweet and innocent?'

I thought of Jean's screaming fits when the wet-nurse was late to feed him. He could be a little tyrant at times. 'I don't know about that. But I suppose a baby is . . . unspoilt. Fully themselves.'

'I see.' She wetted her lips. 'Yes. That must be what makes them so attractive.'

'Oh, no.' I smiled. 'I know what makes them attractive. Their pudgy little arms and tiny feet! Jean has rolls of chubbiness on his legs. Folds and folds of soft skin. When he's freshly bathed, he smells so creamy and sweet, it's like warm milk with a touch of cinnamon—'

Lucy pushed back her stool with a sudden scrape. 'You'd better go outside.'

I frowned at her. 'What? Why?'

'The . . . the wind, last night.' Her voice sounded suddenly hoarse. 'There will be . . . leaves in the drinking trough. Go and clear them out.'

'But—'

'Please!' Lucy raised her hand to her choker and turned away. There came a short hiss, a drip of fat sizzling in a pan. Had she made that sound? I didn't think it had come from her mouth . . . 'Why are you still here?' she demanded, harsh.

'Very well.' I rose from my stool and left as she asked. What had I said to offend her? For a moment I'd thought she was interested in getting to know me and becoming friends.

Last night's gale seemed to have brought autumn to Felwood at last. All the foliage was dropping beneath its chill breath, making a funeral pyre on the forest floor. One of the rams watched me, his lower jaw rotating, as I picked my way across the paddock and towards the trough. Lucy was right: I found the animals' drinking water bobbing with vegetation; not only the oak leaves turning to mulch but acorn cups and the spiky carapaces of chestnuts. How was I to face the coming season in a bedroom without a fireplace? Without even a glazed window? The thought made me shiver, and maybe it was something else – a presentiment, a sixth sense, call it what you will – for I chose that precise moment to turn my head and gaze across the river to where the purple flowers blew. They looked sparser today, depleted by the wind, but it wasn't that which drew my notice; it was the hillock Bridget called a root-cellar. Large black birds gathered there. They perched along the crest, not squabbling or pecking for worms, just . . . sitting. Waiting.

Even as I watched, the door to the cellar opened, and the whole flock started up to join the dark clouds overhead. Instinctively, I ducked behind the trough. The ram opened his mouth, emitting a weird little cry. I didn't know whether it was a warning or a greeting, for the person who emerged was as familiar to the ram as she was to me. The very woman who told me she had no key to the cellar was using it now, to lock the door firmly behind her. Bridget.

*

All through the walk back, my mind was turning, staging conversations inside my head. In some of them I asked Rowena and Bridget calmly for the truth; in others, I demanded it. But even in my imagination I couldn't force their confidence. Just like the cellar, they were locked to me. In a book by Mrs Radcliffe there would be a skeleton hidden inside there, or else a portrait of a murdered relative. Maybe real life wasn't as interesting as all that – but if not, why had Bridget lied? None of it added up.

Lucy traipsed sullen at my side. She'd barely breathed a word. Even when she glanced in my direction, it was only at my moonstone necklace, never my face. Surely *she* must know what was going on? Some suspicion or other must have brought her downstairs last night.

'Lucy?' I started. 'May I ask you a question?' She made no response, just kept kicking up the leaves. I plunged on. 'Last night . . . do you know what my godmother and Bridget were whispering about in the kitchen?'

'Yes.' A downward note, closing the conversation.

The silence grew painful as I waited for her to elaborate. Distantly, a wood pigeon called.

'Well?' I demanded at last. 'What did it all mean? Bridget's "work" and "experiments", something about your future?'

She turned her head from me and trailed her fingers along the fronds of the bracken. The dew was still upon them. 'That's private.'

'Then why did you let me listen at the door with you?'

Lucy sighed and pulled off a leaf. 'Look, Camille . . . my mother is trying her best to make it safe for you to stay here. But the fact remains that it *isn't* safe. It never will be. She needs to send you home.'

Why did she keep saying that? The nearest I'd come to harm was a falling tree, and that could happen anywhere. 'I *can't* go home. Not until my sister is engaged, or I am.'

She swivelled round to me, owl-like. '*You?*'

I shrugged, trying to control my expression, to wipe the image of Mr Randall from my mind. I didn't know how much Rowena had told Lucy about Vauxhall and why I'd come to Felwood in the first place. 'Yes. My engagement to a respectable man would still the wagging tongues at home. But I'm unlikely to meet a beau wandering around the forest, am I?'

'You're too young,' Lucy said gruffly. 'Sixteen is no age to be tied down with housekeeping, accounts, and child-bearing. You'd be stifled in marriage.'

I was taken aback. She barely knew me, she was always finding fault, and yet she had this insight into my character. It was probably accurate. I couldn't picture myself organizing weekly menus or reprimanding servants. I'd lose the key to the tea-caddy for certain. But if I didn't marry, how would my life ever change? It was the only alteration I had to look forward to.

'I'd be no more stifled than you are here,' I pointed out. 'In fact, much less. At least I'd be allowed to leave the grounds of my husband's estate.'

Rusty trees parted, revealing the lodge at a distance, reduced to fairytale proportions. The weather-stained turret stood sentinel through the gusts of autumn wind. To me it was charming, the kind of picture to be hung in a gallery. Yet, as Lucy raised her chin to view her home, sadness crept into her expression.

'Everyone is relatively free, compared to me,' she said. 'That's no argument at all.'

We found Rowena waiting for us upstairs. She'd swept all the glass from my little chamber and stood with her hands on her hips, appraising the yawning window.

'How will we fix it?' I asked her. I doubted she'd bring a glazier into the house, even if she could afford one; the fiction of Mrs Talbot and her invalid sisters must be maintained.

'There is a carpenter in Deepbeck. You must ask him for some wooden planks and I'll use them to board this up.'

So now my room was to be dark as well as cold, with no treetop view. I pouted. 'But it's too late to set out for the village today. And tomorrow will be Sunday.'

'Yes. We must find somewhere warmer for you to sleep in the meantime.'

I expected she was about to suggest the parlour sofa, but I could still see the lodge as it had appeared at a distance, romantic and picturesque. I'd always longed to be Adeline in *The Romance of the Forest*, exploring castles and ruins. This was as close as I was likely to get. 'Can I sleep in the turret? Like the heroine of a novel?'

An expression of alarm crossed Lucy's face. 'No, don't be silly. *My* room is in the turret.'

'I know. But couldn't we share it, like sisters?' I felt hot, suddenly, too big. If I could only get her to accept me, to welcome my company, just the once . . . 'I sleep in the same bed as Marie at home,' I tried. 'My godmother shares a chamber with Bridget. It is not so unusual . . .'

Rowena expressed no opinion but bit at her fingernail, watching Lucy for an answer.

'No,' she said flatly.

It was no more than I expected; no great snub, in the grand scheme of things. But that one word fell with a weight that crushed me, like a daisy between the pages of a book.

CHAPTER SEVEN

When Bridget returned from the farm, she requested my help in the kitchen. She taught me to muddle herbs in the pestle and mortar: pressing, crushing, watching the juices run. Her tea might taste dire, but it smelt divine to make, wet and green like summer rain.

Bridget enjoyed playing the apothecary. She had all the paraphernalia: a miniature scale, a set of measures and a dosing spoon. While I made the everyday tea for us, she mixed Lucy's tisane as if it were a fine art. There was none of my reckless bashing; she'd sift and weigh the same ingredient repeatedly. Last of all, she added drops from a glass-stoppered bottle. The liquid inside was purple-blue.

'What goes into Lucy's medicine?' I asked.

Bridget concentrated on transferring the tea to its pot. 'Herbs,' she replied obtusely.

I clicked my tongue. 'I know that. *Which* herbs? Special ones?'

'Yes. That's why we use separate pots, separate spoons, separate cups for our teas. So there is no risk of contamination.'

Contamination seemed a strange word to use. 'Did you pick these special herbs?' I probed. 'Or do you perhaps store them . . . elsewhere?'

She took the bowl of fragrant mush that I'd ground up. Her face remained closed. 'What do you mean?'

'I thought maybe you'd made a trip today, on purpose to get these herbs.'

'What?' She stirred a pot over the fire. 'I haven't been anywhere.'

She was lying through her teeth. She *had* been down to that root-cellar. I'd get her to admit it.

'Oh,' I said with mock puzzlement. 'How very strange. Because I saw you by the vegetable patch this morning and then you seemed to . . . disappear, all of a sudden?'

She pressed her lips together, staring into the flames as if looking for an answer there. 'We're running low on water,' she said at random. 'I still haven't boiled the potatoes. Be a good girl and fetch me a bucketful, will you?'

So that was her tactic: avoidance. Sending me away. Scowling, I left the smoke and steam of the kitchen and set off towards the farm once more.

At that hour, the meadow was a haven of calm, blanketed by thin wisps of fog. No corvids hovered over the root-cellar. There were no cries, no sounds at all, save for a dunnock shuffling in the bushes and the constant murmur of the river. But I hadn't imagined what I'd seen earlier. There *were* fewer purple flowers growing in the physic garden, and some of the deadfall from the cellar door had been cleared aside, showing someone had entered recently. What had Bridget been doing down there?

I was tempted to go and examine it for myself. But the sun was starting to set, saturating the clouds with ochrous hues and stretching the shadow at my heels. Exploration would have to wait for another day, when there was enough light to see.

Chill water bit at my fingers as I filled the bucket. Carrying the load with both hands, I began to stagger back the way I'd come. Pain pulled along my shoulders, into my neck. A breeze rattled dry leaves upon the ground; they sounded like footsteps, following in my wake. If something really had been stalking me, it would have caught up easily. My progress was achingly slow. When I caught the roof of the turret jutting above the trees, I couldn't believe it was still so far away. Surely if I strayed from the beaten path the distance would be shorter? Instead of taking the track to the front door, I could go as the crow flew, through the thicket. It was worth a try. I shambled on, crashing and blundering through the bracken as I approached the house from the rear.

The bucket's handle wobbled in my grip; I felt my wrists beginning to weaken. For a moment, I set it down to stretch my arms and catch my breath.

These trees arching above must be the oaks that I saw from my bedroom window. I could hear a clicking, rhythmic and steady, flowing from the direction of the lodge itself. Hoisting up my bucket once more, I followed the beat. Verdure began to clear, and I saw the house was right there, with one of the casements on the ground floor propped wide open. The window to the parlour. The clack was the handloom, which Rowena and Lucy were using to weave their wool.

I dodged left, beneath the cover of the trees, not wanting them to see me struggling. But they weren't gazing out at the sunset. They were intent on their own heated conversation.

Suddenly, the loom fell still. Rowena's voice rose in its place. 'Do reconsider. It would be good for you.'

'*Good* for me!' Lucy returned hotly. 'To be tested, you mean?'

'Certainly. Only practice will help you gain control. That was one of the reasons I invited Camille here in the first place.'

Abandoning my bucket, I slunk through the oaks, closer to the open window and pressed myself flat behind a trunk to listen.

'And what if I fail? Is that a risk you're willing to take?'

'You won't fail. The moon is waning and we'll put precautions in place. I trust you,' Rowena said steadily. 'You are stronger than you think.'

'It's my strength that worries me. You don't understand what it's like. There's a reason the rest of the family succumbed. The battle is exhausting. It would be so much easier to embrace it . . .'

'Which you *never* will. But you heard what Bridget said. She can only do so much to help. Unless she has a breakthrough, the only option is to strengthen your will, as you would strengthen a muscle.'

Lucy made a reply that I couldn't hear.

'But what will your life be like, when Bridget and I have gone? You can never marry . . . You would be so alone. At least if you grew accustomed to Camille you could have a friend. Someone to correspond with, if nothing else.'

Lucy's volume rose then, in pique. 'Just because you're bosom pals with Susannah, that doesn't mean I will be friends with Camille!'

'Why not? What is wrong with Camille? She seems a sweet girl to me.'

A pause. I held my breath, straining for the answer.

'She smiles too much,' Lucy pronounced, and then the loom began again.

I was not smiling that evening, as I struggled to change into my nightdress. The temperature in my small room had plummeted. No candle would stay lit, with the breeze flowing through the broken window, and so I had to fumble half-blind. When at last I'd undressed, I stripped the bed of its musty linen. The prospect of sleeping on the sofa held no appeal. Even in my dreams, I'd hear Lucy's cruel words lingering around the parlour. Her refusal to accept me lodged as a splinter beneath the skin. I wasn't usually inclined to self-pity, but it really was going beyond the pale when even a housebound, friendless girl rejected you. Of all the people in the world, it felt as though only Mr Randall sought my company – and even he had fled twice.

With my pillow tucked under one arm and the sheets dragging behind me, I opened the door. Rowena was coming from the direction of the turret, carrying a candle. She smiled. 'I have good news, Camille. Lucy has just agreed to let you sleep in her room, until your window is fixed.'

I stared in surprise. Her smile faltered.

'Is that not what you requested? To stay in a turret room, like one of your favourite Gothic novels?'

'Yes. I'm just . . . astonished that Lucy has changed her mind, that's all. She seemed so . . . decided.' I could hardly say more without confessing to eavesdropping.

'Lucy can speak rashly at times,' Rowena said. 'She's set in her habits. Change can be a little frightening, to us all . . . But she has thought better of it. Come along, I'll take you up. I know you've been dying to see the turret.'

In bare feet, I followed her across the muttering floorboards to the door at the end of the hallway. It opened upon a case of spiral stairs, worn in the middle from countless treads up and down. Now that it came to it, I was apprehensive. What had Lucy meant earlier when she'd spoken of her strength and being tested? She'd definitely mentioned a risk . . .

Rowena began to climb, her candle playing over the rough walls, and I dragged my bedclothes in her wake. Everything smelt of old stone, like a church. The staircase terminated in another door, far sturdier than the one below, with iron hinges and a ring handle.

Rowena knocked once. Crockery clattered inside. 'Come,' Lucy said, and she sounded breathless, afraid.

The door creaked slowly open. My first confused impression was that I'd entered a mausoleum. Wrought-iron candle-holders rose from the floor, illuminating a circular room. The walls were painted black and the windows smothered in thick brocade curtains of the same colour. The drapes were so long that some of the fabric trailed in puddles; there was no hope that even a glimmer of moonlight would find its way in.

A tester bed loomed in the centre of the chamber. It must have been an antique, for the wooden posts were scratched and chipped almost to pieces. Little console tables sat either side of the pillows. The one closest to me bore a silver cross, just like an altar.

Curious. I'd expected tapestries and arrow-slits, stained glass and trapdoors. This was different, but pleasing in its own way. There was certainly more space than in my little closet.

Lucy perched upon the mattress, sipping at a cup of her dark tea. She spoke no word of welcome, but pointed. 'There. Close by the door.' Evidently that was where I was to set up my bed.

She went on drinking as Rowena and I spread my sheets out. This was a concession, I thought, something to appease her mother, not a change of heart towards me. Rather than sharing a room in the fashion of sisters, I'd be curled up at the foot of her bed like a dog.

'Mama,' Lucy said suddenly. 'She's not wearing her moon-stone.'

I glanced, puzzled, at Rowena. She jerked up from arranging my pillow. 'What did I tell you?' she barked. 'You must wear it *always.*'

'Even to sleep?'

'Yes! Go and fetch it right now.'

Apprehension followed me down the stairs and into my room. I pulled out the necklace from my hanging pockets. Lucy's protests were waltzing round my mind. *What if I fail? Is that a risk you're willing to take?* It wasn't clear to me what that risk actually was. Another seizure? While I had no medical knowledge, I was pretty certain a fit couldn't be controlled by sheer force of will. It was troubling to think Lucy believed every convulsion was some sort of failure on her part.

When I returned, Rowena was seated beside Lucy on the mattress, whispering. Only one word carried as I squirrelled into my makeshift bed beside the door: *smell*. Every inch of me tingled. Did Lucy think I smelt bad? I wiggled down further. Even with blankets, the stone paving was cold and hard beneath me. I was afraid I might cry. Why hadn't I stopped to consider that my Gothic heroines spent most of their nights in turrets awake with misery? But when I placed my head on the pillow and saw the ceiling above, the gnawing inside me stilled.

Stars. Little needle tips pressing through black satin. But no, the sky behind them was not plain black; there were subtle graduations of indigo and grey. Thin white lines joined the constellations into shapes: Orion the hunter, *Canis Major*, Cassiopeia's chair. With painstaking detail, someone had stood upon a ladder to draw a work of art and of beauty.

The paint gleamed bright. This was no heritage that came with the lodge; a recent occupant was responsible. Could it really be Lucy?

A cloud of fragrance thickened the air. Turning my head on the pillow, I saw that Lucy was also in bed, laid upon her back with her eyes squeezed shut. Rowena was pouring lavender water on to a handkerchief. Once she'd finished, she pocketed the bottle and spread the handkerchief over Lucy's face like a shroud. What with the candelabras, and the cross, it felt as though she was performing some kind of ritual, burying Lucy from all sight, scent and sound.

'I'll leave this door, and the one at the bottom of the turret, open,' Rowena said. She collected her own candlestick and began to puff out the other flames. The constellations winked from my sight. Her feet sounded upon the stone, and then she was crouching beside me. 'Camille, if you are even slightly alarmed, you must come straight down. You will find me awake, sitting outside my room.'

'Why would I be alarmed? Will my being here make Lucy ill?'

'No.' The light danced beneath her breath, making hollows of her cheeks. 'No, Lucy will be fine. I am sure of it. I would not leave you if I had any doubts.' Impulsively, she kissed me on the forehead. Before I could say a word, she was pattering down the stairs, leaving us to the darkness.

Well, I had asked for this. I'd no one to blame but myself.

Lucy breathed deeply, regular but hoarse, tide washing against shingle. Her presence seemed to press close, to take up all the space in the room.

'Lucy?' I whispered.

The breathing stopped.

'Lucy?' I tried again.

Her voice came thickly from behind the handkerchief. 'Can't you be quiet, even at night?'

'I can – I will – I just . . . I wanted to thank you, for letting me share your room. What made you change your mind?'

She sighed. 'Mama said it was your dream, to sleep in a tower like one of the silly heroines in your horrible books. It wouldn't be fair to deny you something you wanted that badly. Now don't make me regret it. Go to sleep.'

But the darkness made me bolder. Lucy wasn't so imposing without her piercing amber eyes and haughty expression. She was only a voice in the night, disembodied.

'What's *your* dream, Lucy?'

'I'm sorry?'

'What will you dream of tonight? There must be *something* you've always wanted to do, no matter how impossible.'

She made a noise in her throat. 'No one's asked me that before.'

'I'm asking you now.'

There was a pause. When she spoke, it was so softly that her words barely penetrated the handkerchief. 'I'd look at the stars.'

All those books on astronomy downstairs. I hadn't put the pieces together. Moonlight wounded Lucy, but, in shutting it out, she'd never have a chance to behold the majesty of the night sky. So she'd made one for herself, here. In a way the turret was her fantasy too.

'Stars are a good dream,' I said.

'Maybe. But my dreams don't matter. They can't come true. It's better not to have them in the first place.'

Such a melancholy thought to launch into the night. I wished I had the words to make her feel better, to take the cold sting out of this black space. But instead I said, 'Why don't you like me?'

She gave a splutter. 'I do – I mean I don't – I don't *dislike* you. I've no feeling towards you at all. None whatsoever.' I heard her turn over in bed. 'But I might change my mind if you don't hold your tongue. Please, let me go to sleep.'

'All right. I'm sorry. Goodnight.'

'Goodnight,' she said tightly.

But I didn't sleep. The hours passed and I lay, silent and unmoving, upon the chill stone. Somehow, I could sense Lucy still. She had not drifted off. Without seeing, I knew that her consciousness hovered, restless like mine. We were both wide awake in the dark.

CHAPTER EIGHT

The next day was Sunday. We sat at breakfast in the dining room, eating porridge. Light filtered through the oaks outside to dapple over the silverware spread upon the table before us. It would have been a pretty sight, if my eyelids weren't drooping shut of their own accord. I'd barely slept, and here there was no pot of bitter coffee to perk me up. I sipped instead at the herbal tea – maybe its sheer repulsiveness would keep me awake?

'You don't work at the farm on the Sabbath, do you?' I asked hopefully.

Lucy raised her eyes to heaven. 'Animals need to be fed every day.'

'Yes, of course I know that, but . . . don't you mainly rest? Don't you go to church?' Hope leapt as I imagined spotting Mr Randall across the pews and sharing a long, secret look, made all the more thrilling by the fact it would be improper.

Rowena dabbed her mouth with a napkin. 'Sadly not. We can't risk being seen in the local parish. But there is a small, rather derelict chapel some two miles' walk south – a remnant of the old Talbot estate. We've often used it. Shall I take you there today?'

Lucy's spoon clanged against her bowl. Bridget paused,

seemed to be swallowing something unpleasant down with her porridge.

I looked from one to the other, perplexed. 'Yes, I'd like that. If it's no trouble?'

'None at all. Perhaps we should all go.' Rowena watched Lucy, whose fingers were clenching around the stem of her spoon. The silver had tarnished there, turning it brassy and dull. 'What do you say?'

Lucy said absolutely nothing.

Bridget expelled her breath. 'I suppose it is high time we returned.'

'There is no obligation. If you don't feel ready—'

'*I* am perfectly prepared.' Bridget pushed back her chair from the table. Her small, dark eyes sought Lucy. 'It all depends on *her*.'

Lucy proceeded to stir her porridge, anticlockwise. Her pale lashes were swept down. There was a dimension to this conversation that was beyond me, a context I wished they would explain. 'I can stay here,' Lucy said at last. Her words were directed to the lumpy mess of porridge. 'It doesn't matter where I say my prayers.'

Something shifted inside my chest. Echoes of last night, the weight of Lucy's despondency pressing down upon us both in the darkness. She had no friends, no kindred, no hope of her wishes coming true. Rowena had told her she could never marry; she must always be alone. No one should be denied so much. Denied even church!

'No,' I said firmly. 'That's not right. A family goes to worship *together* on a Sunday. That is how it's done.'

Lucy stopped stirring. 'You wish for me to come?' she asked, her voice softened by surprise.

'Yes. I do.'

Lucy took a breath, lifted her spoon. 'Then I shall.'

Was she pleased? Cheered? It was so difficult to tell. Though she sat right by my side, Lucy seemed veiled from me; in some ways the handkerchief of last night was still covering her face. It reminded me of the servants who waited upon us at Martingale Hall. When we sat down to eat, they would draw into the corners, their gazes carefully averted, their expressions blank no matter what passed at table. They shared my life and yet they were unknown. Dolls of people, forced to play a part inside a world to which they did not truly belong.

Bridget continued to eye Lucy with suspicion. 'You must promise me—'

'I shall take responsibility for Lucy's behaviour today,' Rowena cut in. 'Trust me, Bridget. She will not leave my side.'

Lucy swallowed the last of her porridge and set the silver spoon down. The palm of her hand looked as though it had been scalded.

That morning, we found the Felwood pungent with decay. Our footsteps crunched over dropped conifer needles and empty chestnut shells. True to her promise, Rowena linked her arm through Lucy's and held her daughter tight to her side. I followed behind with Bridget. She was uncharacteristically pensive. Rather than telling me about the fungus or the berries as she usually did, she breathed not a word.

'What did you mean at breakfast?' I urged her. 'What was it that Lucy did last time you went to the chapel?'

She shook her head. 'I shan't speak of it. Things in the past are better left buried there.'

I sighed. It was easier to open an oyster than Bridget's shell.

At first we appeared to be following the route to the village, but, when the blackthorn hedges ended, we turned instead towards the fells. Our track rose steeply then petered out on to moorland. In place of the well-trodden dirt path, there stretched heath and bog moss. The palette was sombre: dull purple heather, bilberries, spiny gorse the shade of egg yolk. Beautiful, in a stern way, like Lucy herself.

As we crested a rise and began to descend, I saw the chapel waiting for us at the bottom of the slope, a tiny, rectangular building made of stone with a bellcote on top and a graveyard stretching behind. Remnants of an iron fence enclosed a wizened rowan tree and gravestones that jutted at odd angles. It was a far cry from the medieval churches of Stamford. I thought of my family, all gathered there without me, and that image stung more than the wind.

We descended, blown along, our feet trotting downhill faster than our bodies were ready to go. A flock of birds took wing and murmured overhead. Clearly, no one had been inside the chapel for some time, for a vine of ivy stretched over the thick wooden door.

Lucy twitched free of Rowena's hold and ran forward alone.

'Lucy . . .' Rowena warned.

She didn't listen. Falling on the door, she ripped the ivy away with an almighty crunch. It left small marks like stitches behind.

While Rowena searched for the key, Lucy leant her weight against the panels, eager to get inside. Once the lock clicked, she wrenched open the door and slipped through.

Bridget gave Rowena a dark look. 'Lucy is too excitable.'

'Perhaps you're making her nervous.'

All *I* could feel inside that dim, musty chapel was a sense of peace; the peace of the dead, perhaps. Mullion windows filtered weak light on to a pulpit. The altar bore a plain wooden cross – I expected it had been swapped for the silver one in Lucy's bedroom. Only half a dozen pews filled the space. Even in its golden age, the congregation could not have been a large one.

Lucy stopped near the altar, looking from left to right. Worry furrowed her pale brow. 'Someone's been here,' she announced.

I frowned. 'Really? That doesn't seem likely. You had to pull ivy off the door just to open it. And then there was the lock.'

Lucy shut her eyes, sniffed the air. 'I know that. It doesn't make any sense. But something is . . . wrong.'

Rowena paced down the aisle and lay a hand upon her daughter's shoulder. 'Be calm. What is it you detect?'

'There's a scent. I can't put my finger upon it. It's familiar, but . . .' She shook her head. 'It's like a face I once knew, but I've forgotten it since.'

Bridget heaved one of her disapproving sighs. 'Perhaps this was a mistake.'

Perhaps it was; maybe I'd been wrong to insist on Lucy accompanying us. This church smelt like every other in the world: wood, stone and dust. And did it really matter if a stranger had stumbled across the place in their travels? No harm had been done. Why was she so distressed?

'Sit down, Lucy,' Rowena soothed. 'I'm sure all is well. Let us have a moment of quiet reflection.'

'But, Mama—'

'I know. Whoever it was, they are long gone now.'

There was a creak as she made Lucy take a pew with her. Bridget and I sat the other side of the aisle. Whatever was going on between mother and daughter, we had no part in it. I gave up straining to hear their whispers and drank in the atmosphere of the chapel instead.

Cobwebs drifted up in the rafters. Below my feet, ledger stones proclaimed the names of Talbots long since departed. Everything was tranquil and still. I preferred this to an organ and preacher. At home, church was a place to see and be seen. My spiritual epiphanies happened outside its walls, for it was difficult to contemplate the meaning of life with the galleries chock-full of eager faces, Pierre fidgeting beside me and a couple of elderly gossips in the row behind, dissecting Mrs Granger's new hat.

Bridget gently scuffed the toe of her shoe over the ledger stone in front of us. 'This was Rowena's maternal aunt,' she whispered to me.

'Really?' I squinted to make out the name and dates carved

on the stone. Cassandra Talbot had died at just twenty years of age. So young. 'She fell from her horse here,' Bridget went on. 'Terribly sad. That was why the family never used this place again.'

I turned and reached in the back of the pew to see if there were any prayer books. I found only the tiny, dried shapes of dead moths. 'What do you do here?' I asked. 'Do you read the scriptures, do you sing hymns, or do you just pray quietly?'

Bridget nodded towards Rowena and Lucy. 'They can sing.'

My own voice was poor. Marie refused to perform duets with me; she said I sounded like a toad being trampled on. But I had a fancy to hear a melody; it felt an age since I'd had the chance to enjoy music.

'Godmother?' I called.

Rowena turned, harassed. 'Yes, Camille?'

'Bridget says you might sing us a hymn.'

A pause. 'Well, it is Lucy, really, who sings. I am but a sorry accompaniment. What do you say, my love? Will you sing Camille one of your Psalms? Would that put you at your ease?'

The lines seemed to smooth from Lucy's brow. The thought had steadied her somehow. She looked at me for a long moment, her eyes two dancing flames. 'If that's what you wish.' Then she faced the altar again, her hands upon her knees.

'By the time it's finished, you will have forgotten all about this intruder.'

Lucy squeezed her eyes shut. 'Perhaps.' She lifted her chin. Weak light dribbled through the window on to her upturned face. She inhaled deeply through her nose. Then she opened her lips wide.

The sound that poured out held me motionless. Such a voice as I had never heard before, at the opera or in any drawing room; a voice that shivered along the nerves and crept into the deepest recesses of my ear.

Rowena looked on, smiling sadly.

This was the other Lucy, the girl who talked kindly to the sheep. Her entire posture changed when she sang. Her neck extended, the hunched shoulders sloped away. How was it possible? No master could have trained her out here, but every note rang perfect through the dusty recess of the church. Her pitch was low, for a girl. It added a touch of wistfulness to her song, a longing that couldn't be put into words.

Bridget shuffled beside me. I hardly dared to move in case I broke the spell. Many young ladies in society were praised as having the voice of an angel, but this was the genuine article. Enchanting. Bewitching.

Why did she never sing at home? A talent like this ought to be encouraged. Whichever angle I considered Lucy from, there seemed to be a restraint, a tie or gag upon her, holding her back from what she could be. It wasn't fair. At that moment, more than anything, I yearned to see her turn her face to the sun and bloom.

But when Lucy fell silent, her divine spark dwindled. The hush no longer held the comforting quality of before. I felt cold and bereft.

'Can you sing another?' I pleaded.

She opened dull eyes and stared fixedly ahead at the window overlooking the graves.

Disappointment soured my mouth. This was the way she'd looked at me on the stairs, when I'd scratched my arm: as if she'd left her body behind and travelled miles away. I wanted her back.

'Lucy? What is it, child?' Rowena asked.

A light gust of wind. Ivy tapped against the back wall of the chapel. Lucy shuddered as though she were one of the leaves.

'Are you ill?'

'No,' she said mechanically. She ran her tongue over her lips. 'No . . . But someone *has* been here. Searching. It all feels . . . it all smells . . .'

Suddenly she convulsed. I started to my feet.

'She's going to take a turn!' Bridget warned.

Lucy drove her fingernails into the wooden seat to steady herself. Rowena felt the temperature of her forehead. 'Lucy! Lucy, stay with me.'

'We should leave.' Bridget rose beside me and seized my arm. 'I'll take Camille outside.'

Had she been expecting this – was it what happened last time they'd come to the chapel? Ashamed, I let Bridget pull me away. I should never have insisted on bringing Lucy. I'd only caused more trouble.

Yet I was glad that I'd heard her sing.

The sky outside hung malignant and heavy with clouds. One last glance over my shoulder showed Rowena, removing her moonstone necklace and pressing it into Lucy's palm. Then Bridget pulled the chapel door shut. 'We'll wait in the graveyard.'

'But will Lucy recover? Was she taken ill like this when you came before?'

'Not like this. That was . . . different. She was here alone.' Bridget shook her head. 'We gave her too much freedom. The sad fact is, that girl doesn't belong anywhere near a church.'

There was something uncharitable in the way Bridget spoke of her, a meanness of spirit I'd never expect from a woman who'd watched her reared.

'Why would you say that? *Everyone* should be welcome at church.'

Bridget scoffed, seemed on the point of saying something more. But then she drew back. 'Never mind. I spoke rashly. I'm out of temper, don't listen to me.'

Slipping away from her and down the side of the chapel, I entered the silent graveyard alone. The whole place was hopelessly overgrown. Wood sorrel stretched unchecked over the burial mounds. Each memorial stone bore a fuzz of lichen: some green, some yellow, some black. What strange angles they slanted at, like crooked teeth in a beggar's mouth. No doubt changes in the soil had pushed them askew, but it looked to me as though the dead were trying to climb from their graves.

Bridget's footsteps sounded close behind. 'Is there anything there? A moorland pony broken through the fence?'

'No. I don't know what disturbed Lucy so much.' I strode on. At that moment, the wind changed direction and suddenly I tasted what she had smelt: old earth, disturbed.

Strange. Stopping, I scanned the graveyard for something that could cause a stink, but I was at a loss. There were only piles of russet leaves, bird droppings, dirt . . . a lot of dirt, in fact. A whole mound of it sat over by the rowan tree.

Cautiously I stepped closer. A cavity gaped by the roots. Could it be a rabbit burrow there, a badger den? That might explain the animal pungency . . . I paced slowly forward, the stench building with every step, until my boot knocked against something hard that rolled alongside me. I glanced down and nearly lost my footing.

There on the ground was a tiny skull, picked clean of flesh. No one could mistake the shape. Miniature, but undoubtedly human.

Bridget cried out behind me.

I couldn't turn to her; I couldn't look away. I stared into the small eye sockets, willing the picture to change. It didn't. The disturbing details only became clearer. A crack across the cranium. Other fragile, barely formed bones scattered among the wilted leaves. Some were snapped jaggedly in half; others bore tooth marks.

Bile rose in my throat. The poor baby's grave hadn't just been exhumed; it had been rifled through, like a wardrobe the night before a ball.

CHAPTER NINE

'Miss Camille's fever has reached its crisis. This is exactly as I planned. Now we will cool her off.'

I wish they would. I am hot, so hot, with a thirst I cannot slake. The physician, Mr Leiston, places a palm on the top of my head. 'We will cut her hair. All of this must go.'

There's a gasp of horror from Marie. It would break my sister's heart to lose her own prized mahogany locks. 'Must we?'

Mr Leiston nods gravely. Part of me expects he's enjoying the chance to punish me for his failures. 'See how thick it has grown?' He pulls at a lock. 'It will only serve to inflame her mind and cause hysteria.'

'And the bezoar stones have done nothing for her?' Mama interjects. Her hands worry at an embroidered handkerchief, unpicking the stitches one by one.

'No. Quite frankly, madam, if this were rabies I would expect your daughter to be dead by now. Mark my words, this malady is something else.'

In this, at least, we are agreed.

The physician and his assistant manhandle me from the bed.

Propping me in a chair, they bind my wrists to the arms with ribbons so I can't break free.

'Stop! You're frightening her. Step aside, sir. *I'll* cut her hair, if it must be done.'

A mouthwatering scent wafts towards me as Marie approaches. She must have been in the nursery playing with baby Jean, because I can smell him. Plump arms and legs. Folds of chubby flesh. Such tender, tender meat.

No. I will *not* think like this. I shake myself violently and everyone takes a step back.

'It is too dangerous for you, Miss Garnier,' the physician rules. 'See how your sister flings herself about? And as for the mattress, look: she has clawed it almost to pieces.'

'She's just in pain,' Marie pleads. 'Let me crop her hair tidily. I don't want her looking like a . . .' She doesn't have a word to finish the sentence, but Mama nods her agreement. They are trying so hard to keep a part of me alive.

While Marie fetches the scissors, the physician orders Mama to douse the fire and crack open the window. Air feels blissful. Hundreds of tastes and nuances are carried on a single breath of wind.

'Is that better?' she asks me. 'Are you more comfortable?'

'Moonstone,' I gasp. I sound like Pierre the summer his voice broke.

Mama leans closer. 'What's that? Do you want your necklace?' She retrieves the moonstone from its place beside my bed and drops it into my lap. 'There. It is just like the heirloom Rowena used to wear when we danced at balls together, her mother's moonstone . . .' She frowns and shakes her head, unable to comprehend. 'Did Rowena give that to you? The girl I knew would never let you come to harm. If you would only explain why she sent you away!'

I wish I could. I'm fluent in two tongues, but no one has taught me the language for matters like these.

A blue sheen winks up from my lap and steadies my breath. 'Moonstone restores . . . tranquillity,' I say haltingly, parroting Rowena's words, 'to a soul in . . . turmoil.'

The physician titters. 'I have told you, madam, your daughter won't be lucid until the fever leaves her. Only nonsense will pass through her lips.'

I can't see how my reliance on a gem is any different from him trying to treat rabies with bezoar stones, but I don't have the energy to argue. The truth is, I don't know if what helped Lucy will help me. My illness isn't taking the same path as hers; I was not born with it. My body fights against the infection in its bloodstream. I can almost feel the contagion spreading, pushing organs aside, making way for itself. My very essence is altering.

Marie returns with two pairs of scissors, one large and one small. She moves stiffly to stand behind my chair. 'I don't like doing this,' she reasserts, lifting a tress off my shoulder. Again, that tantalising scent sweeps across me. I grit my teeth, keep focused on the necklace, but a thread of drool escapes from my mouth. 'It reminds me of those frightful stories Grandpère used to tell us. Were you aware, Mr Leiston, that women had their locks cut short like this to bare their necks for the guillotine?'

Bitterly, I remember what I told Lucy about the French Revolution. *Changes can go too far.*

'There is no need to be dramatic, Marie,' Mama sighs. 'The task must be performed for your sister's health. If you cannot do it, I shall.'

'No, no, I'm quite capable.'

There's a harsh, rasping sound. Hanks of matted hair drop. Most fall to the floor, although some land on my lap, my shoulders, even plunge down the back of my nightgown. There's so much of it. I feel monstrous, coated in a pelt of fur. Marie steps forward, smaller scissors in hand now. 'I can make it prettier,' she promises. 'Just . . . just hold still a little longer, Camille.' The blades flutter, metallic flies around my head. 'That's right,'

Marie coos. 'Sit nice and still. It's looking better already. I'm going to touch the side of your face. Don't jump. Let me . . .' She tucks a strand of hair behind my ear. Stops.

It's so quiet you could hear a pin drop.

'Whatever is the matter?' Mama asks.

Marie lets out a dry sob. The scissors crash to the floor. 'Oh, Mama, her *ear*!'

'Her ear? Do not tell me you have cut her ear by accident—'

Forgetting the ties around my wrists, I lift a hand. The restraint snaps as though it were nothing but straw. I touch the skin on my earlobe, which feels more or less the same, but at the top . . . This must be what upset Marie. At the top there is a definite point.

Mama draws in her breath. 'Good God. Look at that! We ought to send for a specialist.' She sounds dull, in shock. 'Mr Leiston, you will accompany us to London. We will find someone who – who—'

'I have this under control!' the physician shouts, actually forgetting his station and bellowing at a gentlewoman. His fear is consuming him faster than the illness is taking me. 'I know what I am doing!'

'With respect, sir, you clearly do not. My daughter's life is at stake. I will not have you toy with it.'

Marie weeps fit to break her heart. 'Please, Mama. Don't let her die like the babies. Don't let Camille die too!'

I wish I could tell her that death isn't what I fear. I would rather join my little siblings than hurt one like them. If my terror had an image, it would be that of the tiny skeleton unearthed in the chapel graveyard.

I didn't realize, back then – how could I? – that wickedness seeks to devour the light. Whatever is true, whatever is pure, whatever is lovely, tastes delicious in the jaws of evil before it's destroyed.

*

When we returned to Felwood Lodge, Bridget and Rowena banished us girls to the parlour while they argued in the kitchen. Lucy sat next to me on the velvet sofa. She flung her cap aside and burrowed both hands into her thick hair, covering her face.

I had no spirits to comfort her. Whatever dug up those bones had exhumed my past too, all of the sad times I endeavoured to forget. Gabriel and Emilie. I'd never considered how small their remains must be; I'd liked to imagine them both as I'd last seen them, resting peacefully on white satin. But now I knew the reality was much harsher. My little siblings were dust and bone.

'I don't understand,' I said numbly. 'What do you think did it? An animal? One of those . . . foxes we hear?'

'A fox might burrow to get at dead meat,' Lucy said from behind her fingers. 'But it wouldn't seek out old bones.'

I shuddered. 'What animal would? Dogs like to chew on bones, don't they? But again . . . it would be a strange type of dog to prefer musty old graveyard bones to fresh ones.'

Lucy didn't answer. Maybe there *was* no answer.

'Could you really *smell* that something was wrong, even when we were inside the chapel?'

She exhaled. 'Yes. My sense of smell is painfully keen. The stench of death in particular is . . . rich. Complicated.'

My stomach turned, remembering. Lurid details were all very well in a story, but in real-life tragedy there was no thrill, only this nauseous weight.

Lucy tugged at the roots of her hair. She'd been ill at church. I should probably let her alone and sit in silence for a while. But I couldn't. To do so felt like putting a lid upon a boiling pot. My thoughts wouldn't be contained; they must burst free.

'There was no headstone nearby. Isn't that strange? I suppose some local woman – a poor, grieving mother – must have placed the infant in the ground herself?'

Mama had told me about the unmarked graves in the church-yard back at home; how some people were so desperate to see their loved ones interred on hallowed ground that they snuck in and buried them secretly by night. Mostly they were babies who had died before they could be baptised, but some were suicides. There was still a custom in parts of the country that required people who committed suicide to be entombed at the crossroads with a stake through their heart. I understood why their family would prefer a secret, unmarked grave to that fate.

'That's exactly what happened.' Lucy swallowed. The silver choker bobbed on her throat. 'A grieving mother . . . The remains you found were of Bridget's child.'

Shock knocked the breath from me. Bridget's *child*? But it all made a terrible kind of sense. She'd spoken of a soldier, of squatting alone here. The man she'd loved must have gone off to war, leaving her pregnant and unmarried, disgraced.

'Good God. Did she tell you that herself?'

Lucy sniffed. 'She ought to have done. She told my mother about the stillbirth sixteen years ago, when we first arrived. But no one mentioned it to me.'

'Then how do you know?'

Lucy leant back on the sofa suddenly, casting her hands down. The eyes she'd been hiding were bloodshot and tortured. 'Haven't you been listening to that racket in the kitchen? Don't you hear what they're saying?'

I shook my head. I hadn't been able to make out the words.

'Bridget thinks that I did it. That I dug up her son.'

I stared at her. She returned my gaze steadily.

'Why would she suspect you of defiling a grave?'

There was no defiance now, only pain; a pain that could be hidden no longer. 'Because I did it once before.'

The room seemed to tilt around me as everything slid into place. This tension between the two of them. Bridget's fury at Lucy's digging. The claim that she shouldn't be at church.

Lucy dropped her eyes to her lap. Her fingers played a nameless melody upon her knees. Again I saw how short her nails were, bitten ragged. 'Go on, then. Scream. Call me wicked. Run home to your mother.'

I was tempted to. But the girl sitting beside me didn't look like a lunatic who disturbed the dead. She resembled the porcelain doll of my childhood, the toy I'd nearly snapped in half by mistake. These days it slumped on a shelf in the room I shared with Marie, lop-sided and hopeless.

'Tell me why you did it.'

Her fingers stopped. 'It wasn't . . . intentional,' she admitted. 'I didn't know it was a grave. There were no markers, you said so yourself.'

'But what were you digging for?'

She shook her head. 'Why does it matter?'

'Because I want to know.' I indicated the bookshelf. 'You have all that literature on fossils and ruins. Is that what you were doing? Were you excavating?'

Her cheeks turned beetroot. 'They . . . interest me,' she said haltingly. 'Things buried in the earth. They always have. All that we've forgotten or hidden away.'

'Have you ever found anything?'

'Yes.' Her fingers worried at her skirts. 'I've found arrowheads, from hunters long ago. Pottery.' After a long pause, she added, 'Did . . . did you ever read that pamphlet on the ichthyosaurus?'

I'd glanced over it. A skeleton unearthed from the cliffs of Lyme Regis that pre-dated time as we knew it. There'd been an illustration of a gigantic creature with a beaked nose, sharp teeth and a large, staring eye. 'Yes. An awesome find. Quite fascinating.'

The tip of her tongue appeared through her lips. 'It was . . . strange,' she said. 'Monstrous. The kind of creature no one expected to uncover. Something that should only exist inside a myth.'

I frowned, wondering where this was leading. 'Yes, I suppose it was.'

'I thought that if I could find something like an ichthyo-saurus . . .' Lucy swallowed.

'That you'd make your fortune? I'm sure you would.'

'No, not that. I thought that I'd feel . . .' She struggled, seemed to be fighting with her words.

'Feel how, Lucy?' I asked gently.

'I'd feel less . . . less . . .'

'Less what?'

'Alone.'

The word dropped like a pebble into a lake. There was a moment of silence and recognition as the ripples fanned out to reach me. Lucy felt alone and monstrous. Who could understand that better than I?

My lips parted. I wanted so badly to tell her. To confess that my cheerful manner hid the hurt of being judged by those closest to me; that I too knew what it was to be branded by one heedless action you could never take back. She was not on her own. But, before I could speak, Lucy surged to her feet and crossed the parlour with quick steps, knocking the spinning wheel in her haste to flee.

She was the loneliest person I'd ever seen, and yet, there seemed to be a darkling voice telling her that it was better this way.

CHAPTER TEN

The handcart trundled along behind me, its wheels sliding through the mud like a knife across butter. Monday was at least dry for a walk and not as cold as it had been of late. A fast-moving breeze pushed clouds across the sun, ricocheting light and shadow over the fells. I wished Marie could see it. The heath and blasted trees were equal to any of Mr Gilpin's paintings, which she so admired. But I didn't have my sister, or any companion at all. Still overcome with grief, Bridget had refused to leave her room, so the task of walking into Deepbeck for wooden planks was mine alone.

I was glad of an excuse to quit the house. The pinched faces and bruised silences of my companions had been making me feel morbid too. But now I trotted forward, buoyed by a taste of freedom.

Two ducks and a drake swam under the arches of the stone bridge as I clattered into the village. I watched them until they were out of sight, then my eyes roved about the square for Mr Randall. The sight of his dark, tousled head would be a tonic for my spirits. All I saw were servants and farmers' wives chatting around the well.

Fewer people glanced at me today. Even those that did

appeared distracted, as though I were nothing more than a mild curiosity to them, in my bonnet with its spray of flowers. The well was in constant use, the bucket clattering up and down on its rope. I caught the words of a bearded man who worked it. 'Six head o' cattle, they told me. Torn every which way.'

The bone-thin woman next to him tittered and shook her head.

Clearly, there was no tantalising gossip to overhear in Deepbeck.

I had letters to send home, but I didn't want to face the insufferable postmistress straight away. Nor was I eager to weigh down the handcart with planks for my broken window quite yet. I looked up the steep hill towards the church. There came the sound of hammering and a dog barking in the distance. I'd explore what Deepbeck had to offer first; it might be my only chance to wander alone, at liberty.

As I toiled up the long, sloping street, an aroma reached out to lure me on: something sweet that made my mouth water. Burnt sugar. I was sure of it. My legs found a new burst of energy. The change in my diet was one aspect of Felwood Lodge to which I wasn't growing accustomed at all – I dreamt of whipped syllabub at night – but here, perhaps, I'd find some real food.

There. A bow window jutted into the street, exhibiting iced cakes upon a stand. I'd never hoped to find a confectioner in a small Yorkshire village, yet here it was, advertising peppermints and bergamot chips. Leaving the handcart, I hurried inside.

The man at the counter was already occupied with a customer. Others loitered over the array of jellied fruit winking from silver trays, or the liquorice sticks crammed into jars. Jewel-like colours enticed me from every side, but I'd have to wait my turn. It seemed that the people of Deepbeck, like me, had a sweet tooth.

Some of the customers were dressed plainly as maids. Their mistresses must have sent them out for violet pastilles. As I considered the various merits of chocolate nonpareils over lemon drops, I listened to their chatter.

'My master's set a watch by night. He can't afford to lose any livestock.'

'I heard a lad two farms over took a shot at it. From a distance, mind, he didn't get a good look, but he said it were a great hulking thing, bigger than a mastiff.'

'How did the daft 'ap'orth manage to miss it, then?'

They shared a strained laugh and then I heard no more, for another dog began to yap outside, and the confectioner was dusting off sugar-powdered hands, calling the next customer forward.

I'd not come to a decision, so I ordered both the nonpareils and the drops, along with a slab of marchpane besides. It was as well to stock up. There wasn't so much as a loaf of sugar or a pot of honey in the kitchen at Felwood Lodge. I found myself wondering if sweet food had ever passed Lucy's lips. Did she actually know what chocolate *was*? I paused, my gaze hovering over the display. A row of candied apples glinted back, their translucent coating a warm gold. Like looking into Lucy's eyes.

'And a quarter of toffee,' I decided suddenly. 'For a friend.'

The confectioner raised his brows at my largesse but was happy enough to take my money.

When I regained the street, the dog was still barking. It was a rough-coated black and tan terrier, straining at his leash, much to the embarrassment of his master.

'Stop it! Hold your whisht, Blighter!'

Diverted, I followed the dog's line of sight, expecting to see a cat or the butcher's boy. But he was barking at a man. A man staring straight at me with an intensity that took my breath away.

Mr Randall reached up to remove his cap. In the cold sunlight, his hair was blue-black like the plumage of a crow. He inclined his head, never breaking eye contact for a moment. 'Miss Garnier.'

I had to gather myself. I wanted to seem poised and in control, not a girl who'd been looking desperately for a glimpse of him. I swallowed, raised what I hoped was a flirtatious half-smile. 'So *there* you are, Mr Randall. I had begun to think I'd imagined you after all. Why ever did you run away before?'

He turned his cap in his hands. 'I apologize for that, I didn't wish to involve you in further trouble. I thought you might be scolded by your companion for talking to young men.' He gestured to an alleyway between the shops, dark and dank. 'May we speak for a moment, without this incessant barking?'

I choked back an instant agreement. It wasn't appropriate; I mustn't give him the impression I was loose. 'Perhaps . . . not there? My good name has been compromised enough.'

There was a hint of self-deprecation in his crooked smile. 'How thoughtless of me. Will you sit awhile instead? There's a wall that runs around the forge, in plain view, where nothing can be misconstrued.'

He returned the cap to his head, offered me his elbow. Trembling, I took it. Every inch of my skin was fizzing like champagne. The dog refused to be quieted; its master was forced to pick it up and carry it away.

Mr Randall led me over to a brick building, hunched low to the ground, which was spewing acrid smoke. This then, was the forge, and the place where the sound of hammering originated. With easy grace, Mr Randall detached himself from me and perched upon the wall in front. I didn't climb up beside him, just rested one hand upon the uneven bricks. I had to remind myself to keep breathing. Had he somehow grown *more* handsome since I'd last seen him?

He cast about for a moment, looking up and down the hill. 'Where is the lady who accompanied you before?'

'She is at home, sir.'

'You don't mean to tell me that you've walked to Deepbeck quite alone?'

I could concentrate on nothing, nothing at all, save the space where my hand rested on the wall, close beside his leg. Even through the smoke, I could smell his sandalwood cologne. 'The distance is not so far—'

'It is utter madness, with this rabid beast roving around!'

I stared at him, recalling now the strange snippets of conversation I'd heard. 'Rabid beast?'

'Why, yes. Can it be that you haven't heard? The whole village is abuzz with the news.'

I shook my head.

'There is a mad dog, or some other creature, scouring the countryside and slaughtering the livestock. No wonder that little terrier was so distraught just now. Animals can always sense these things.' Swiftly he caught my wrist, held my hand upon the wall. There was electricity in his touch. 'I must entreat you, Miss Garnier, to take the utmost care of yourself. Who knows where the monster will strike next?'

His story explained so much. The beast must have been to the chapel and dug up Bridget's son. It could even be making the eerie calls that I'd heard by the root-cellar! That was a little too close to home for comfort. I shuddered.

'I had no idea! Is it really dangerous for me to be alone? I still have to go to the post office, and then to the carpenter, before I walk all the way home . . .'

'My dear madam, you can't imagine I'd let you out of my sight at such a time? Of course I shall accompany you on your errands.'

My heart throbbed. 'I'd appreciate your protection, if it's not too much trouble.'

'Trouble?' he repeated, leaping off the wall. A cloud of black smoke plumed from the forge behind him. 'This doesn't even rate as an inconvenience. I already told you, I've travelled over a hundred miles just for the sight of your face.'

'To what end?' Blushing, I glanced down, afraid I'd sounded

too blunt. 'I am very glad to see you. But what, exactly, do you hope to achieve by being here in Deepbeck?'

Gently, respectfully, he laced my arm back within his own. 'Why, to court you, of course. It's been my secret intention ever since we first met. I was too shy to speak of my feelings back then, and you were so young ... I always meant to visit Martingale Hall again, when you were a little older, and pay my addresses formally. After the quarrel with Pierre, I told myself it was not meant to be, but then fate brought us together again at Vauxhall. It was a sign. Destiny. So here I am. Hoping for the opportunity to converse with you frequently, hoping for a chance to win your heart.'

He pulled me forward and we began to walk; I knew not where. I hardly cared. A foolish smile spread across my cheeks. This was exactly what I'd hoped. He'd noticed me all along. Even though he'd been too well-bred to let a sign of it slip, he'd felt the same longing as me when we first met at Martingale Hall. I peeped up at him coquettishly. 'And on the slim chance that you are successful in your suit, Mr Randall?' I teased.

'Should such happiness befall me, I would write to your father at once.' His eyes sought mine. 'Between us, I'm certain we could persuade him to overlook Pierre's objections to our union.'

This gave a check to my glee. I'd let my feelings run away with me at Vauxhall and it hadn't turned out well. Little as I valued Pierre's judgement, I ought to know what his grievances were. 'Excuse me,' I said, a little hesitant, 'but ... you haven't explained quite how the disagreement between you and my brother originated. For all I know, he might be *right* to object.'

'Ah.' Mr Randall's shoulders sagged and he frowned at the cobbled pavement under our feet. 'Yes, you've caught me there, Miss Garnier. I don't dispute Pierre's right to hate me. I used him badly. But there was no harm intended! I hardly think a few boisterous pranks at Oxford should leave an indelible stain upon my character ...'

'What manner of pranks?'

'They were never played at his expense,' Mr Randall stressed. 'But your brother, you know, is not swift upon his feet. A whole group of us planned the larks: letting a horse loose in the dining hall, smuggling a dog into the dormitories, forging love letters to the master's daughter . . . But Pierre always seemed to be the fellow who copped the blame.'

He was right: Pierre wasn't quick. Though seldom clumsy like me, my brother was rather ponderous, bound to lag behind his companions.

'And *this* is all he holds against you?'

'No,' Mr Randall said slowly. 'Matters rather came to a head over a horse. And here I must admit to being dishonest. My mare Shadow was a sure thing, bound to beat any other in the student races, but only I and your brother knew how fast she really was.' He wet his lips. 'I hatched a plan to hold her back on purpose for the first few races, thereby raising the stakes against her. When they were high enough, we'd both gamble a large sum, and of course she would win, making us rich.'

'So you were fixing the betting odds? You cheated?'

'I did,' he admitted, shamefaced. 'And not that it excuses me, but your brother was ready to cheat too. Only he mistook the race where Shadow was to triumph. Evidently there was some miscommunication between us and . . . he lost a good deal of money.'

'Oh.' This was more serious. I remembered, now, Pierre selling some of his favourite dogs, and wondered if he'd done it to repay debts.

'I tried to apologize, but you know his temper. He attacked me, physically, and was sent down that term for fighting.' Mr Randall turned to me, his expression more curious than repentant. 'It hardly seems fair, does it? Your brother only had to rusticate at home for a while when he gave me a black eye, yet you've been sent all the way here for . . . what? A stolen kiss? And for how long do they mean to banish you?'

'A whole year!' I was gratified to hear his little puff of disapproval. Mr Randall understood; the punishment wasn't proportionate to the crime. Had I been a boy, my misdemeanours would be dismissed as high spirits. 'Or until my sister Marie is safely engaged to her long-term admirer. Do you remember Marie?'

His brow wrinkled as he considered. 'Oh, yes. I took her out riding when I stayed at Martingale Hall, didn't I? I'd forgotten her name . . . I remember that lovely dapple-grey pony, though.'

My jealous heart crowed for joy. He'd stayed in our house with Marie for a whole week and he only recalled her horse! Neither her charms nor her accomplishments had made a conquest. They didn't seem likely to secure her a better match in the future, either. What was drab Adam Ibbotson, after all, beside such a fine young man as Mr Randall? The girls we went to school with would envy me, not her.

'And you give me your word that this courtship is not just another elaborate prank designed to irk Pierre?'

'Good God!' he cried. 'Of course not. In fact, I'm putting aside a small sum each quarter to try and make amends for what your brother lost. I may be a rogue but I am not a fiend, Miss Garnier.'

I could object no more. He must be speaking the truth. Everything was working out in my favour, and perhaps there would be a happy ending after all. Mr Randall's sins were relatively small and he was endeavouring to correct them. I saw no reason to believe he'd make me a bad husband.

Lucy's words sprang up unbidden: *You'd be stifled in marriage.* But what did she know? She'd never felt this breathless agitation, never seen any man, let alone one as handsome as Mr Randall.

'Well, this is the carpenter's shop. You mentioned you had business here?'

He pulled open the door for me. A vague haze hung within. I inhaled the warmth of sawdust, heard the workers in the back making furniture with great rasps and bangs.

One man stood behind a bench, sanding a handle smooth. He fixed me with large, soulful eyes as I entered the shop. 'How do?' This seemed to be a greeting in Yorkshire, so I bid him good morning while Mr Randall followed me inside. The man laid aside his work and wiped his hands on a cloth. 'Staying with Mrs Talbot, aren't tha?'

Alarm bells clanged inside my mind. How did he know? News must spread fast in a village like this. Both he and Mr Randall watched me intently for an answer.

'Yes,' I admitted. 'Mrs Talbot is my godmother.' A white lie, but clearly no one in the village knew Rowena.

The carpenter nodded. 'Strange ways, that woman.'

I returned a bright, false smile. 'Anyhow . . . I am hoping you can help me? A tree smashed one of our windows and we need to board it up. I have the measurements of the gap somewhere here . . .' Opening my reticule, I pushed past the bundles of wrapped confectionary, filling the workshop with a frivolous, sugary scent.

'Here it is,' said Mr Randall, plucking out the scrap of paper and handing it to the carpenter.

The man frowned at the numbers. 'What type of wood?'

I hadn't thought that far ahead. 'Um – ash, perhaps? There's ash panelling in the house.'

Mr Randall grimaced. 'Is there? I never did care for ash wood myself. What about a nice elder or aspen? Apple wood?'

The carpenter shook his head. 'Ash or oak will do best, sir. Sturdier.'

'Well, there, you see, the lady knows far better than I!' Mr Randall laughed at himself with good nature. His smile made me light-headed. I would have chosen any kind of wood, the flimsiest of sticks, if only to please him.

'Let it be oak, then,' I decided. 'It was an oak tree that broke the window, so an oak tree can repair it.'

'Oak planks,' the carpenter nodded, inspecting the piece of paper again.

A sudden realization hit me. My face must have dropped, for Mr Randall's expression sharpened with concern. 'Is something the matter?'

'Oh – I've been a goose, that's all. I brought a handcart with me to transport the planks and I've gone and left it outside the confectioner's.'

He dipped me a little bow. 'Say no more, madam. I am at your service, I shall retrieve it at once. Did you not say there were also letters to post?'

'Yes, I have them here . . .' They were squashed and dusted with sugar from my reticule, but the directions were still legible and Mr Randall took them without seeming to notice.

'I'll send them for you on my way. I've met the postmistress – I daresay you won't be sorry to forgo her . . . sparkling company.'

I grinned. 'Truly, you are very kind.'

'It is my honour.' He inclined his head and left at a quick trot.

How pleasant it was to have someone wait upon me again! Mr Randall behaved as though I were valuable, not an annoyance. I wished Lucy, who rolled her eyes at every one of my mistakes, could see me now.

I waited as the carpenter set about his work, flooding the shop with the harsh, rasping voice of the saw. Autumn sunlight slanted through the windows and caught the dust teasing around him. It hardly seemed possible that the oaks waving outside Felwood Lodge could be reshaped in this way. Mighty trees, so alive and vital, reduced to dead, uniform slats.

By the time the carpenter was finished and I'd paid his fee, Mr Randall had returned. He loaded the cart for me and insisted on pulling it himself. I felt quite the pampered lady as we approached the square and the well. Little stalls were laid out with all the fruits of the harvest for sale: shining nuts, fat marrows, apples ready for the cider press.

'Now I'll escort you home,' Mr Randall announced. 'Perhaps you can introduce me to your godmother, Mrs Talbot? What kind of woman is she?'

I nearly stumbled. Beneath the brilliant sky with this frisky breeze, I'd forgotten about the cares I'd left behind. 'Oh, no! I'm afraid I can't do that, Mr Randall. My godmother is so . . . reclusive. She'd never consent to my receiving visitors.'

He stopped. 'None at all? Surely once we explain that I'm known to your family, and that you needed an escort on account of this mad dog roving the fells . . .'

I shook my head sadly, rustling the ribbons of my bonnet. I trusted Mr Randall – or at least, I wanted to. But Rowena's secrets weren't mine to share.

'Alas, no. It's as the carpenter said: she has strange ways. Eccentricities. If she even saw you walking me up to the door, she'd be furious.'

His dark eyes widened, showing the golden speckles. 'You are not in earnest? But of course you are, I see it in your face. Confound it! Why must there always be some foolish impediment keeping us from one another?'

I was vexed too. But everyone at Felwood Lodge was upset enough over the baby's grave; I wouldn't add to their sorrows by bringing home an outsider and putting them at risk of discovery.

'I'll come to you,' I suggested. 'Whenever I can. Either here or at The Grey Lady inn. We can still talk.'

'You shall do no such thing, while the country remains so dangerous! I'd never forgive myself if something happened to you. Indeed, Miss Garnier, you must permit me to walk you *part* of the way home, at least. You are a slow target, moving with the cart, and you're carrying half the sugar of the Indies in your reticule. Any predator would find you . . .' he drew a breath, fixed his gaze on my lips '. . . irresistible.'

I swallowed. '*Part* of the way,' I conceded. 'If you would be so kind as to take me back to the inn, I can make it alone from there.'

He rewarded me with another beatific grin and bowed. 'Madam, it would be my pleasure.'

CHAPTER ELEVEN

The sun was bobbing low in the sky by the time I saw Lucy's turret rising above the treetops and knew I was nearly back at Felwood Lodge. In my fluster, I'd almost lost my path back from the inn. The forest had never appeared so perfect. The sun was a flaming ball, glowing orange between silver birch and washing the grass with gold. A flock of swallows flew overhead, migrating for the winter. I felt I could soar with them. My feet seemed to tread upon the air, the loaded cart to weigh nothing at all. I was fit to burst with all I had to tell, and all I must conceal.

Leaving the handcart by the front door, I tried to arrange my face, to look less absurdly glad, before I ventured inside. If Lucy thought my smiles were excessive before, what would she make of this? But surely she would have to smile too, when I told her my news. The village gossip of a wild animal would vindicate her. Bridget must accept Lucy's innocence now and we could put the sorry episode of the baby's skeleton behind us.

The kitchen stood empty and swept clean. I heard the steady clack of the handloom, a faint click and hiss from the spinning wheel. They must all be in the parlour. I flew straight there and burst in, unable to contain myself.

'Lucy! You'll never guess – it *was* a dog!'

Rowena removed her foot from the treadle of the spinning wheel. Bridget had finally risen from her bed and sat stiffly at the loom with her back towards the others. Although she didn't turn around, her hands stopped their work.

From the sofa, Lucy raised her honeyed eyes. 'Take a breath,' she said, still sewing the pieces of my new clothes together. 'Why are you jabbering about a dog?'

It was as I'd feared: I was too happy, too bright for this dimly lit parlour where they spun their dull grey wool. I tried to rein myself in. 'A dog was responsible for . . . what we found yesterday. The news is all over the village. There's a mad beast on the loose killing livestock. That *must* have been what was at the chapel, digging.'

Nobody spoke. Nobody moved. Silence curdled, thick and oppressive. The smile wilted on my lips. 'Isn't that good? I thought Bridget would like to know.'

Bridget remained perfectly still. It was Lucy who put aside her sewing and rose to her feet. 'I'm going to check on the sheep.'

Rowena nodded. 'Yes, that's a good idea, love. I am sure it cannot be . . .' She trailed off. 'It is a coincidence. These things do happen in the countryside.'

'They've only happened here once before,' Lucy said darkly, brushing past me as she went to leave the room. At the door she caught her breath, glanced back. 'Camille, where did you go in the village?' She sniffed. 'You smell . . . strange.'

'Lucy, remember your manners!' Rowena protested.

'It's all right, Godmother, I *was* standing by the forge for a while, I suppose I'm a little smoky.'

Lucy regarded me. I couldn't meet her eye. If I did, I was sure she'd see the truth plain on my face: the way Mr Randall had wrapped me in an embrace as we parted, cloaking me in his masculine scents of sandalwood, shaving soap and pomade.

'Hmm. Smoke. That must be it.'

Just after Lucy closed the door behind her, Bridget stood wearily. 'I think that's all the work I can manage for today.' Her voice sounded gruff, as though she'd been crying. 'I'm going for a rest. I *am* glad you told me about the dog, Camille. I only hope . . .' Just like Rowena, she didn't finish her sentence. She walked slowly to the door, weighted down by her grief, leaving me standing there in my bonnet and pelisse, utterly bewildered. I didn't know what I'd expected – some kind of gratitude. But I only seemed to have caused consternation.

I turned to my godmother at the spinning wheel. She was chewing on her lower lip. 'What's wrong?' I asked. 'I thought you'd all be glad. This proves Lucy was not to blame for the grave!'

'Yes,' she said quietly. 'Yes, it does. You were right to bring the news home. But I'm afraid it raises . . . other concerns for us.'

'About your sheep? I'm sure we can protect them. Lucy just said this happened once before? What did you do last time? Forewarned is forearmed, my father says.'

Rowena gave a sad little smile. 'Indeed. We were able to keep our sheep safe from the last worrier. But it's not possible to be prepared for every eventuality . . .' Her hand rose to her moon-stone necklace, turning it between her fingers.

I took Bridget's place at the loom and removed my bonnet. 'Tell me, Godmother,' I entreated her. 'What has made you all react so strangely?'

She hesitated. 'Memories. My past experience with my husband's family, the Alaunts. I didn't tell you, Camille, that they have a great affinity with everything canine. They are hunters, with many hounds at their command. Every time I hear of vicious dogs in the vicinity, I imagine them scouring the moors in search of me, with a bloodhound trained on my scent.'

Though she kept her voice level, fear radiated from her. She twirled her moonstone as keenly as Lucy twirled her yarn. But she was letting terror cloud her judgement.

'I'm sure this isn't connected to them,' I reassured her. 'It's a lone dog, not a hunting party. And if your husband had found you, wouldn't he just come straight here? Why would he go to other farms?'

'It is the Alaunt way,' she said bitterly. 'Even hunting a fox, they will not kill it outright but toy with the poor creature, relishing its agony. Or perhaps they mean to scare me into making a mistake, to flush me out of hiding as a spaniel drives birds out of a bush, straight into the guns.'

What must she have suffered in that marriage? These Alaunts, as she called them, had clearly injured her in ways I couldn't even imagine. 'I see. Well, I don't blame you for being scared,' I said softly. 'But I do think it's unlikely this has anything to do with your husband. It is not . . . rational.'

She nodded again. For an instant, in her uncertainty, I saw a flicker of Lucy in her face. 'I am sure you are right, Camille. That part of my life is over. Finished with.' She tried a smile, but it was pained. 'Anyway, how did you get on in the village? Did you find some nice sturdy planks for your window?'

I fought to keep my expression neutral, to keep Mr Randall's raven curls out of my mind. 'Yes. The carpenter was very helpful.'

'Good.' She took a steadying breath. 'I think I'd better get to work securing that window sooner, rather than later. Just to be safe.'

So this was my last night in the turret. My spine would be thankful for that. It had been uncomfortable sleeping on a hard stone floor, and as I climbed the spiral staircase, carrying my little paper parcel I was aware of pain dragging down the backs of my legs. But part of me would be sorry to leave. Lucy's room really did belong inside a story book.

I pushed the door open with a creak. All the candelabras were lit and running with wax. Light danced across the ceiling, illuminating the constellations Lucy had painted there. If I squinted, I could almost imagine the roof of the turret had been removed and left open to the night sky.

Lucy sat on the side of her hearse-like bed, ghostly in white. She did not ignore me as usual. On the contrary, she set her cup of tea down upon the console table and motioned for me to come closer.

'I want to know what they're saying about this dog. Tell me everything you heard. What breed do they take it to be?'

At last, I could say something that would interest her. I perched myself on the end of her bed. The mattress gave a little moan beneath me, releasing the warmth of Lucy's musk to mingle with the damp, woody scent of her tea. 'A mastiff dog, I think. Someone mentioned it was about that size. It took down cattle, so it must be pretty large.'

'And where was it spotted?'

I wasn't used to her looking at me like this: attentive, fully present, open to my response. It made my hands clammy. 'I'm – I'm not sure. I only heard bits, in passing. But some of the farmers are setting a watch by night, so it can't be long before the dog is shot dead.'

She gave a small shake of the head. 'They're field labourers, not marksmen. Unless they shoot it through the heart, they'll probably just make it angrier. They might even be killed themselves.' Her brows knit together. 'Perhaps Mama will send you back home now. I told you: you'd be better off there. Safer.'

I pouted. 'Don't be silly, there's no real danger. I'm just as likely to be chased across a field by an angry bull as attacked by a stray dog.'

'You don't know what you're talking about,' she said, frustrated. 'You're too . . .' She ran her tongue over her lips as she searched for the word. 'Innocent.'

'That's not what my parents say. They banished me here because I am not innocent enough for their taste!'

Her head twitched away from me in irritation. 'Ignorant, then. Do you not see the scars on my mother's face? Do you think this is a jest?'

'Not at all! But, Lucy . . . I don't believe for a second that your father is seeking you out with this dog. It's too absurd! And after all this time . . . it cannot be him.'

'No.' She sighed, becoming pensive. 'No, it isn't Sir Marcus. But I don't like it, all the same. You were walking all alone. Anything could have happened to you.'

My chest gave a kick. She sounded like Mr Randall. Maybe she didn't want me gone; maybe part of this was her strange way of looking out for me?

I fidgeted with the parcel in my hands, unsure whether to give it now. Lucy inhaled, her nostrils tremulous as eyelids, and then she saw what I held in my hand. 'What's inside that package? It smells . . .'

'Delicious,' I finished for her. Making my decision, I untied the string. 'It's something I brought back from the village. A "thank you" for allowing me to share your room.'

She looked a little stunned, as if I'd hit her between the eyes. 'A . . . gift? For me?'

'Yes. Take it.'

Our fingers touched as I passed the parcel over, and Lucy flinched. She appeared lost for words. Cautiously, she unwrapped the paper and stared at the contents, puzzlement creasing her brow. Then she held a fragment, so similar to the colour of her eyes, up to the candlelight. 'What *is* it?'

'Have you really never seen toffee before? I did wonder – there is nothing sweet in this house!'

'You eat it?'

I compressed my lips, trying not to laugh at her; she was too proud to bear that. 'Yes. It's sugar and butter.'

She shifted on the bed, embarrassed. Our roles had been reversed. 'Mama says my diet must be kept plain. Because of my . . . condition.' She turned the piece of toffee over in her fingers. 'But it does smell . . . wonderful.'

'One small bit won't hurt you, surely? Everything is good for you in moderation, that's what my mother says.'

Lucy deliberated, her focus trained upon the sweet as it'd been trained upon me that day on the stairs. For some reason I couldn't explain, I was desperate to see her eat. But I spoke with more restraint. 'If you really don't want the toffee, I won't be offended—'

Before I could finish, Lucy thrust the toffee into her mouth. It cracked loudly between her teeth. She made a little moan.

A grin spread across my face. 'Isn't it good?'

Lucy gobbled up another piece, her eyes wide like a starving man. It had barely passed her lips before she was raising yet another.

Something sped up inside of me. 'Not too much, if you're not used to it!' I warned her. 'You won't sleep tonight.'

Her head snapped to my voice. For an instant she stared, and my heart skipped. There was pure power in that glance, an energy so strong that it held me captive. Her pupils had dilated, black flooding the amber irises. Suddenly, she lurched.

My breath quickened, but she didn't plunge towards me, only the console table. The remaining toffee clattered from her lap and skittered across the floor as Lucy grabbed at her cup of tea and tipped it desperately. Her hands quaked while she gulped it down.

'Are you all right?'

Gradually, her panting stopped. Cradling the cup in one hand, Lucy touched her silver choker with the other. A flush had crept from beneath, up her neck and towards her face. It felt as if something had been narrowly avoided, something I desired and dreaded in equal measure.

I cleared my throat. 'Are you better now?'

'I'm fine,' she said gruffly. 'It was as you said. Too much . . . sugar.'

'I didn't mean to make you ill.'

'I'm not, I'm fine.' Then she added, incongruously terse, 'Thank you for the gift.'

'You're welcome.' I peered over her shoulder into the nearly empty mug. The dregs were bluish-purple. 'What *do* they put in your tea?' I asked, to release the pressure between us. 'It's a different colour from the one Bridget makes for me. What is it?'

'Medicine.'

'Can I try it?'

'Absolutely not.' She raised her eyes up to the ceiling, refusing even to look at me.

I followed her gaze. Above us was a constellation shaped like a hook with a daisy sprouting off the end. 'What's that one?' I asked softly.

'It's called Scorpius.'

Here was a path back to normality: a trail lit by stars. I knew all the legends of classical antiquity, because Pierre used to tell me the passages he was translating for school. 'Oh! Scorpius was the only creature able to defeat Orion the hunter,' I announced. 'The constellations all have myths behind them . . . were you aware of that? Or are myths too much like novels for your taste? Do they make you feel ill?'

The corner of Lucy's mouth quirked; there was some joke I wasn't privy to. 'Oh, I know my fair share of myths. I can manage little tales like those. People and animals, turned into stars by the gods . . .' She sighed. 'That's a lot nicer than your novels about ghouls and murderers.'

I couldn't argue. 'Tell me, what is it about astronomy that you like? Is it just that stars are something . . . forbidden? A sight you can't see in real life without risking your health?'

She shrugged. 'No. It's more than that. They're so ancient, so huge. When I read of Mr Herschel's telescope finding the moons of Saturn, far, far away, I feel . . . small. Insignificant. A little dot compared to the vast universe. That's comforting.'

I thought it was rather morbid. I wanted to feel important, not tiny. Special. The way I felt when Mr Randall looked at me.

I rose from the bed and went over to my makeshift bunk. Lucy kept looking upwards. What exactly was it that she sought? Whether she was gazing high up to the heavens or burrowing deep down in the earth, she was desperately seeking something. To feel less alone, she'd said. But also unremarkable. Perhaps she wanted an ordinary life, where she wasn't ill or in hiding; to fit into society as neatly as a piece of a jigsaw puzzle. The life I always complained wasn't magical enough for me – that was a life she dreamed of.

'I am sorry,' I said as I settled down. 'About the sweets. I hope you won't be ill during the night.'

Lucy cast her cup aside and lay back on her pillows. 'It's not your fault. My nerves are different from everyone else's. Sometimes I think, if other people could feel the things I feel, it would kill them on the spot.'

I pictured my sedate family: their nice manners, their sheer lack of wonder. Hadn't I chafed among them, as though I were cut from a different cloth entirely? If anyone could sympathize with Lucy's strong emotions, it should be me.

'You can always talk to me about it,' I offered softly. 'If it will help.'

There was a beat of silence. 'No.' Her vocal cords sounded hoarse, choking something back. 'No, I can't tell you.'

And abruptly she rolled away, pulling the covers over her head.

CHAPTER TWELVE

The days passed, yet I didn't abandon my mission to make a friend out of Lucy. Mr Randall might be close by, but I'd have precious few chances of sneaking out to see him. I needed a confidante in the meantime. None of the girls I'd grown up with in Stamford would serve; their careful mamas would never allow one of my letters within a mile of them, lest they be tainted by association with my scandal. And, while I hoped Marie would soften towards me, that hadn't happened yet. No; my mind was made up. I must win over Lucy. That was my challenge, almost an obsession. I'd make her like me in spite of herself.

As we walked together through the trees that morning, with the sky cold, hard and bright above our heads, I was struck by the realization that this moment wouldn't come to me again. The summer was already spent; the mellow autumn haze would soon give way to frost. By the time the leaves died, and budded, and grew once more, I'd be back in society, no longer free to wander in a dirty gown or scrape my hair back any which way. This was only a brief interlude in the first volume of my life before the pages turned, the lodge vanished and its inhabitants faded; all part of a back story in a book which I could never reopen.

There would be new milestones to look forward to, of course: marriage, an estate of my own, maybe children. Every stop laid out on a prosaic, predictable road until I rested as dust and bone with my little siblings in the graveyard. I'd never be this young again, meandering with Lucy at my side, drinking in the smell of wild grass. I had to seize the moment. I had to live.

I grabbed Lucy's arm. She gave a little jump.

'Come on, I'll race you.'

'Why?'

Pulling her with me, I started to run.

A group of magpies scattered cawing from our path. I charged on, not even stopping for puddles but splashing us through them and coating our skirts in mud. The thought of my mother's face made me laugh all the harder.

A bush vibrated in the undergrowth, its leaves trembling and fluttering. As we drew close, a hare shot out and bounded ahead of us. I whooped. Lucy jerked free of my grip and flew forward, her white cap falling to the dirt behind her.

She ran like the wind. I had no hope of catching up with her. Her long legs seemed to swallow the distance at a lope while I puffed behind, choking on breathlessness and giggles. 'Wait for me!'

She didn't. Lucy careered until she disappeared from my sight. Of course she would win the race. Her skirt was looser and shorter than mine, her boots made for work. These slippery leaves and muddy tracks were more familiar to her feet than carpet. She'd been allowed to run every day of her life . . . But she didn't. I realized now that I'd never seen her unfettered like this. She usually kept herself on the tightest of reins.

My lungs were burning by the time I reached the meadow. I had to stop and lean against the paddock fence. Lucy stood inside the enclosure, by the trough, her skin healthy and glowing for once. She wasn't even slightly winded.

It took me a second to realize what she held in her hands.

The hare quivered between her palms, nose twitching wildly. Its long hind legs hung down, not kicking but motionless, as if it knew it had been mastered.

'How on earth did you catch him?' I cried.

'Isn't he beautiful?'

He was. Two panicked brown eyes regarded us. His velvet ears lay flat, plastered to his back. Shades of taupe, umber and tan made up his coat.

'We won't harm you,' I crooned. 'We just want to look at you.'

Lucy passed her tongue over her lips. Giving the hare a squeeze, she bent and set him gently down. He whipped away before I had time to blink. Lucy watched him, all the way to the bracken, looking as though she yearned to run with him. Her hand tugged at her choker. My brother Pierre did the same thing when he'd tied his cravat too tight.

'Is your necklace hurting you?' I asked.

'A little, today.'

The silver sheen was mottled with black dots, like smuts from a fire. 'Why don't you take it off for a while?'

'I can't,' she returned, too fast. Seeing my puzzlement, she added, 'It's medicinal.' Then she turned and began to clean the leaves from the trough.

I folded my arms and leant them on the top rung of the fence, watching her. 'Your mother thinks silver has some kind of power, doesn't she? That it fights infections?'

'It's true! Don't laugh!' she flared up.

'I'm not laughing!' I wasn't, but I had to admit I was sceptical. 'I just want to understand. You don't *have* an infection, do you?'

Lucy's brows lowered. The breeze blew one of her mousy curls over her shoulder.

'Silver is pure. It reacts to anything impure.' She paddled her

137

fingers in the water. 'My necklace works like a barometer. I can tell when my illness is relapsing, because the silver hurts me more. But let's stop talking about that.' She pulled her hands from the trough and shook the droplets free. 'Come into the barn; I've thought of a good task for you today. A chore even *you'll* be able to manage.'

Was it my imagination, or was there less rancour in her voice? A note of teasing, rather than disdain . . . But perhaps that was wishful thinking.

I noticed the stench of the barn less and less every day. When Lucy opened the door and ushered me inside, the warm, earthy aroma was almost like coming home. The chickens squabbled at my feet, but I was ready for them now, flinging their feed far from me to get them away. 'Go on with you, Firetail! Why must you always be the difficult one?'

He gave me a swift peck before skittering to join the others. Although I didn't hold him or the hens in high esteem, I was warming to the sheep and their funny sounds as they watched us with square pupils. Lucy went over to Queenie and scratched her under the chin, murmuring affectionate words I couldn't hear. I felt a little pang, wishing she would look that kindly upon me.

'So what was it you wanted me to do?'

'We're running low on wool to spin. It's time to sort and wash the fleeces we sheared in the summer. If you go into the hayloft you'll find them all folded up, ready. Bring one down.'

Hitching my skirts, I went to the ladder and struggled up. The hayloft reminded me of the attics at Martingale Hall: a place of tired items, faded memories and hidden spiders. My footsteps stirred the dust and I sneezed as I made my way across the boards, towards the corner where the fleeces were carefully rolled and stacked. They looked dirty, ragged, a far cry from the felted material Bridget wove on the loom. Stooping, I reached for the topmost roll and slung it across my shoulders.

It was tacky, sour-smelling. The weight of it nearly unbalanced me on the climb down. I slid rather than stepped on the last two rungs.

'Careful!' Lucy said. She shook her head at me, her curls frizzling. 'Did you really make it to the village and back all by yourself yesterday? I can't picture it. Every time I take my eyes from you, you're falling over or tripping on something.'

I had no defence. She was right. Compared to Lucy I always felt weak and frivolous, gauze beside hard-wearing cambric. 'Well, I've been bred gently, haven't I? We don't get much practice climbing up ladders at Martingale Hall.'

'Do you . . . dance?' she asked, uncertain.

'Yes. Not well, but I do it.' I hesitated. 'Would you like me to teach you?'

She blinked the image away as if it discomforted her. 'No. Never mind your clumsiness; you'll be able to sort wool with ease. There's nothing to it.' Taking the fleece from me, she untied the neck wool that held the roll together and spread it out on the floor. 'There, this is a nice, open fleece. You want to skirt it – rip off the edges, and the dung tags, any bits of straw or hayseeds. Mind for thorns – they need pulling out too. Don't prick yourself on them and get blood near me. Just take off any bits that look too dirty, or matted.'

'That's all?'

'That's all. Then roll them back up; we'll wash them another day.'

I nodded, relieved. Even I would struggle to bungle this.

Lucy left me to it while she mucked out the sheep pens. I drove my hands deep into the fleece. They were reddening from manual work, the skin peeling from my knuckles. I noticed a callus that wasn't there before, and a broken nail. What would Mr Randall think, if he saw me without my gloves? A lady's hands should be as white and soft as snow. But mine had never been good at delicate tasks. They were better at things like this:

tearing, or digging for potatoes. With a gentle pull, the woollen fibres gave way beneath my fingertips, sometimes crackling, sometimes making a clean twang. The breeze snatched up little wisps that floated like the hen's feathers. Lucy sang softly from the stalls and I fell into the rhythm of my work, learning to ignore the grease on my palms. The smell wasn't bad, once I grew accustomed: like fields warming beneath the sun, and a rusted gate that opened on to them.

A feeling of contentment spread over me. I was useful, I had purpose and I could hear the sweet balm of Lucy's song. She sang so rarely, for one with such a beautiful voice – did this melody mean she was happy too?

Snap. A staple tore off in my hand as a harsh, metallic chomp made me flinch. The sheep bleated in protest and Lucy's song died.

'Lucy? What was that?'

'I don't know,' she called back. 'My mother and Bridget are out there. They must have dropped something.'

My curiosity was roused. Rowena and Bridget, outside alone, up to goodness knew what. *Experiments.* I remembered how dishevelled they'd appeared that night when the tree broke through my window – as if they'd been dragged through a hedge backwards. Then the day Bridget emerged from the root-cellar, after she'd told me there was no key to open it. Maybe that *snap* had come from there?

I had to know. Wiping my oily hands on my skirt, I went over to the barn door and poked my head outside. Across the river, Bridget stood by the crops with her arms folded. Rowena bent over something nearby. I couldn't see what.

'Have you ever been in the root-cellar, Lucy?'

She stopped forking the dung. 'No, of course not.' It didn't sound entirely truthful.

'Why "of course"?'

'It's old. The structure isn't sound. It's falling apart.' She reeled off the excuses Bridget had given me in a rush. 'You must never go near it yourself.'

'I know I'm clumsy, but—'

'Camille.' Her voice arrested me. A cold fire burnt behind her eyes. 'I'm serious. You must promise me you won't go there.'

I nodded. I didn't dare do anything else. Her expression was as sombre as it had been when she'd told me about Bridget's dead baby. Even the sheep were edging away, unsettled.

'Good. I'll hold you to that,' she warned. Giving me one last, earnest look, she bent to her work once more.

Lucy *couldn't* hold me to account. I'd promised her nothing – not really. A mere nod of the head didn't constitute a vow. Lucy's emphasis only convinced me of one thing: not that the root-cellar was dangerous, but that she knew its secrets. Well, I'd be staying at Felwood Lodge for many months yet, and I'd be hanged if I didn't find out what was in there for myself, before my time was through.

'Here,' I offered. 'Your barrow's almost full. I'll take it to the dung heap.'

'You haven't finished sorting the fleeces yet.'

'I'll do it in a moment.'

Before she could protest further, I grabbed the handles of the wheelbarrow and steered it, pell-mell, through the door into the yard. I wanted to get a closer look at what my godmother was doing.

As it happened, Rowena was already crossing the river, stalking towards me with a lopsided gait. She carried a heavy, rusted object. Some kind of tail dragged behind it.

'Godmother? What is it you have there?'

She waited until she was a little closer before she answered me. Her face was flushed. 'It's a trap, Camille. We're setting them to protect the animals against that mad dog. Bridget is making a map of where they are laid and you must study it carefully. I don't want you or Lucy stumbling into them and hurting yourselves.'

'A trap?' I repeated, running my eyes over what looked like a torture device, all jagged teeth. The trailing length I'd mistaken for a tail was a heavy chain. 'Like a poacher's snare?'

'Stronger than that. Here, I'll show you how it works.' She knelt and prised the mouth apart. 'Stand back a little. Where is a stone? There, that will do.' Straightening again, she tossed her pebble at the centre of the metal disc. 'When the beast steps onto the plate—' The jaws leapt up and closed with a clang. I flinched. 'See? The dog will be caught fast.'

Objectively, that was a good thing. The sheep would be safe and the dog lamed if not killed. But Rowena was a vegetarian; she didn't want to hurt animals.

'Where did you get these traps?'

Rowena stooped to collect it. 'You forget this was a hunting lodge, long ago. We still have much equipment at our disposal.' The wind blew a strand of her grey hair from its tight braid. 'Lucy mentioned the trouble, once before. This is what saved our sheep back then. We baited the traps and caught the beast.'

Bile filled my mouth as I realized that the stains I'd taken for rust were, in fact, dried blood. These metal teeth had broken flesh. 'Did it die?'

'No, it was only stunned, incapacitated for a time.' She rose to her feet. 'Bridget subdued it with some herbs and we were able to move it . . . The entire episode was nothing short of a miracle. Providence was on our side.'

'But where did you move it to?'

She bit her lip, as if she'd said too much. She didn't answer my question. 'This time may be different, of course. Another type of predator entirely. Perhaps we'll tip the teeth with poison to make sure.'

'Poison!' I regretted leaving the barn. My morning had been mellow, with leaping hares, the bleat of sheep and Lucy singing;

now a fog seemed to descend, sucking out all the light. 'There are kinder ways to put rabid dogs down, aren't there? Quick, humane methods. It need not suffer?'

Rowena shot me one of her wistful smiles. I could see she thought me a child, that I knew nothing of the real world. 'My dear, I don't like to do this, believe me. But the sad fact is, some creatures are harder to kill than others. There are beasts that simply . . . refuse to die.'

CHAPTER THIRTEEN

Marie has brought me the medicine I need, the palliatives no one else will fetch: wax to plug my ears later tonight; smelling salts that will blast away baby Jean's scent. The silver-backed toilette set from Mama's own dressing-table lies upon my bed. Gritting my teeth, I clutch the hairbrush with both hands. As I feared, it reacts to my impurity. Every pore on my palms tingles and they emit dark wisps of smoke. If silver acts as a barometer, this means the pressure is plummeting fast. A storm is rolling in.

Wincing, I shift on the mattress, feel the slashes I've made in the ticking. My hands are on fire with pain. Well, at least if the agony forces me to vomit, that will carry more of the corruption out – just like Mr Leiston wanted.

But to judge from his expression of dudgeon, and the hands fisted on his hips, the physician will only be happy with a recovery on his own terms.

'This is lunacy. The elder Miss Garnier is indulging the ramblings of a fever patient. Please, madam. Come to your senses and make your daughters cease their folly.'

My mother continues pulling back the dimity curtains and raising the window sashes. Damp air flows through and flutters the short hair around my ears.

'We have tried your *learned* methods,' she replies briskly. 'Now we shall test my own. And if it comforts Camille to keep certain objects about her person, she may have them. A *hairbrush* will not impede her convalescence.'

'Perhaps not. But this quack cure you insist on administering may.'

She rounds on him, her colour high, earrings jangling. 'It is no quackery, sir! I will have you know this is a valued family remedy, proven to heal the bite of a mad dog. Liverwort and black pepper dissolved in warm cow's milk. Where, pray, is the harm in that?'

Mr Leiston mops his brow with his handkerchief; it's becoming a nervous habit with him. He is a large man with a belly that swells his waistcoat and small, hot eyes. It would be unkind to describe him as porcine, yet to me he has begun to smell like bacon, sizzling in a pan. 'We have no evidence that Miss Camille was bitten by a rabid dog.'

'Then explain her scar! Explain any of these symptoms, Mr Leiston, and I shall double your fee, but I know you cannot.' Mama presses a hand to her side. Her chest is heaving beneath her stays. 'I have watched enough inept physicians tend to my children. I have trusted their educated opinion and paid the price for it. This time, I am taking matters into my own hands.'

Little does she know that I'm doing the same. My plan may cause distress if it goes wrong, but taking no action at all would result in horror. I must try. Anything is preferable to forcing my family to witness scenes like the ones at Felwood Lodge.

Gasping, I finally drop the hairbrush. My palms are scalded lobster-red.

As luck would have it, the maid chooses that moment to shoulder her way in. She's carrying Mama's family recipe in a porcelain cup with two handles. Marie slips through the door behind her, chin tucked against her chest. Delicate brown ringlets form at the nape of her neck from the rain outside. Although she's shrugged off her bonnet and cloak, she still wears the gloves and shoes she donned for her trip into Stamford. Her right hand clutches the tiny parcel I asked her to fetch. So small a container for such a desperate remedy. My heart gives a stutter. This *is* the right thing to do, isn't it?

The maid passes me the cup, repressing a shudder as my raw, peeling hand touches hers. 'That will be all,' I say. Curtseying, she beats a hasty retreat.

The mixture looks noxious, herbs turning the milk to sludge, but its steam smells pleasant enough. Mama and the physician are still arguing as Marie steals to my side.

'It's not the right season,' she whispers. 'I could only get dried ones. Will they suffice?'

'I think so. You remembered what I said – you didn't touch them, did you?'

Marie frowns. 'No. The apothecary was most insistent I should not. Whatever *is* this, Camille?'

By way of answer, I ease open the packet and crumble some of the dry flowers into my mug. Little stars of purplish blue – one of the few remaining colours I can distinguish. Their nutty aroma transports me back to another time.

My lips flutter in a secret prayer. 'I'm trusting you, Bridget,' I whisper.

I've caught Mr Leiston's attention. 'What do you have there?' he snaps. I hurry to push the packet under my pillow. As he paces heavily towards us, he sees the top of my drink and his eyes bulge. 'Aconite! She must not take that! She must not consume—'

Quickly, I raise the cup and gulp the mixture down. Searing heat, a bitterly foul taste. Mr Leiston knocks the cup from my grasp; it falls to the carpet and one delicate porcelain handle snaps clean off. But it's too late. I've swallowed.

Mr Leiston stands aghast. A long look passes between us: his disbelief, my defiance. But then his fleshy face appears to melt, like wax. It's taking effect.

'It was just a flower,' Marie protests. 'A herbal remedy she asked me to fetch for her tea . . . '

Weak and numb, I drop back on the bed.

'A *tea*!' the physician spits. 'Aconite is a poison, madam. Even a small dose can prove fatal.' Marie and Mama cry out as he dives for his bag and begins to rifle through it, babbling about emetics. 'If we can force her to vomit . . . There might still be time.'

Marie's terrified countenance floats into my field of vision; she is warped, all haunting eyes. 'Did you make a mistake? Did you ask for the wrong plant?'

'I'm not going to die,' I insist weakly. But in truth I'm not so sure. My stomach writhes and I can feel a torpor spreading through my bloodstream, heavy as lead. My eyelids shut. It's hard to open them again. In fact, I cannot.

Mama's shouting from underwater. I can't smell at all. For all the bodily discomfort, my relief is immense. Finally, I've found a way to dull my razor-sharp senses. Perhaps I'll sleep at last.

Something pushes at my lips, tries to prise them apart. With my remaining strength, I keep my mouth shut. The flowers are working, I don't want to throw them up. If I die . . . This doesn't seem such a bad way to go. Pain cramps my stomach, but it's nothing like the agony that's kept me awake and howling at night.

My heart beats a faint, discordant rhythm. With every pulse I see a flash of purple.

'What have you done?' Marie hisses close to my ear. 'Camille, what have you asked me to do?'

CHAPTER FOURTEEN

My chamber was dim, now Rowena had nailed the planks across the window. Even in the middle of the day there was a whisky-coloured tint to whatever light managed to seep through. I sat upon the bed, my mouth full of marchpane, squinting at the text of Ovid's *Metamorphoses*. Daphne's tale had drawn to a close and now I read of poor Inachus, weeping in the depths of a cavern for the daughter he could not find. It touched a chord. Did Lucy's father mourn like this, searching for her? I thought not. Yet, as the words passed before my eyes, the two began to blur together in my mind. The maiden Io became Lucy. I saw Lucy lured into the shade of the wild beasts, Lucy disguised as a heifer and pursued by demons. It was Lucy who sank to her knees by the river and lifted her face to the stars for mercy.

Then there was a tap at my door. 'Come in,' I said, closing my book and brushing the crumbs from my skirts.

The hinges whined open. Lucy herself stood there, summoned from my imagination, although to judge from her posture she'd rather be anywhere else in the world. Her chin was tucked against her chest, her shoulders stiff as she clutched a package tight to her stomach.

'Lucy!' She'd never knocked on my door before. Was she finally seeking out my company? I blustered to make her welcome, afraid she'd slip through my fingers again. 'Sorry, there's not much space with my luggage . . . but you can come inside.'

She hesitated on the threshold. 'It smells so sweet in here.'

'Yes! That's the marchpane I've been eating. I would offer to let you try some, but—'

She shook her head, clearly remembering the toffee as I did. 'Best not. Just how much confectionery did you buy in Deepbeck?'

I gave a laugh of self-deprecation. 'Too much. You should never go to market when you're hungry, and I've been famished here. The food at Martingale Hall is . . .' I didn't want to cause offence, but I could already feel my nose wrinkling at the thought of Bridget's thin gruel. 'Different,' I finished, inadequately.

Lucy scoffed. 'I daresay. I'm sure you can't wait to get back home.' But it wasn't true. Right now, this was exactly where I wanted to be. Awkwardly, she proffered the parcel. 'My mother said I should give you this.'

I rose from the bed and took it eagerly. 'What is it?'

'Can't you guess?'

I tore at the paper. Something grey began to emerge, something at once soft and prickly against my skin. My dress for the farm. 'Oh! How . . . lovely.'

In truth it was an insult to fashion: undyed, loose-fitting, with long sleeves that attached at the shoulders and laces down the front of the bodice. Rather than gathering around the bust, the waistline settled at the hips. Once, I would have compared the colour to dirty dishwater, but now it reminded me of the clouds brooding over the moorland. Stark, yet oddly beautiful.

'You hate it,' Lucy declared.

'No, I don't! It's just so different from what I'm used to wearing.' I shook out the gown, held it up against my shoulders. 'But it will be much easier to move in. Warm for the winter, too. Once I'm dressed in this, the four women of Felwood Lodge will all match. Like sisters!'

'We're *not* sisters,' Lucy said with a touch more force than she needed to. 'Why do you keep saying that?'

I gathered up the coarse material and folded it. 'It's just an expression.'

'Well, now you can save all your fancy dresses to dance at balls with your *real* sister.' Lucy gestured to my piles of luggage. 'To . . . attract the gentlemen, or whatever it is you do.'

She wanted to nettle me, but I couldn't help laughing instead. She sounded like a sulky child. This was my room, my territory, a portal into my strange world where *she* was the one on the back foot.

'Why do you despise finery so much?' I asked her. 'Come and have a look at my wardrobe. You've clothed me for *your* life; let me show you how I'd dress you for Martingale Hall.'

Before she could object, I'd pulled open my trunk, revealing ribbon and lace, Spencer jackets and fine lawn cotton. A thrill ran through me as I imagined Lucy arrayed for Stamford Assembly Rooms. A diaphanous muslin gown would show her figure to such advantage. I'd put topaz at her throat to catch the colour of her eyes, coax her thick curls into ringlets. She'd be irresistible, a girl *nonpareil*.

'I could never wear any of that,' Lucy protested as I rifled through. 'I don't want to. I'm not pretty like you. I'd look ridiculous.'

With my face buried in the trunk, she couldn't see my flush of pleasure. She thought me pretty! That one word of approval from Lucy, my severest critic, hit with more force than a stream of Mr Randall's compliments ever could.

There. I'd found the item I sought: my most expensive shawl, its Paisley pattern of saffron and oxblood warming even in this weak light. I drew it out and turned to Lucy. 'What about this? It came from India, where your mother was born, all the way across the sea on a ship. Like the moonstone. When it first arrived, it smelt like spices.' I buried my nose into the fabric. 'They're still there, faintly, beneath my scent.'

I'd caught her. Cautiously, Lucy leaned forward and touched the fringe of the shawl with a fingertip. 'It looks so soft.'

'It is.' Taking a step towards her, I wrapped it over her shoulders and pulled the cashmere up against her cheek. The colours suited her; breathed vitality into her skin and made her amber eyes ignite. 'There! That's what a young lady of your birth would be wearing in society, not dull dresses made of wool.'

She stood for a moment as if stunned. Then, slowly, she fed the fringe through her hands. 'No,' she said, her voice thick. 'No . . . it's too fine for me.'

'But why shouldn't you have something nice? You're a baronet's daughter!'

She shrugged her shoulders. The shawl slithered off and she caught it fast between her hands, as she had the hare. 'You speak of my heritage as if it's an honour, but it's not. I'm ashamed to be a baronet's daughter – I don't *want* to be his daughter, or caught in the trappings of his wealth.' She plucked at the worn bodice of her gown. 'This reminds me of who I really am: a shepherdess with a simple life. I am not like the Alaunts.' Her mouth was tremulous but resolute. 'I'll *never* be like them.'

Wasn't she a little curious about her father's family? How did she know they were all so very bad? 'And what *are* they like?' I asked.

She looked as if she'd swallowed something sour. 'Very rich. Decadent. Extravagant. They think they own the world. It doesn't matter to them who suffers for their pleasure. They may powder their hair and drip with diamonds, but inside they are black and cold.'

Her vehemence took me aback. 'Oh. I see.' Awkwardly I began to close up my trunk. I ought to have known from all my novel-reading that titles and wealth were no guarantee of good nature. I ought to have known from my own father's past. These Alaunts sounded like the French aristocrats whose behaviour had fanned the flames of revolution. Wretches who cared nothing for the starving, who told peasants to feed their children grass. I'd forgotten that privilege could bring out the worst in people. And now that my dream of Lucy arrayed in her finery had dimmed, other aspects of the ballroom came to mind: whispers behind fans, insults disguised as compliments, everyone always jostling for position and grasping for more.

Lucy set my shawl gently on the end of the bed. 'You weren't to know. I'm not angry at you. Don't be upset. My anger's against *him*.'

'It's difficult for me,' I admitted from my position kneeling on the floor. 'No one will talk about your father, and I understand why, but . . . it leads to all kinds of mistakes. All I've heard is that he shared your illness and he was violent.'

Lucy took a breath, seemed to be weighing her words carefully. 'It's like this: I feel unwell if I'm overstimulated. I nearly lose control if any emotion is too strong, or my senses are flooded with something too sweet, too bright, too . . .' She met my eyes for an instant then glanced away. 'So I avoid those things. But my father let the illness consume him. He embraced it.'

'Is he mad?'

The words had shot out without thought. I bit my lip, wanting to take it back. But, rather than rounding on me, Lucy just raised her eyebrows.

'Insane? No. I think he is wicked, not sick.'

'How do you know?'

'Because of what he did to my mother. You see the scars she incurred in her escape from Moyset Chase. And they aren't as bad as the reason she had to run away in the first place. My father ordered her to do terrible things. She wouldn't obey him, so he threatened to rip me from her belly and devour me whole. His own daughter.'

My lips moved, but no sound came out.

'A diseased body or a clouded mind are misfortunes. But a corrupt spirit, a distorted soul, is infinitely worse. A lunatic doesn't fully understand what harm his actions cause. My father . . . he knew.'

It meant something, that she was confiding this to me. Surely it signified a level of growing regard? I swallowed. There was no better time to roll the dice, to make my bid for a real place in Lucy's affections.

'Thank you for explaining. It all makes a little more sense now. But I want you to understand something, too.' Climbing to my feet, I gathered my courage. 'Pretty things aren't always about self-indulgence or corruption. Sometimes they can symbolize goodness. Fondness.' I touched the moonstone at my neck. 'This is gorgeous, but Rowena says it's also holy.'

'I suppose.'

Picking up the shawl from the bed, I pressed it into Lucy's hands. 'I want you to keep this. Not to be fine or decadent, but as a token of my friendship. Don't wear it, if you don't like to.'

She looked utterly lost, as she had when I'd given her the toffee. Afraid to trust either me or herself. 'But—' She glanced down, alarmed at the closeness of our fingers as we held the shawl between us.

I pressed on. 'Whenever you see it, remember there's a life beyond today. Your father won't live forever. When you reach twenty-one, he'll have no legal claim on you anyhow! You'll be free. You can even come and visit me. You're *nothing* like him or his horrible family, and no clothes that you put on will ever change that.'

I was rather proud of my little speech. I'd put my heart into it and it sounded like something from a play, spoken by a benevolent heroine. But as I waited, breathless, for Lucy's answer, the reserve swung back into place like a curtain across her face.

'You don't understand,' she said stonily. 'Even when my father is dead, his shadow will cover me still.'

Pulling away from me, she turned and left my room.

But she took the shawl with her.

CHAPTER FIFTEEN

I'd washed the silverware; now I had to dry it as thoroughly and quickly as possible. Moisture sped up the tarnishing process, or so Bridget said. Picking up the plate on top of the stack, I wiped it in small, circular motions. A blurred version of me, an almost-me, squinted back from within the metallic surface.

In truth I felt like that reflection: wispy, not quite solid. It had been a week since I'd seen Mr Randall. No matter how hard I hinted, even suggesting letters from my family might be waiting for me at the post office, Bridget refused to go to Deepbeck, and she wouldn't let me travel alone because of the mad dog. My boredom would be easier to bear if I could win Lucy to my side. But her reaction to the shawl had left me shy of pushing further.

I put my frustration into buffing the plates. 'Softly,' Bridget warned.

Now I'd finished at the sink, she emptied the water out and refilled it with a pot freshly boiled over the fire. Carefully, she placed Lucy's teapot, cup and spoon in to soak, then added a pinch of soda. It fizzed. I watched the water bubbling gently like a witch's cauldron and took up another dish to dry.

Bridget moved back to preparing herbs on a chopping board: plump, straw-coloured capsules with seeds like peppercorn.

'What's that one?'

Quick as a flash, she dropped the knife and slapped my reaching hand away. 'A poppy head. Mind your own chores.'

She was so protective over her work! 'I'm not being nosy,' I said, though I was. 'I'm interested in learning. Can't you teach me a little something about physic?'

That was the right card to play. Bridget gave half a smile. 'You want to be my apprentice, do you?'

'I may as well, while I'm here.'

'Well, you can't mix Lucy's medicine. I've told you before, her condition tests even my skill. But there are plenty of other things you can learn.' Reaching up to a shelf, she drew down a worn leather book. 'This is my catalogue of plants. It explains all the herbs and their medicinal uses, which ones can be found in the Felwood season by season, and how I distil them.'

'May I look at it now?'

'After you've finished your work.'

I fell on the stack of wet silverware with renewed speed, my curiosity sharpened to one focus: Lucy's disease. If I looked up the ingredients Bridget used for her tea, surely there would be a clue to the mysterious illness she and her father shared?

Once the service was dry, I grabbed the book and spread it out over the table. Written inside the cover, in a hand so elegant it would have sent my governess into raptures, was *Bridget Barber, Plants and Receipts*. I sat and flicked through, stopping here and there to inspect the detailed illustrations. 'Did you draw these yourself?' I marvelled.

Bridget preened a little from where she chopped. 'I did.'

I found the poppy heads first. *Toothache, catarrh, to induce sleep.* Then *willow bark, useful for the treatment of nerves and general pain.* The paper whispered as I turned pages back and forth, reading with increasing concern. Here were the herbs I watched Bridget crush every day, faithfully represented. They all had one property in common: *soporific effect.* Again and again.

Red valerian, feverfew, mandrake: each ingredient designed to sedate. I told myself that there were occasions when Lucy really did need to be tranquillized. She'd said that she had trouble sleeping. But this was an awfully large amount of narcotics to administer on a daily basis.

The oaks behind the house groaned as if they, too, were awakening from a long slumber. At the same moment, footfalls sounded on the stairs. I glanced up to see Lucy enter the kitchen, wearing her outdoor things. Not the shawl I'd given her – but it would hardly be appropriate for the farm anyway.

'Hello,' I chirped, mortified at how desperate I sounded.

Bridget turned around in surprise. 'Lucy? What are you doing down here? I thought you were feeling ill.'

Lucy ducked her head, avoiding Bridget's gaze. 'I was. But the air will do me good.' She glanced at me. 'I'm going to scour those fleeces you sorted. Will you hand me a washboard from over there?'

Pushing back my stool, I closed the book and rose from the table. The pair of washboards were leaning against the far wall, beech wood with deep grooves. I picked up one in each hand.

'Do it another day,' Bridget urged. 'Don't go getting all out of breath and bothered. You should rest. Look, I'm just making your tea for you now.'

'I'll drink it when I get back,' Lucy insisted. 'I'll be fine. I need to get out.'

'You *need* to do what you're told,' Bridget cried. 'Why do you bother to ask for my help if you never listen to my advice? You've been getting worse and you'll come crying to me again before today is through, saying you feel unwell.'

Lucy glowered, worked her jaw. 'I want to do this. You can't cage me.'

I handed Lucy one of the boards, but held on to the other. 'Why don't I come and help you?' I suggested. 'Then it won't be as much work.'

The question seemed to surprise her. 'Well . . .' I thought she was about to refuse, but then she caught the entreaty in my eyes. 'You can. If you like.'

Such a small crumb of acceptance and yet I gobbled it up, hastening to put on my outdoor things.

'No! That's not going to make it better!' Bridget huffed. 'You'll be even more stimulated with company. And what about your work here, Camille? A poor apprentice you'd make me! I counted all of five minutes that you were reading that book.'

I rolled my eyes at Lucy and she actually smiled. Her smile was always a surprise. Precious, because it was rare. You had to earn it. Bridget bristled.

'I see you, saucy miss. The pair of you may laugh at me all you choose. But it'll be tears before bedtime and I'm the one who will have to put Lucy back together. You're spoiling all my hard work.'

'Nothing's made me feel so ill today as your incessant nagging!' Lucy burst out. 'For heaven's sake, let me be!'

Bridget threw up her hands in frustration and turned back to the chopping board, punishing the herbs with rapid slices.

Leaving her to her ill humour, we set off into the bonfire of Felwood's autumn together. My feet knew the path well by now. I was starting to recognize some of the birds: jays flashing bright tails, wagging chiffchaffs, and goldfinches with their tinkling call.

'Why was Bridget so grumpy?' I asked Lucy. 'You don't look ill to me. Have you really been feeling worse?'

She shrugged. 'Don't worry about it. Everything I do is wrong in Bridget's eyes lately. My mere existence offends her.'

It certainly did seem that way. I remained silent for a while, watching the forest, reminding myself where Rowena had set the traps. My habitual clumsiness carried a price now: it might cost me my foot.

Flames of bronze and copper lit the foliage above us. Below, the leaf mulch moved with spindly harvestmen and mice hoarding nuts. 'Bridget's behaviour isn't natural,' I said at last, unable to let it go. 'She's lived with you since you were a child; she should be like a family member, fond of you.'

Lucy considered this as I watched the light dapple through the branches across her head. A lock of hair had fallen loose from her cap, flicking with a curl at the end; I wanted to reach out and tuck it back up for her.

'Bridget probably resents me,' she decided. 'She resents that I lived and her baby didn't. She resents that my mother takes my side. Most of all, she resents that she can't cure me. She's been trying my whole life.'

I hadn't thought of that. To Rowena, Lucy was a symbol of hope, the only good thing to come of her disastrous marriage, but to Bridget Lucy must appear the walking embodiment of all her personal failures. However, that wasn't an excuse. None of it was Lucy's fault.

'She's wrong, to blame you for her own problems. And she ought to be a little more careful how she speaks to you. She's entirely dependent on Rowena's charity. If someone talked to *my* daughter like that, I'd throw her out of my house.'

Lucy smirked. 'Would you? But you're thinking of servants and Martingale Hall, not life here. Losing Bridget would be a disaster for us. She makes my medicine, she knows crops, she can walk into the village on our behalf.' She held aside an over-hanging bough so I could pass. Paper-dry leaves dropped as she let it snap back into place behind us. 'No, I'm the one who should be more careful in what I say. As my mother's pointed out many times, we need Bridget a good deal more than she needs us.'

None of that had occurred to me, either. In a way, they were in Bridget's power here. Distantly, a wood pigeon called with its gentle *hoo-hoo-hoo*. 'So no one questions what Bridget does?'

Again, Lucy's lips curled. 'Only you. You question everything.'

It sounded teasing, almost fond.

We reached the meadow. The river slipped clear as a crystal champagne flute across the pebbles lining its bed. Froth rose to the surface, skirting and playing around the rocks. I stood on the bank, peering down, wondering where the water had been and where it was flowing to.

Lucy laid her washboard by my feet. 'Stay there,' she said. 'I'll get the fleeces.'

I dropped my washboard too. Tossing pebbles into the current with a soft plop, I pictured the river unspooling in a silver thread across the moorland, down dizzying slopes and crags until it came to the village of Deepbeck. It might catch a glimpse of Mr Randall there, but it couldn't stop to admire him, for it would be off again, maybe to the sea where white sails bellied in the wind and people scoured the clifftops for Lucy's ichthyosaurus.

One day she'd see the bones of that giant lizard. I made the vow to myself there and then. When I was married to Mr Randall, and Lucy's father was dead, I'd commandeer the carriage and take Lucy off to Lyme Regis where she could hunt unchecked for fossils.

But for now, Lucy went to and from the barn, fetching three buckets full of wool tied into little hanks. Then she sat on the riverbank beside me, spreading her skirts over the clover.

I picked up one of the bundles, soft as a cloud. Its odour was more waxen than greasy out in the air. 'What do we do with these?'

'You take one at a time and let the water run through it. Use the washboard only on the tips if it's needed – and gently, Camille, for pity's sake. The more you bash the wool about, the more it will felt.'

I squatted down. 'And then?'

'We put them back into the buckets and let them soak over-night.'

I thought of Lucy's tea set, bubbling and hissing in soda. 'What do you soak them in?'

'Just cold water, and vinegar, if we have any. If we don't – urine.'

I spluttered and threw down the hank of wool. 'Urine! That's disgusting.' A horrible thought struck me. 'The wool in my dress! Did you soak it in urine?'

Lucy laughed, the most genuine sound of joy I'd ever heard from her. 'Your face! Why are you so *delicate*?'

I wasn't offended. I grinned back. '*Is* it being overly delicate, to want to keep the chamber pot separate from my wardrobe?'

'I can't remember how we soaked that fleece, but it doesn't matter, because I always give it a hot rinse afterwards. So settle yourself down. There's no need for hysterics.' The smile stayed upon her lips. It lifted my heart to see it. A thought seemed to strike her. 'Do you know, my mother once told me about a lady of her acquaintance, back when she lived in society. This lady had set her cap at a gentleman who only cared for blonde hair. So she used to bleach her own locks with horse urine, just to please him.'

'She put her *head* in it?'

We erupted into giggles. I hadn't known Lucy could laugh like that, so freely, almost as beautifully as she sang. It was like being with a different girl altogether. But the moment couldn't last for long. She caught hold of herself suddenly and climbed to her feet, all business once more. 'One piece of wool at a time,' she reminded me. 'Don't go dunking the whole bucket in; fleece is heavy when it's wet.'

The clover grew sparser towards the riverbank, giving way to tacky patches of mud underfoot. Taking a bucket and a washboard, I knelt beside the rushes and the meadowsweet. Stones pressed through the dirt into my legs. I grabbed my first clump of wool and let it soak slowly into the water. A muscular current threatened to tug it from my grip.

'Gently,' Lucy cautioned from upstream.

'I know!'

The river ran so clear that I could see dirty ribbons spiralling out of the fleece and into the flow. From the side of my eye, I watched Lucy with her washboard. She'd assumed I knew what to do with one, but I didn't. I'd just have to imitate her.

My hand was already going numb in the water. As I switched to the other, there was a harsh caw from beyond the crops. I raised my head. Rooks wheeled above the root-cellar in a column of black smoke. What was it that drew them there, time and again? What was it that drew *me*? I had to admit the place was becoming a preoccupation, a constant scratch at the back of my mind. Those uneven stones, the weathered door . . .

Lucy glanced up from her work. 'It's just a cellar,' she said, harshly. 'Why can't you let it alone?'

Because it wasn't 'just a cellar'. It was a secret. So dark, hunched there near the treeline, like a predator waiting to pounce.

'It makes me feel strange,' I answered. 'It gives me goosebumps.'

She fell to scrubbing. 'That's the cold river water.'

I knew better. Just as I knew that the sounds occasionally rising up from its direction weren't foxes, or deer rutting.

Lucy sang, presumably to distract me, but now I'd looked at the cellar I couldn't tear my eyes away. I barely heard her voice or the merry plash of the river, only the hoarse croak that came from the rooks as they spun into dark shapes. A lone bird perched above the door. He started to peck near his feet, tugging at something. There was a mark on the panels I hadn't noticed before. Four white grooves like the slash of claws . . .

I bent forward, trying to see, but I hadn't accounted for how soft the bank was. Everything seemed to crumble beneath me. With a cry I lost my balance, toppling headfirst into the frigid clutches of the river.

Burning cold filled my lungs. I seemed to be spinning, turning like the rooks, and I couldn't tell which way was up. Water rushed past my ears, flooded my nostrils. All I could do was kick blindly for a foothold. Surely the river wasn't this deep . . . But I'd fallen topsy-turvy and my woollen skirts clung, oppressive as guilt, dragging me down, down . . .

Strong hands seized me by the shoulders and brought me gasping to the surface. The light was too bright, too hard.

'Camille! Are you hurt?'

Spluttering, I smoothed the dripping hair back from my face. Lucy stood there, holding me firm as I listed in the current. Her wild locks lay slick across her shoulders, making the panic on her features more prominent. Those sharp, chiselled cheekbones. Water dribbled in silver threads from her ears, the end of her aristocratic nose.

'Camille!'

Digging with my feet, I managed to anchor myself in mud. The water only came up to the bottom of my ribcage but it rolled, splashed and frolicked about us, a living thing.

'I'm fine. No harm done.' I tried to laugh but it came out like a gurgle.

'I thought you were going to drown!' Lucy's teeth were chattering.

I shook my head, feeling the damp hair slither across my neck. 'I can swim. Papa taught us how in the lake. I just got . . . turned about.'

Swimming in the lake at Martingale Hall was one thing, but this river was a fiercer creature. I hadn't realized it was so strong. The current was tugging me irresistibly, inch by inch, closer to Lucy.

'You need to be more careful!' she yelled. Her chest heaved where her woollen dress was plastered against it. 'You are so heedless! What would I tell my mother if something happened to you? What would I *do*?'

She was beside herself. I'd given her a fright and now she couldn't hide the fact: she *cared* whether I lived or died. Triumph filled me to the brim. This was worth almost drowning for. I ought to apologize, to speak words of comfort, but I was too drunk on glee. Instead, I splashed Lucy in the face. 'Whoops.'

She froze, stunned, blinking the water from her eyelashes. 'You . . . you did that on purpose!'

I giggled and splashed her again.

Suddenly, the sun broke out on her face. 'Why, you little . . .' She paddled both hands furiously in the water. Droplets flew around us, made rainbows in the golden sun. I shrieked, more from joy than the cold. I didn't feel the chill any more – I felt free.

Just then something answered our cries of merriment. Not the wail I'd heard before, though it came from the same direction. High-pitched, like nails on a chalkboard. A whining that rose above the river's song to put my teeth on edge.

Lucy stopped dead. 'We need to leave.'

'Why?' I glanced over my shoulder at the root-cellar. The rooks were scattering in fright.

Lucy seized my wrist and began to tug me towards the shore, as firmly as she'd pulled me from the river's churn. I was powerless to resist her. 'We need to go. *Now*.'

Our moment together had been spoiled. We sat huddled on stools before the kitchen fire, towels wrapped around our shoulders, while Bridget poured us cup after cup of hot milk. My woollen dress steamed as it dried, made it look as if I was burning from within.

'You'll catch your death,' Bridget fussed, taking my empty mug. 'Fancy falling in!'

I was more worried about Lucy. Gone was the wide smile, the merry laugh. Crimson brushed the tops of her cheeks and her eyes glowed feverish.

Jerkily, she summoned Rowena to her side and whispered in her ear. I couldn't hear the words, but Rowena's face changed by the light of the flames. I knew in my bones that it must be related to the root-cellar. To whatever lurked, concealed within, behind the sere ivy.

'It's too soon,' Rowena announced, straightening up. 'You must be mistaken, my dear.'

Bridget stopped refilling my mug and became alert. 'What's that?'

'Lucy thinks she heard . . . foxes.'

Each woman held the other's troubled gaze. The fire cracked and quivered. Lucy sipped at her milk in little spasms, as if moving against her volition.

'Lucy's telling the truth,' I said. 'There was something whining like a dog in pain. It was coming from the direction of the root-cellar, the same thing that keened like the souls of the damned before.'

Rowena pulled out her almanac, rapidly scanning the page.

'It definitely sounded . . . *animal*?' Bridget specified. 'You're sure? It couldn't have been a person crying?'

'A person!' I scoffed. 'Impossible. That was an animal. We should have gone to investigate the sound, not come running back here. You might have caught the mad dog in one of your traps!'

Bridget's frown smoothed out. 'You're right. That must be what you heard: a creature in our trap. It makes more sense than . . .'

As she trailed off, Rowena glanced up from her almanac. 'I agree. The moon is only at waning crescent today, as I thought. It shouldn't be strong enough to . . .' Again, she stopped. Why could no one finish a sentence in this house?

'What does the moon have to do with anything?' I demanded. 'This isn't about Lucy's sickness.'

'Camille, please hush.' Lucy put a hand to her forehead. 'I'm getting a headache.'

I gritted my teeth. The last thing I wanted to do was make Lucy ill – but I wouldn't have to ask so many questions if people were less cryptic. My imagination was conjuring up possibilities too terrible for words. Something in the root-cellar that enthralled the corvids and startled them in equal measures. Bridget's work. An experiment. I'd read *Frankenstein* and maybe Bridget had too. Maybe she'd sewn a monster together from dead bodies, a poor creature unable to communicate in human language . . . Unlikely, of course, but I couldn't quite shake the image.

Rowena put her almanac away. 'I'll check the traps. Bridget, can you listen by the root-cellar?'

'I'll come too,' I said, going to rise, but Bridget's hand clamped on my shoulder and held me on the stool.

'You and Lucy will stay here and change your wet clothes. The last thing we need is for the pair of you to come down with influenza.'

I groaned.

Lucy beckoned Rowena back to her side. This time I made out a few of her whispered words. '. . . more powerful than before. I can *feel* it.'

Rowena nodded gravely. 'All right, dear. Leave it to us. Change your clothes and have a lie down. Lock your door behind you.'

'Do you feel very unwell?' I asked Lucy.

She shook her damp head, the ends of her hair still rat-tailed, and set down her cup. 'I don't know. I've never felt quite like this before.' To my surprise, she took my hand. 'Come on, let's go upstairs and get out of Mama's way.'

We rose and made for the door. My gown had stopped steaming, but Lucy's hadn't. Translucent white vapour rose from her neck.

'Do you know what it really was, whining like that?' I whispered. 'I think you must! You were so afraid . . . I know you have your secrets, but can't you just tell me *one* thing? Were we truly in danger, by the river?'

She gripped my hand a little too tight for comfort. 'I thought *you* were in danger,' she said through clenched teeth. 'I didn't save you from drowning only to have a wild predator carry you off instead.'

My cheeks glowed. 'You were frightened only for me?'

She pulled me up the stairs, each of them emitting their own shriek of fear. 'I've been frightened for you since the minute you arrived. Now more than ever.'

'But *why*?'

We reached the landing outside my room. Lucy dropped my hand suddenly, as if it had burnt her. 'Because my illness is getting worse, even before the moon grows. I'm so . . . unsettled. Nothing soothes me, nothing distracts me. My emotions are out of control.'

I touched her shoulder, peered into her averted face. 'You worry too much. Of course I hate to see you ill, but your sickness can't hurt me. And you don't give yourself enough credit! You don't seem "out of control" at all. Even when you scolded Bridget this morning, you were perfectly restrained.'

Without warning, she embraced me. I trembled, caught by surprise, overpowered by the scent of wet wool. Heat burned beneath, heat that seemed to be building, radiating from her throat. 'You have no idea what I'm holding back,' she whispered into my hair. With that, she flung away from me, hastening towards the turret and slamming the door behind her.

CHAPTER SIXTEEN

Of course they told me nothing. Bridget and Rowena returned from their escapade tousled and winded, but they hadn't discovered the origin of the noise – or, if they had, they kept it from me. All I established was that the traps lay empty, still smiling their crocodile smiles, while the mad dog stalked between the trees.

Deepbeck remained off limits for safety. I wasn't sure I could have faced the walk, anyhow, for I had caught a slight chill in the river, leaving my nose blocked and my head sluggish.

Following the short golden days of her acceptance, Lucy seemed reluctant to be in my company again. She stopped waiting for me to walk to the barn, going alone before breakfast and doing all the chores by herself. It might have been kindness, allowing me to nurse my cold, but it still chafed. Sometimes I caught her staring in my direction, yet when I tried to meet her eyes they slipped guiltily away.

She'd laughed with me, she'd hugged me, but now she only had time for Bridget, of all people. They were always together in those days, their private whispers like thistles in my ears.

Seeing my despondency, Rowena asked me to help her make butter. She'd been skimming the cream from our milk over the past few days and now she poured it all into a churn. We took turns twisting the plunger, watching it go round and round, up and down until my head began to spin with it. Slowly – achingly slowly – a transformation took place. The milk membranes ruptured; small grains floated on top of the liquid. Without quite seeing how it happened, I noticed the grains had become clumps. Our butter finally emerged as white and craggy as a snowy mountain; my hands were blistered raw.

Rowena gave me a salve for them. 'All changes worth making hurt a little, my dear,' she said kindly. 'Remember that, as you grow up.'

My spirits rallied at the end of the week as September drew to a close. Michaelmas was here: the feast of the angels. At Martingale Hall it would be a Quarter Day, with all the tenants paying their rents, servants hired or dismissed and the harvest gathered in. We'd eat a roast goose for dinner. Afterwards, the kitchen staff would examine the breastbones and declare if it was going to be a bad winter or not. I didn't expect the same level of celebration at Felwood Lodge, but surely there would be *some* fanfare?

As it turned out, I'd raised my hopes in vain. The morning routine was the same, and dinner that day proved nothing more than a bowl of lentil and parsnip soup. I swallowed it grudgingly. Were there to be no holy days here at all? Would Christmas, Twelfth Night and Easter all pass with the same tedious food?

But when I laid my cutlery down, Bridget rose from the table and began to gather our bowls with a smile on her face. 'There's a treat today,' she announced. 'I had to use up the last of the blackberries.'

There was a tradition not to pick blackberries after Michaelmas day. Legend had it that, when St Michael pushed Lucifer down to earth, he landed on a blackberry bush and spat over the fruit – and it did seem they turned sour from October onwards.

I sat forward on the edge of my chair. 'A treat?'

'Can't you smell it?' Lucy said, thrumming her fingertips on the tablecloth. 'It's been cooking for ages.'

'Indeed, it's the labour of many days,' Rowena said to me. 'Yours included. I know you were vexed that the butter gave you blisters. But I think you'll agree it was worth it when you taste Bridget's blackberry pie.'

Pie was beyond my wildest dreams; at best, I'd expected some kind of jam. Bridget returned, using a towel to hold the hot dish, and the whole room flooded with the fragrance of warm pastry. Even I could smell it through my stuffy nose. It looked perfect, golden brown and steaming.

'I make this every year,' Bridget told me proudly as she set it down. 'Following my mother's recipe. There's no sugar in the crust, so it might not be as fancy as some of your Martingale Hall desserts—'

'You won't hear any complaints from me,' I jumped in. 'Right now I think I'd trade my arm for a slice of that pie.'

Gratified, she picked up a knife and cracked the top of the pastry. The blade passed slowly through, releasing steam and a satisfying squelch as it pulled berries asunder. 'It's only right our guest should have the first slice.'

Manners had been so firmly drilled into me that I sat with my hands upon my lap, waiting for everyone else to be served before I started. Lucy fidgeted, swinging her feet under the table as Bridget doled out a slice for Rowena, then set one in her own place.

Finally, Bridget passed behind me with the fourth plate for Lucy.

I didn't quite see what happened. Lucy moved; Bridget cried out and then slammed into the back of my chair. My chest bumped against the table.

Winded, I looked up and saw Lucy was eating – but the way she ate! Mouthful after mouthful shovelled in rapid succession, slopping juice on to the tablecloth.

'Really!' Rowena cried. 'What has got into you? Apologize to Bridget at once.'

She might as well have been speaking to the wall. Lucy didn't even stop to chew.

'She's getting worse.' Bridget's voice sounded strangled. She backed away, towards Rowena at the other end of the table, clutching one of her hands to her chest. 'I feared this would happen.'

Rowena rose to her feet. 'Did she hurt you?'

Bridget showed her. 'Not badly. It'll bruise where she grabbed at me.'

A berry flew in my direction, splattering on the cloth beside my plate. Purple dribbled out, lurid as a bloodstain against the white.

I regarded Lucy with dismay. My laughing girl from the river had gone. Now she was a puppet being moved by unseen hands, scraping her plate clean and sucking greedily upon her silver spoon. After a moment, her mouth puckered around the stem. She groaned, retched, and pulled it out with a loud pop, sending the utensil clattering to the table. Her lips were left peeling. A livid red mark stretched across her palm. I stared in disbelief. So silver really *did* have a physical effect on Lucy when she was ill.

'I need to increase her dose,' Bridget said. Rowena gave a slight shake of her head. 'I *need* to – look at her!'

Tears filled Rowena's eyes, one milky, one blue. 'Very well. But just a little! Fetch it now.' Bridget scurried from the room. 'Camille, come away from the table, there's a good girl. Lucy is not quite . . . herself.'

I could think of only one thing to do. If Rowena was right about silver, moonstone should work too. Fumbling at the chain, I removed my necklace and set it on Lucy's empty plate.

'Camille! Come here.'

I obeyed my godmother, but I could see the stone was having

an effect on Lucy. Her gaze sank to the plate, the fire simmered lower in her bright eyes, and her jaw unclenched.

Bridget returned with the teapot and thrust it at Rowena. 'You pour. I'm not going near her again.'

What were they so afraid of? Lucy had been a little rough taking the plate from Bridget, but she was ill, not dangerous . . .

Rowena gathered herself, took a deep breath. 'I need you to drink this, my dear. It'll make you feel much better.'

Lucy scrubbed her sleeve across her lips as her mother approached. A ghost of purple-red remained on her chin, like a birthmark. With steady hands, Rowena poured a dark stream into Lucy's cup. A flicker of aversion crossed her face. I remembered with a sick plunge that first day, when she'd fought against the tea. I didn't want them to force her like that again.

'There is to be no discussion. You *will* drink it.'

To my relief, Lucy reached for the cup. Watching the moonstone, she drank in hesitant sips, each swallow making her wince. She'd scarcely set the empty vessel down when Bridget piped up behind me. 'Another.'

Rowena glared at her.

'Make her drink another cup,' Bridget insisted. 'We've already had one . . . unexpected change.'

Reluctantly, Rowena refilled the cup. 'You can bear this,' she murmured to her daughter. 'I know you can. We must make sure Camille is quite safe.'

Lucy's gaze reached for mine like a hand. It was her again, fully present behind those golden eyes. They were brimming with urgency. She tipped the cup back and emptied it in one large gulp.

For an instant, nothing happened. Then she dropped forward, just as I'd tumbled into the river, her head landing with a crack on the plate before her.

Rain tapped on the roof. A soft, crackling sound filled the room as the oak trees and the ivy began to drip. The rhythm grew faster, stronger. Soon the wind had joined the orchestra, picking up raindrops like pebbles and flinging them through the boards across my window. Tired and poorly as I was, I couldn't sleep.

I lay there, turning the moonstone over and over between my fingertips, trying to make sense of all I'd seen and heard. The struggle between Bridget and my godmother, invisible but strong enough to charge the atmosphere. *I need to increase her dose*, Bridget had said. *We've already had one unexpected change.* Only now did it strike me how odd her speeches were, how many questions they raised. There was a heaviness in my chest and a rawness in my throat that had nothing to do with the chill I'd caught.

Again I saw Lucy gobbling up the fruit pie: a girl hungry for more. Was her behaviour so very unacceptable, in the grand scheme of things? Did it merit such panic? No matter how long I stared at the ceiling, I couldn't reconcile her conduct with the response. Deep down I felt Bridget had done something wrong. A line had been crossed and I'd just stood there and watched it happen.

I must have drifted off eventually, for the next thing I knew, drab light was trickling in between the planks on my window. Feet paced somewhere in the house. Groggily, I opened my eyes. It was barely dawn; early for anyone to be up and about, even at Felwood Lodge. I nestled back down, keen to disappear into dreams and imagine myself back in the river with Lucy, both of us laughing, rainbows arcing through the spray . . .

A rough clip of boots passed my door. I heard the turret unlock. Someone was climbing the stairs. Rowena's voice echoed, far above me, and Lucy's came fretful in response. She was awake, then. The *increased dose* had worn off, but something was going on. Crawling out of my warm nest, I fished beneath the bed for the chamber pot.

That was when I noticed the blood. My nightgown was stained. A small, rusty patch marked the bedclothes. Damnation.

I'd been so busy getting used to my new life that I hadn't prepared for my monthly course arriving. Now there were no housemaids to boil away my accidents; everything would be washed here. Everyone would know! Mortified, I reached for my portmanteau, trying to remember where I'd put the rags I'd brought precisely for this purpose.

'Stop!' Rowena called from above.

Footsteps rapidly approached. 'I told you, something is wrong with Camille!' Lucy's voice.

Too late, I realized I'd forgotten to lock my door. 'Wait—' I started, but, before I could finish, Lucy had burst into the room like a firecracker.

Dismay knocked my vision askew. I saw them in flashes: Rowena in the doorway, stricken with absolute horror, and Lucy's nostrils flaring like a spooked horse. She took in the blood. Then she began to scream. At least, I thought it was a scream. A guttural, haunted sound, horribly familiar.

'Lucy,' I stuttered. My face burned hot as a coal. 'It's – it's – all right – I—'

Rowena lunged, pulling Lucy's arms behind her back as Bridget came clomping up the stairs. Shouts rang in my ears. I couldn't distinguish the words. Lucy's scream was echoing, reverberating dreadfully.

This couldn't be happening.

Lucy thrashed about in her mother's grip, her lovely features mottled and contorted. With Bridget's help, Rowena managed to heave her back across the threshold. They kicked my door shut; I heard a key turn in the lock.

'Wait! What are you doing?' I called, but no one answered.

Scuffling in the corridor: blows against the walls, squeaking over the floorboards. They were grappling, wrestling with one another. Somebody snarled. There came the sound of an open-handed slap, skin against skin. I gasped. Had one of them *struck* Lucy?

The hubbub moved off down the corridor, towards the turret room, leaving me shaken and alone.

I cleaned myself up as best I could. Tying on my belt and clouts, I dressed for the day, even pinned up my hair, but the house remained unsettlingly quiet.

Once, when we were small, I'd wet the bed I shared with Marie. My sister had been revolted and refused to speak to me for two days. The same feelings of dirtiness and shame returned now, even though none of this was my fault. Natural bodily functions were not a crime, so why was I locked in my room?

All the while, the rain whispered on.

A dragging pain started in my lower back. I sat wearily upon my bed and took up Ovid to amuse myself. Time alone was, at least, time to read, but I found the story of Lucy concerned me more than any myth. Had she recovered from that horrid convulsion yet? What was happening to her now? The way she had screamed . . . no, *bayed*. The realization struck me cold: it had sounded like the noise that came from the root-cellar.

By and by the door unlocked and Rowena entered the room, holding a cup. She looked drained, pale, her scars standing out more starkly than ever. 'I am so sorry for everything that's occurred this morning, Camille. You must be confused and afraid. I ought to have known that this would happen soon. I didn't consider the matter of your monthly courses, obvious though it should be.'

'How's Lucy?' I demanded, throwing the book aside.

'Resting.' She kicked the door closed behind her and offered me the mug. 'Now, Bridget tells me the tea she's made you today is a little different. Ginger, turmeric and raspberry leaf with shepherd's purse. She says it makes your courses lighter and cuts them short by a few days.'

Warily I gazed into the murky liquid. Notes of ginger zinged out – Bridget had told the truth about that ingredient, at least.

But I kept remembering the way Lucy's head had slammed into the table after her second drink yesterday. I saw again the sedatives in the book, and those purple-blue flowers, jingling bells I was forbidden to touch. I accepted the cup, but only cradled it.

'Bridget drinks it herself,' my godmother went on, seeing my hesitation. 'Although I have to say, her courses have never produced such a marked reaction in Lucy. This is something . . . unprecedented. I did not expect it.'

Fine vapour blew on to the back of my neck through the window. I sat forward. 'Is Lucy very ill when her own curse arrives?'

A hard spatter of rain. Rowena's hands balled into fists, then stretched again. 'The fact of the matter is, Lucy hasn't bled yet. It is full late, I know, but her condition . . .' She trailed off. Didn't look directly at me. 'Your mother was there with me when Lucy was born. I don't suppose she's told you anything about my travails?'

I shook my head.

'No . . . that is for the best. Suffice to say I suffered terribly and . . . well, I, also, have not bled since. So you see, Lucy has had little exposure to the way of women.'

Rowena twitched her gaze away.

'I must keep her from all the factors that aggravate her symptoms. It is imperative for us all. So, I've decided that Lucy will have to stay in the turret until your flow has stopped.'

She couldn't be speaking in earnest. 'That could be a whole week!'

'Indeed.'

'And the situation will recur. I'm staying here for a year; she can't possibly be confined to her chamber for seven days every month!' Her silence turned my voice into a pathetic thread. 'She *can't*, Godmother. That would be absurd.'

'Then we will have to be absurd,' Rowena said sadly. 'To

protect her health. To protect us all. I do not expect you to understand.'

The wisps of steam rising from my mug were growing fainter and fainter. The tea seemed to have cooled along with the atmosphere between me and my godmother. She was right: I didn't understand, and no one would take the trouble to explain Lucy's illness to me fully. In society, infirmity was often glossed over, treated as a matter of secret shame, but why should that be so here? There was no reputation or marriage prospects for this family to protect. And as for the symptoms – the *irritants*, as Rowena called them – they grew more outlandish by the day. No moonlight, no meat, no digging, no sugar, no blood . . .

'Now, drink your tea,' she ordered. 'It's time I prepared breakfast. We will have more chores to share between us, with Lucy ill.'

I waited for her to leave and shut the door. Then I emptied the concoction Bridget had made me straight into the chamber pot.

CHAPTER SEVENTEEN

It wasn't like the last time Lucy fell sick. The indifference I'd felt towards her then was gone. Now I craved her presence in the barn. The animals knew I wasn't their mistress and they wanted none of me. Queenie kicked the bucket over as I tried to milk her and the chickens took umbrage again, reproaching me with their harsh squabbles.

The barn had been starting to feel like a pleasant place, but Lucy's absence reduced it back to a stinking shed. Her milking stool leant against the wall, forlorn. There was no song to distract me as I worked Queenie's udders. I even missed the teasing snipes.

What would Lucy do with her time, up in that tower, gazing at the stars? Perhaps she blamed me for her imprisonment. She might be revolted after what she'd seen. Even now, the remembrance of it made me choke. Everything I did in front of Lucy was wrong, or embarrassing or stupid.

As I forked the endless piles of dung, I considered writing home. Telling my mother about the sedatives and the confinement. Would Mama just think I was meddling in Lucy's treatment, being fanciful as usual? Pierre would call me a busybody, starting baseless rumours—

I stopped, leaning upon my pitchfork as inspiration struck. Maybe for once gossip could prove to be my ally. Because of my Vauxhall scandal, there was someone nearby willing to help me. Someone who'd be only too delighted to listen – and I to see him.

I just had to find a way to get myself to The Grey Lady inn.

'I'm going for a stroll.'

'A *stroll*?' My godmother glanced up from darning a stocking as I poked my head into the parlour. Her hands dropped when she observed my appearance.

Perhaps I *had* made too much of an effort, coaxing the short hair at my forehead into curls, pinching my cheeks for colour and dressing once more in my flowered bonnet and blue pelisse. I'd known it would raise suspicion, but I couldn't face the thought of Mr Randall seeing me in a frumpy, shapeless dress.

Bridget kept clacking her knitting needles. 'How many times must I tell you? My orders at the apothecary won't be ready yet. Leave it a week or so and then we'll go to Deepbeck together, I promise.'

'But I want the exercise now!' I complained.

'I'm not happy with the idea of you out walking alone,' Rowena said. 'Have you forgotten the mad dog on the loose?'

I almost had. 'Would it be abroad in daylight? I highly doubt it . . .'

'Even so.'

'I promise to stick to the paths!' I exclaimed. Then I fished about my pockets. 'Remember my father gave me this penknife, to defend myself with.'

Rowena tied off her stitch. 'No, I'm afraid I cannot permit you to walk into Deepbeck, Camille. It would not be responsible of me.'

Frustration spurted. She wasn't my parent; she had no right to forbid me. 'I don't mean to walk all the way to Deepbeck!

I was going to head somewhere nearer. Just, say, to the inn and back? Please, I'm bored to death without Lucy.'

Rowena exhaled. 'Well, the inn *is* closer to home. Yet still . . .'

'I suppose it might be good for Lucy, to get Camille out of the house for a while,' Bridget put in. 'Take away the scent of blood.'

As if my blood could have any effect upon Lucy from down here, when she was two flights above! But Bridget's nonsense helped my case, so I nodded eagerly. 'You might even let Lucy out of the turret for a spell. Poor thing, I'm sure she's clawing at the walls by now.'

Rowena frowned at my turn of phrase. 'This is not about Lucy. It's about your safety. And your visiting the inn would be sure to draw attention.'

'I won't go *inside*!' I wasn't adept at lying. My voice jangled false and bright. 'What would *I* want in a coaching inn? I won't even go out on the road, Godmother. I'll just walk within sight of The Grey Lady and return straight home.'

I tried to veil my expression, to look blank and innocent beneath that piercing blue eye. My heart was beating so hard that I was sure she must hear it.

Finally, she picked up her stocking. 'Very well. But you must promise to take care, Camille. And if you glimpse anything odd at all, man or beast, I want you to turn back at once.'

Again, I had to fight against my face – this time to look less wildly happy. 'I will.'

Anticipation and the chill October breeze propelled me along. I barely noticed the martins migrating overhead, or the red toadstools that sprouted at the roots of the shivering birch. After a whole two weeks, I had the chance to see Mr Randall again. Assuming he hadn't lost hope in my absence and returned home. Lord, I dearly hoped not.

Nothing tripped me or tangled in my skirts as it had on the night I'd first arrived and taken this path in the opposite direction. It wouldn't dare; today I was unstoppable. I waded through the mud, ignored the drips that fell from the canopy above to make polka-dots on my pelisse. Dregs of rosebay willowherb lined the verges of the road. Michaelmas daisies flared purple here and there. In this part of the wood, the leaves of the oaks wore galls like tiny buttons. I pushed one of their branches aside and there before me stood The Grey Lady with its smoking chimneys, just as I remembered. Now it was my turn to emerge from the trees, as Rowena had, and be the formidable woman who walked alone through forests towards the inn.

But as I started out along the road, my assurance began to fade. A group of servants were clustered in the courtyard, near to an open door that must be an entrance to the kitchens. Ostlers, waiters, maids and the boot boy all talked over one another, gesturing wildly. Their faces looked pale and strained. Not wanting them to see me, I ducked back into the cover of the trees. Their words didn't carry, but the energy of them did. Electric. Something was afoot at the inn today and maybe that would work in my favour. I might be able to slip in unobserved, and thereby keep the spirit, if not the letter of my promise to Rowena. I was bound to draw *some* attention. A young lady didn't usually go wandering into taprooms alone . . .

Creeping on a little farther behind the fretwork of the oaks, past the main entrance, I came to the stable-blocks on the far side of the courtyard. No carriages stood waiting for assistance. I couldn't even spot the grooms moving to and fro. They must all be over by the kitchen, seeking the gossip. If there was any place to sneak nearer, it was here.

I crossed the road, dodging puddles and dung as I went. The dusty-sweet aroma of horses percolated through the damp air. I could hear them, shifting in their stalls, whinnying low. There came the steady *crack crack* of a hoof kicking against wood.

181

My eyes followed the sound. A jet-black mare was tossing her head over the half-door. I'd listened to enough of Pierre's orations to know that this was a hot-blooded creature; she had an Arabian arch to her neck and a slender nose, better suited to the winner's circle at Newmarket than pulling a chaise. And she seemed to know her worth; she wasn't happy here.

Bang, bang. She kicked on, neighs juddering from deep in her chest. I stole a step closer. She was magnificent – frightening in her power. Her coat shone black as obsidian. She must be one of the pair I'd spotted, pulling the fine equipage the night I'd arrived. That had been a while ago now, but I couldn't imagine two very wealthy visitors crossing this inn in the space of a month. It was so remote and off the toll roads.

The whites of the mare's eyes showed. Her delicate nostrils flared, but she didn't flatten her ears; they were flicking back and forth.

'Can I help you, miss?'

I jumped. With the horse kicking at her door, I hadn't heard the man sneak up to my side. He wore the felt hat and stout shoes of a groom. His shirt sleeves were rolled back to the elbows, showing arms coated in thick hair.

'Oh! No, thank you. I was just admiring the horse. One does not expect to find an animal of such quality in a coaching inn.'

He grinned. His teeth were discoloured at the base either from rot or tobacco. 'Nay. You'd travel the breadth of England without finding her equal. Thanks be *she* wasn't hurt last night! Mr Randall would never have forgiven us.'

My mouth dropped open. 'Mr Colin Randall?'

'Aye.'

I daresay I looked very foolish, gaping at him like a fish. 'This is his horse?'

'It is, miss. One of a pair. Would you like to see the other? She's almost as bonny.' He looked at me askance, crinkling his eyes. 'Are you a friend of the gentleman?'

I shook myself. I was rousing curiosity, exactly what I'd promised not to do. 'It doesn't signify. I'm returning inside now. Good day to you.'

I turned from him, all aflutter, and headed for the dull stone building. My mind was dancing waltzes. Could this mare be the famous Shadow, who had caused the rupture between Mr Randall and Pierre? I'd imagined a fine horse, but not a king's mount! I hadn't realized Mr Randall's family were so affluent – no, *rich*. With a horse like that, another equally fine and the carriage I'd seen them pulling, he must be a second Croesus. But he'd never entered the village dressed as one of the *bon-ton*. He wore simple clothes, blended modestly in among the citizens of Deepbeck. That only spoke more to his favour.

Mr Randall was too good to be true. Like a fairytale. How was it he favoured *me*? I wished now that I didn't have muddy petticoats or damp curls to see him.

A warm fug of tobacco, boiled mutton and wood smoke reached out to greet me the moment I entered the inn. Ducking beneath a stout beam, I saw the landlady barking orders to an underling. She was no longer rosy and cheerful, as she'd been when I came with my father. Her face was lined with harassment.

'Good day.'

She didn't recognize me from before. 'Yes?' she snapped.

I drew back slightly. She wasn't supposed to speak to a gentlewoman like that. I found myself compensating for her rudeness, my voice suddenly refined and cut-glass. 'I do beg your pardon. I am here in search of my dearest kinsman, Mr Colin Randall. He told me he was staying at this establishment and I should be most welcome to call upon him. But perhaps I am mistaken?'

The landlady coloured and straightened her cap. 'Mr Randall? I'm ever so sorry, miss. I didn't mean to speak hastily. There has been a dreadful to-do with the mail . . . but that is not your concern. Mr Randall is in the parlour as we speak, taking his breakfast. Shall I show you in?'

Breakfast! It was past eleven o'clock. But I was forgetting the fashionable hours of society. The day was long when you were forced to rise with the dawn. Back home, I'd eaten later too.

'If you please.'

As I followed the landlady inside the parlour, I spotted him instantly, at a table near the sofa where I'd drunk tea with my father. He rose swiftly to his feet.

'Miss Garnier! What a delightful surprise! I was beginning to despair of ever seeing you again.' Bustling forward, he shook me heartily by the hand. There was a tightness in my stomach, a shift beneath my ribcage. He wasn't fully attired; he wore no coat or even cravat. His silk waistcoat hung open and his black curls tumbled as if he'd only recently climbed out of bed.

'Good morning . . . cousin,' I invented, breathless.

The landlady seemed to swallow my lie – or rather, she was too preoccupied to care about our youthful romance. 'Shall I bring another pot of coffee, Mr Randall?'

'Yes, thank you. My *cousin* will be joining me for breakfast.'

He pulled out a chair so that I could sit. For the first time I noticed the breakfast spread. Marmalade, honey-cake and cold pork. Lumps of sugar and warm cream for the coffee. It would take all my self-control not to behave as Lucy had with the blackberry pie, and inhale it all in one gulp.

He poured me a cup, toasting the air around us, and began to pile my plate high. 'You must excuse my state of *déshabille*,' he said, plopping sugar into my cup. 'I was awake uncommonly late. That terrible business with the mail coach. The place was in uproar, not a wink of sleep to be had.'

I watched his elegant hand, stirring the coffee anticlockwise. 'What happened to the mail coach?'

His dark eyes widened. 'Did you not hear? Upon my word,

Miss Garnier, you told the truth when you said your godmother was the reclusive sort. She must be living beneath a rock. The coach was attacked in the early hours of the morning! The entire vehicle overturned, spilling letters, cracking skulls. They carried the driver here, but I don't know whether the poor fellow is still alive or has perished of his injuries.'

'Good God! And was it highwaymen?'

He rasped a palm over his chin. The shadow of stubble there suited him more than clean-shaven skin. 'No, that's the worst of it all. You must recall the beast we spoke about, when we met in Deepbeck?'

With a sinking feeling, I dragged the cup of coffee towards me and held it in my palms. 'An animal did this?'

'Yes.' Reaching for a piece of toast, he began to butter it. 'It would appear the creature is much larger than we first supposed. Wily, too. It lurked by the side of the road and then pounced on the horses – tore them quite to shreds, I understand. Animals always sense these things. My own mares have been jittery all morning.' He took a large bite of the bread.

This was terrible news indeed. Rowena would be beside herself – she certainly wouldn't let me go wandering through the forest alone again. But it was too strange. I'd never heard of such accidents happening. The drivers of mail coaches were armed with a blunderbuss; surely they could stop a dog with ease?

I sipped at the coffee. Its bittersweet taste gave my senses a wonderful kick.

'My godmother said there was a rabid dog in these parts once before. But there was nothing like this – devouring horses! What do they suppose the beast is?'

Colin swallowed and dabbed at his lips with a napkin. 'This you will not believe. Passengers of the coach said they saw a wolf.'

'Impossible! We've not had wolves in the wilds of England

since . . .' I did not perfectly recall the date, but I was sure my governess had said it was long ago.

'Quite,' Colin agreed. 'We can only speculate that it escaped from some menagerie or stowed away on a boat. Either that, or the rumours have been blown out of all proportion. But no small animal would be capable of taking down a horse of sixteen hands, travelling at speed.' He picked up his knife and fork. 'And yet here you are, Miss Garnier, setting out boldly to see me. I ought to scold you for putting yourself in danger, but I do so admire your spirit.'

I gave him a flirtatious look. 'Well, I was very hungry.'

We ate for a moment in companionable silence, enjoying the fire's warmth and the glimmer of the horse brasses from the wall. I almost forgot why I was there. The flavours bursting in my mouth were even richer than I remembered, full of texture, awakening all my senses. The resistance of pork between my teeth, the satisfying slip of jam across my tongue. And, there before me, a man who looked good enough to eat himself. I was well contented. It would have been worth the risk of a dozen wolves to come here for this.

'I must say,' he said at last, 'it's a relief to see you so well. I sought you out in Deepbeck, but with the length of time that has passed since we last met . . .' Mr Randall ran a hand through his dishevelled hair. 'At first I worried I'd offended you. But then my anxiety took a different turn. I began to hear the strangest rumours about your godmother, Mrs Talbot. I'm afraid she is not at all liked in the village.'

I fidgeted on my chair, discomforted to think I'd nearly forgotten poor Lucy and my errand here. How easily my head was turned! 'Actually, Mr Randall—'

'Colin, please,' he grinned. 'Are we not cousins this morning?'

Suddenly the fire was a touch too warm. 'Colin, then . . . The truth is, I set out here today not only to see you, but to consult you. To ask your opinion.'

'Then you do me great honour.'

I wanted to tell him everything. Yet Lucy had been so adamant about hiding from her Alaunt family. I was loath to betray her secrets; she'd never forgive me.

'I'm worried about my godmother too. Can you please tell me what it is they say about Mrs Talbot in Deepbeck? Why is she disliked?'

For a moment he just looked at me with those star-studded eyes. Then he blinked and wet his lips. 'I shall certainly tell you what I've heard, but you won't like what I have to say. And I must ask *you* something first. Does your godmother truly have sisters? They say in Deepbeck that there are two other ladies living with her, but no one has ever set eyes upon them.'

I cleared my throat, performing mental gymnastics in an effort not to lie outright. 'There are four of us. The other two do not leave the house.'

'Ah.' Again he rubbed at his chin. It brought my focus to his mouth. The taste of it was still etched upon my memory. 'That complicates matters, indeed it does. For in some circles they believe she is performing some type of scientific experiment upon animals. I'd almost hoped that was the case.'

All at once, I saw the root-cellar, the claw marks, and the cries of despair were ringing in my ears. 'Why – why would they say she's hurting animals?'

'Well . . . it cannot have escaped your notice that Mrs Talbot places many orders at the apothecary. I met you there myself, waiting for her.'

The taste of pork rose at the back of my mouth. 'Yes. She needs . . . medicine.'

Colin dropped his hand and began to toy with his cup, clearly uncomfortable. I was too, but the words must be spoken.

'What does the apothecary say?'

He took a breath. A toby jug leered over his shoulder. 'The truth is, the items your godmother purchases at the apothecary

are . . . unusual. Dangerous, even. Sedatives enough to tran-
quillize the beast that attacked the stagecoach.'

The smack of Lucy's head as it hit the table. I pushed away
the memory. 'Yes. It's true. That's what worries me. I fear that
perhaps she is administering too much . . . But she says her
father was an apothecary himself and she knows what she is
doing . . .'

Colin tapped a fingernail against his cup. 'Well, that's the
other unpleasant rumour. People begin to say that her sisters
are not ill at all. That she poisons them, to keep them needing
her.'

The room seemed to go very still. I could no longer hear the
clink of Colin's nail nor the merry crackle of the fire. Even the
sounds of cutlery and feet moving on the floorboards above
faded away. 'Mrs Talbot has actually purchased poison?'

'So they say.'

I thought of Bridget, friendless and alone. Her only excuse
to stay at Felwood Lodge was to mix Lucy's medicines. Could
she really be keeping her ill, on purpose? 'Good God, this is
monstrous.'

His brow furrowed with concern. 'Do you think it possible?'

I looked up to the window, to the woods creeping close to
the road. 'Yes,' I admitted. Mama wouldn't be able to dismiss
my concerns now. If I wrote and told her the apothecary was
suspicious of Bridget, and had sold her poison, she couldn't
accuse me of an overactive imagination. 'I hope to God I'm
wrong, but this is just what I feared you'd say. Something very
strange is going on at the house and I don't know what to do
for the best.'

'You must leave your godmother, Miss Garnier. That much
is evident.'

Even sitting down, I felt as though I were plummeting from
a great height. He reached for my hand.

'Don't be afraid! I'll take you into my protection and reunite you with your family. I can have my carriage ready in a moment to carry you home to Martingale Hall . . .' He let go of his hold on me, conscious of others looking our way.

My heart thudded. I could have done it. Were his carriage at the door, I might have thrown caution to the wind and climbed straight inside. But, as I glanced down at my plate to see the smear of mustard and the pork bones, I had a sudden vision of Lucy. The way she had dropped, head-first.

'I – I cannot. I thank you, but—'

'My dear Miss Garnier, this is no time for missish scruples. Your godmother sounds dangerous. I am a man of my word; do you not trust me to escort you home?'

'It's not that. One of the ladies is my friend. I cannot leave her.' I drew myself up, suddenly certain. 'I *will* not. If she's in trouble, I must try to help her.'

He blew out his breath. 'You good and excellent creature! I should have expected nothing less of you. But what can you practically do, without putting yourself at risk?'

'I'll write to my mother – no, my father – and explain everything. He's known Mrs Talbot for many years; he'll be able to advise me best. And in the meantime I'll have the comfort of knowing you are close by, Mr Randall, and ready to assist me if the need arises. For that I am eternally grateful.'

His fingernail tapped anxiously against the cup again. My answer didn't satisfy him. 'We could go to your godmother's house now, and sort this sorry business out at once. We could carry your friend back here to the inn! I shall run mad if I must endure another fortnight without sight or word of you, supposing the worst . . . Consider the time that must elapse before Mr Garnier's advice can reach you! The mail coach has just been attacked; all the post is in disarray . . . Will you even be able to send the letter today?'

This gave me pause. Bridget had said we must wait a week before walking to Deepbeck and the post office again. 'I don't suppose, if I wrote the letter here and now, you would be able to post it for me?'

He brightened. 'That's an idea! I will go one better: I will have it sent by express.'

A generous offer, for it would cost him several pounds. 'Would you? That would be wonderful! I can walk to Deepbeck in a week's time. Perhaps, if I'm very fortunate, an answer will be waiting for me by then.'

Colin nodded. 'And, if it isn't, you must come here to me again. In the meantime I'll see if I can find any more information about Mrs Talbot . . . But there is the waiter.' He gestured to the servant. 'Let's have him clear the table. I'll fetch my writing equipment for you.'

CHAPTER EIGHTEEN

The herbal tea Bridget made for me was innocent enough. By the insipid morning light, I checked every ingredient in her leather-bound book. But there was no mistaking the entry I found at the back: the purple-blue bells which nodded by the root-cellar, labelled clearly in Bridget's own hand.

Wolfsbane. Also known as monkshood. All parts poisonous. Toxins may seep into the skin through touch. Symptoms include palpitations, restlessness, convulsions and hallucinations.

I sat cross-legged on my narrow bed, staring at the open page. Willing it to change. But even as the blur of sleep cleared from my eyes and birds awoke in the treetops, the writing remained the same. Indelible. Colin was right, and the rumour breathed upon the air in the village of Deepbeck was true. Bridget had been poisoning Lucy.

The boards over my window pulled and strained in the wind like a horse on a short rein. My mind was struggling too, trying to free itself from a sticky web of lies. Had Lucy ever really been ill at all? Or had every one of her spasms been caused by the tea she drank?

My first instinct was to fly downstairs with the book and show my evidence to Rowena. Yet surely she must know? She wasn't a stupid woman, to be duped by someone like Bridget. It would not have taken her sixteen years to uncover what I'd managed to figure out in the space of barely a month. For some unimaginable reason, she was letting this abuse happen to her daughter.

And then my thoughts began to sink indeed, every surety crumbling to dust under closer inspection. Because if Rowena were not the doting mother she appeared . . . what else had she lied about?

Hearing her footsteps coming up the stairs, I made a hasty decision. Closing the book of herbs, I rose and opened my door just as Rowena was sweeping past towards the turret.

'How is Lucy?' I demanded.

Rowena slowed her step, although she didn't stop. 'Better,' she called over her shoulder. 'But she's still not entirely well, Camille.'

Perhaps she thought I'd leave it at that, but I trailed her all the way to the heavy wooden door. She paused there to unhook the chatelaine of keys from her belt. I watched her in profile, seeking the features of a woman who'd hurt her own daughter, but she looked only pale and tired. The skin on her forehead was drawn taut where she'd brushed back her hair and braided it tight.

'I want to see Lucy,' I said. 'I've stopped bleeding completely now.'

She didn't answer immediately. Threading the key into the lock, she let it turn with a deep-throated *clunk*. 'Well . . . I suppose you may come up for a little while.'

The turret was sour with an unpleasant tang, like when one of Papa's dogs got caught in the rain. Rowena began to mount the stone steps and I followed behind her, watching her gown sweep over each stair. 'What's that smell? Did you burn vinegar for Lucy's illness?'

'There have been . . . many medicines,' Rowena answered vaguely.

I couldn't resist pushing her further. 'Medicines such as?'

'Such as camphor julep and . . . I forget what Bridget calls the other stuff. Nothing yields much relief.' She placed a hand against the wall, guiding her. 'In my experience, silver and moonstone work better on Lucy than any herbs.'

We stopped again as Rowena applied another key to the second door. It felt as though I was going to visit someone in jail. The metallic grate of the lock went straight to my back teeth.

'Godmother, if nothing works, then why don't you tell Bridget to stop giving Lucy herbs altogether?' I studied her for a reaction, some sign of guilt.

'I dare not,' she said simply, and pushed open the door.

It was still night, in there. The only thing deeper than the darkness was the silence. No birds trilling, no branches scratching against the wall; at this end of the house, the whole of Felwood seemed to hold its breath. I was tempted to hold mine too; the bitterness reeked stronger than ever.

'Oh, dear. Your candles have all burnt out.' Rowena stepped forward, reaching in her pocket for a tinderbox. As she brought one of the candelabras flickering to life, I caught a flash of Lucy; not lying in bed where I'd expected her to be, but sitting by the closed curtains in a rocking chair. My shawl was wrapped around her shoulders.

'Lucy . . .'

'Camille!' My name emerged as a wheeze. Lucy tried to rise, but her legs wouldn't hold her. She fell back and the rockers bumped.

'Careful, now!' The light rippled as Rowena rushed to steady the chair.

I stood frozen, appalled at the change that had come over

Lucy in our few days of separation. Her hair fell lank and had been brushed tamely over one shoulder. There was no more colour in her skin than in the wax candles that dripped by her side. Her silver choker had been polished to a mirror sheen, but that was the only glimmer of brightness.

Rowena held the chair firm from behind. 'I'm sorry, did we wake you?'

'Camille's . . . alive,' Lucy choked. 'I thought . . . I saw you bleeding. I've been so confused.' She raised a hand to her forehead. Her fingernails weren't a healthy pink and white; they looked like something carved from horn. 'I thought perhaps . . . I'd hurt you.'

I skewered my godmother with an accusing stare. 'I'm fine. *You* haven't hurt anyone.'

Rowena pretended I hadn't spoken. Moving out from behind the chair, she said, 'Let's get you some lavender water. It's close and stale in here.'

'You could open a window,' I pointed out.

But again she ignored me, spilling the perfume on to a handkerchief and presenting it to Lucy.

Lucy didn't reach out to take it from her. She let the handkerchief drop on to her lap like a dead bird. Her eyelids drooped shut.

'What have you been doing to her?' I hissed at Rowena.

She'd lost weight. Her face looked lean and hungry in the shadows, where once it had been impetuous and proud. Almost overnight, Lucy had become the invalid I'd imagined before I arrived at Felwood Lodge: insipid, spiritless. I didn't like it. I wanted her back.

'I did tell you,' Rowena answered gruffly. 'She's been very ill.'

'She looks half-starved!'

Perhaps she saw the truth of this, for she exhaled. Her expression was at once angry and close to tears. 'She is a little thin. I'll go and fetch her breakfast now. Will you watch her for me?'

I nearly snorted. *Watch her*. She could barely move! Why on earth had they locked her in?

Rowena left the room at a trot without closing the door. I was glad; the turret needed airing. I moved to Lucy's side and squatted down on the stone floor. A great need to protect her swelled within my breast. The shawl was proof that she'd accepted my friendship – and what a fine friend I'd turned out to be, letting her suffer like this!

'Lucy,' I murmured.

Her eyelids peeled back. The pupils were tiny and impenetrably dark. 'I wish you'd go away,' she whispered hoarsely. 'I wish I'd never set eyes on you.'

I flinched, stung. 'I can leave the room right now.'

'But then I should be miserable!' She rocked the chair gently. I didn't understand. Maybe she didn't, either. They were dosing her so heavily it was a wonder she could speak at all.

I brushed aside the curtain. Dust cascaded down, shimmering in the dingy light. Perhaps if I could open a casement the cool October breeze might slap Lucy back to life? But the window glass was smeared, desperately in need of a clean, and instead of a handle there were rusty spots that made my blood run cold. Nails. Iron nails hammered all along the window frame, making it impossible to open even a crack.

They were keeping her caged. Poisoned and trapped like some kind of vermin.

I let the curtain fall. How could this be true? Felwood used to be my land of freedom, where I could neglect the styling of my hair and run wild like a hoyden, drinking in the beauty of nature; now it was a house of locked doors and iron traps. What had happened? How had everything slid south so quickly?

Impulsively, I reached for Lucy's hand resting on the arm of the rocking chair. It felt cold and dead, but it squeezed mine back.

'I was well enough, until you came. Nothing overpowered

me. No feeling was too big to bear . . . But I can't control this and he . . . he is stronger.'

Tears filled my throat. Lucy had been tough and whip-smart; now she couldn't string a cohesive sentence together. Heaven knew if she'd even understand me, but I needed to warn her against the poison. 'Lucy,' I started. 'I have to tell you—'

'Make way there, Camille. Breakfast is served.'

Blast her eyes, Rowena had returned already bearing a tray. I dropped Lucy's hand and scuttled backwards on the cold stone floor.

Rowena carefully set down the breakfast upon Lucy's lap. The candles gleamed on not just a silver bowl, but another cup of wolfsbane tea. 'Come on, now,' she urged, picking up the spoon and jamming it into Lucy's hand. 'Have something to eat, my dear. As Camille says, you are very thin.'

Lucy stared at the bowl of porridge for a moment. Then, wrinkling her long nose, she pushed it away. 'I don't want that.'

'Are you not hungry?'

'I am. I'm famished. But I want . . .' She wetted her lips. 'Something else. Something more . . .' She didn't hit upon a word to explain her craving, but her cheeks worked.

Rowena looked as if she had seen a ghost. 'What a notion! You always have either porridge or gruel for breakfast. These are your only options. Now eat up.'

'What's in the bowl?' I demanded from my position on the floor.

The start Rowena gave told me all I needed to know. 'Whatever do you mean, Camille? You know very well what porridge is. Oats, water and milk.'

I held her gaze. 'Are you sure there's nothing else mixed in?'

She gave a harsh, bruised laugh. 'I don't understand you, child. Go and try some yourself, there is more in the tureen downstairs.'

It was on the tip of my tongue to mention the tea, but at that moment Lucy's head lolled back on her shoulders and she sighed heavily, staring up at the painted sky. 'Sirius. And *Canis Major*, the dog with the blazing face.'

She was still in there, the girl I knew. She was still trying to rise to the surface and gaze upon the light of the stars.

Rowena squirmed uncomfortably.

'I think his name is Laelaps,' I replied softly. 'I read of him. A dog destined to catch whatever he pursued.'

Rowena took a breath, but Lucy spoke again. 'It must be nice,' she said, slurring her words, 'to be made into stars. Taken out of this form. Burning bright. Pure light.'

The silver choker was taut around her throat. Somehow, it had speckled already. A reverse of the stars Lucy loved; dark marks upon the brightness.

There was so much I wanted to say. That to me she was always radiant, the most luminous person I'd ever seen. That even in her sickness she dazzled somehow, and it was a light neither her mother nor Bridget could ever put entirely under a shade.

But Rowena moved in, pulling me roughly to my feet. 'I believe that's enough visiting for one day. Go downstairs and eat your breakfast, Camille, there's a good girl.'

I was not a good girl. The fact that I'd been sent to Felwood Lodge in the first place ought to have warned my godmother of that. I had no intention of buttoning my lip and letting them carry on in this fashion.

But nor was I a stupid girl. Tempting as it was to shout and storm, I foresaw only two outcomes: that Rowena would lock me away in my room, or that Bridget would sedate me, too. I needed to be prudent until I was safely in possession of Papa's advice.

Bridget and I finally set out for Deepbeck under granite clouds. Before we'd reached the milestone, rain started to fall. Snails emerged upon the paths, risking the wheels of our handcart. Raindrops pocked the surface of the river as we crossed the bridge and the ducks beneath us quacked with glee.

'Best we split up,' Bridget said. 'We'll complete our errands faster.'

That suited me. 'Very well.' I surveyed the square. No Mr Randall – but that was hardly surprising on such a grim day. All the eaves were dripping and the kennel carrying waste water ran fast. 'I'll head straight to the post office. Is there anything you want me to send?'

'No. I'm going to the apothecary.'

'Naturally.' I narrowed my eyes at her, unable to hold my tongue. 'You always find an excuse to make sure I never set foot inside that shop, don't you? That the apothecary himself never speaks to me. I wonder why that could be.'

For an instant, she wore the panicked expression of an animal caught in a trap. 'Nonsense. I'm saving time, that's all. I'll meet you by the well.' Turning her back on me, Bridget strode off with the cart clunking behind her; I viewed it as her guilt, rattling close at her heels.

But help might be at hand. I strode to the post office as quickly as I could without actually running.

The postmistress was holding her spectacles to her mouth, breathing on the lenses to polish them. She made me wait until they were positioned back on the bridge of her nose before she acknowledged me.

'So you're still here, *mademoiselle*. Haven't seen you for a while. Thought you might have fallen ill with the *Talbot sickness*.'

It all made sense now: her supercilious manner, the carpenter talking of Mrs Talbot's 'strange ways'. 'No,' I breathed, 'but I'm very eager for a letter. Has anything come for me by express?'

She raised her eyebrows. 'Express! Nothing as exciting as all that. There's this, though.' The correspondence she pulled out of the sack bore Marie's writing. I'd never been so disappointed to see my sister's familiar hand.

'You're sure that's all?'

'I didn't *say* that was all. A young man left this.' Reaching below the counter, she drew out another folded piece of paper and tutted over it. 'We'd be ashamed to give love letters publicly in my day. Very Continental, such goings on.'

I was too flurried to make any answer. She was right: Colin's writing to me was in itself an act of enormity. Correspondence was usually only exchanged after a positive engagement had been formed. But after our last conversation I feared these weren't just overtures of romance. He had something important to tell me. Carefully, I took the letters, terrified my wet gloves would smear them.

There was no room to stop and read here. Outside, the rain would melt the ink into black tears. No, I'd be forced to endure the agony of waiting until I was back at Felwood Lodge. I paused beside the timber-beamed wall to unlace my cloak and tuck the precious bundle under my stays, close to my heart.

Outside, the cobbles danced with plashing raindrops. People hurried past, their collars turned up and their hats pulled low. Dodging puddles, I managed to make it across the street to a milliner who sold me a cheap cane umbrella.

Bridget was waiting by the well, standing slackly against her handcart. A large burlap sack rested there; she'd drawn an oilskin partially across it, but a few dark patches were seeping through. Was I imagining the colour? Purple, with a hint of blue? But Bridget accosted me before I could ask any questions.

'Why didn't you tell me?' She had to raise her voice to make it heard above the rain.

'Tell you what?'

'About the mail coach! You must have caught wind of it being attacked when you walked to the inn last week.'

'The mail coach has been attacked?' I repeated, all innocence. 'How should I hear anything about that? I promised my godmother I'd only walk within sight of the inn, not go inside.'

Bridget frowned as though she didn't believe me, but she had no proof. The rain pattered on my umbrella while she absorbed every drop. 'Rowena will want to know about this straight away. They're saying now that it wasn't a dog haunting these parts at all, but a wolf.'

'People say lots of things,' I replied with impatience. 'You should hear what they're saying about *you*.'

Grunting, she picked up the handle of the cart. 'Come on, let's get back before we start to drown.'

As the wheels jolted, the sack peeped open, revealing a bluish purple mass within. I followed after her, relentless. 'Tell me, was it the rumour of a wolf that made you buy so much wolfsbane? Do you intend to poison the creature stalking the fells, if Rowena doesn't manage to trap it first?'

She paused at the peak of the bridge. The rain plopped merrily into the river. 'How do you know it's wolfsbane in the sack? Have you been reading my book?'

'Yes, I've been educating myself. But there are no wolves in England, Bridget. So you've either been giving that poison to another animal . . . or to a person.'

Blinking raindrops from my eyelashes, I watched her face for a reaction. It remained carefully blank. 'I know what I'm doing, Camille. Each medicine has been painstakingly tested.' She moved on.

'Tested on whom?' I asked, scurrying in her wake.

Ahead, there seemed nothing but a haze of vapour stretching into infinite distance. The fells looked like a watercolour landscape that had blurred across its canvas.

'This flower is only used in the direst of circumstances. It prevents Lucy from . . . taking a turn.'

It might soon prevent Lucy from breathing altogether. There must be some way to stop this! Desperately, I cudgelled my brains for a solution. Bridget sneezed.

I saw a way to get my hands on the poison. 'Why don't you let me wheel the cart? You're struggling.'

'I'm not struggling,' she protested. 'And you can't manage it, with your umbrella.'

'I'll swap you my umbrella for the cart.' I gave her my sweetest smile, seizing hold of the handle. 'It doesn't do to get soaked through at your age, Bridget. You could fall dangerously ill.'

She snorted. 'Such pertness. I daresay I can bear the rain much better than you, young miss. But have it your own way.' She took the umbrella from me. 'We'll swap, and see how long your delicate constitution lasts.'

What now? I would think of something . . . Our path sloped upwards. Little streams of rainfall trickled down past us as we climbed.

'Why have you bought a whole sack, if you only use the wolfsbane in small doses?'

Bridget said nothing, but angled the umbrella against a sudden gust of wind.

'What did you mean by "taking a turn"? You're not talking about Lucy's fits. Wolfsbane can *cause* convulsions, not cure them.'

'Hold your tongue, lass!' Bridget cried, exasperated. 'Everything you've learnt about herbs, you've learnt from *me*. Trust that I know better.'

'But it's a *poison*.'

'Life isn't like your books, Camille. No one is trying to murder people in secret. You're so fanciful that you even think the Queen was poisoned!'

In truth, I did think that. It had seemed too obliging for Her Majesty to die that August, just after the King had failed to obtain a divorce and she'd stormed the coronation. But I wished I hadn't told Bridget of my theory now.

'*This* isn't my imagination, though. The postmistress was surprised to see me alive, the carpenter warned me against you, and Lucy is looking sicker than ever.'

Bridget tilted her umbrella the other way, allowing streams

to run off the canvas right on to my boots. 'You know nothing about us. And quite frankly, it's none of your business. We ought to have listened to Lucy in the first place. It was foolish to take you into our house.' She hastened her step, pulling ahead of me, knowing I couldn't easily catch her up with the cart.

That was the sign of a guilty conscience: running away from my questions. If only she realized how badly I wanted to believe her innocent. Of *course* I didn't understand the minutiae of herbal medicine, but, with the apothecary himself doubting Bridget's methods, it was clear that something was very wrong.

I continued toiling uphill, raindrops needling at my cheeks. The cart I dragged behind me felt as dangerous as the cannons the army horses towed. More so, perhaps. For this weapon didn't kill with an obvious boom, but the quiet slurp of a mouth drinking tea. Lucy's wide, thin-lipped mouth.

Horrible images came to me. Lucy submerged in purple-blue water, her golden eyes fixed open and unblinking in death. Thick hair billowing like tendrils behind. All her light and restless energy gone . . . My foot slipped.

The breath left me in a rush as I skidded backwards. The cart yanked at my arm, its wet handle nearly slithering from my grasp. I dug my heels deep into the mud and tried desperately to stop. There was a horrible slop and hiss as my feet gradually squelched to a halt.

Panting for breath, I glanced over my shoulder. Cold, claggy dirt piled right up to my ankles. If it hadn't caught me like a fly in jam, I might have fallen and rolled, over and over, the slope one great muddy slide towards another cold bath in the river . . .

And suddenly, my terrible imaginings seemed to be a sign. I knew exactly what I had to do for Lucy: drown the poison, before it could drown her.

Looking up, I saw Bridget had already reached the crest of the hill, her back was still turned on me.

I let go of the cart.

It trundled, ponderous. I worried it might stop, or hit a rock, but then the wheels began to gather speed and mud sprayed out on either side.

'Oh, dear!' I called. 'I'm so clumsy!'

Bridget glanced back. She was just in time to see the cart accelerate for a final burst before it launched itself off the bank and into the river.

Dropping the umbrella, she skated and slid downhill, heedless of the danger. 'What have you done?' she shrieked, but she didn't wait for an answer. Plunging down the riverbank, she waded up to her knees in the water. A group of boys gathered on the bridge to watch and hoot.

But of course Bridget was too late. The sack bobbed, rushing fast downstream, the current bearing it far, far away, where it could hurt Lucy no longer.

CHAPTER NINETEEN

A smell creeps through first, guiding me to the surface: a waft of dairy and yeast. Part of me recognizes that it's my baby brother Jean, but there's no mistaking the fact that he doesn't smell like an infant any longer. He's started to smell like food.

I want to stay down. Sink beneath the purple waves that quickly lighten to mauve, to grey, to white. *No, no. Let me sleep.* But the hunger will not rest. It claws its way out of the grave I've tried to bury it in and, all too soon, my eyelids flutter open of their own accord.

A single candle lights the room. Two figures sit praying at my bedside. One is Marie; it takes me a moment to recognize the other. He's taller than when I left home, his hair brushed forward and longer on the top.

'Pierre?'

He starts and nearly falls from his chair. Even by candlelight, I can see his throat bob in fear beneath his loosened cravat. My elder brother, scared of me.

But Marie bursts into a tearful smile. 'You're awake!' she cries, relieved. 'Oh, thank God!'

'But – but—' Pierre gestures, spluttering.

Marie glances at me for a moment before she understands

what bothers him. Her smile wavers. 'Oh. Yes, I forgot that you haven't seen Camille since she returned. Her eyes have . . . done that, recently.'

'Done what?' I rasp.

She hesitates, still trying to spare me the details. 'You mustn't worry. It's quite pretty, actually. But sometimes, in the dark, your eyes . . . shine. Like a cat.'

Of course they do. That's how I can make out every detail of the pair at my bedside in spite of the dark.

Pierre stands up, puts his chair between us for protection. 'Well, that's a deuced strange thing. I'll – I will go and tell the others she's awake. Yes. Mama will want to know.'

It's horrible to see him blustering like this. 'Wait . . .' I start. 'Pierre – I need to tell you—' But he's gone, leaving only the scent of his terrified sweat behind him.

I reach for the smelling salts. One blast and their bitterness fills all the space inside my head. That's better. No Pierre, no Jean. For now.

Marie blots her hazel eyes with a handkerchief. They're swollen. She must have been keeping watch over me for hours; she's still wearing the same sprigged gown as when I passed out. 'Gracious heaven, Camille, whatever were you thinking, asking me to dose you with that . . . detestable weed? No one expected you to survive, I can only thank God that you've been spared!'

Have I been spared? This doesn't feel much like mercy. My guts seem to move with a life of their own and the baby's scent is coming back . . . I swallow. Try not to wonder if an infant's skin would taste salty, like pork crackling.

'I know you're in a lot of pain. I can appreciate the – the temptation,' Marie adds falteringly. 'But self-murder is not the answer! And it was cruel of you to involve me in your plan! How would I have lived with myself if that plant had killed you?'

She's right, of course. It was a selfish, shabby trick to play on my sister. But I suspected deep down that I wouldn't perish. Before this illness began, that drink would have stopped my heart, but my heart has changed, as everything is changing, and my survival is only another proof that I'm too late to reverse it.

'Forgive me,' I say weakly, reaching out for her. 'I was desperate.'

A tear slips down her cheek. She takes my horrible rough hand in hers, so slim and white. 'I know it is difficult, but we must await God's will.'

'God didn't inflict this illness upon me, Marie. My condition . . . I think it comes from the other place.' Marie pulls back, shocked. 'There's evil . . . prowling around me. Circling closer. The flowers you fetched kept it at bay, but I don't know how much longer I can hold it off.'

'How can that be?'

I run my tongue around my aching gums. My teeth are growing, sharpening. 'If the illness takes me, if I'm not myself . . . If people get hurt . . .'

'Don't speak like that!' Marie pleads. She looks suddenly very young, her freckles standing out against her pale, tired skin. 'There must be some remedy. I'll help you. We'll ward off any evil together.'

I can't bear to tell her that I have watched others try and fail. The darkness growing inside me wants to consume all the light, all the goodness, like little Jean; blot it out completely so I can't find my way. But at least the wolfsbane has delayed the inevitable. Now I must use the extra time those purple flowers have bought me.

Pulling my hand from Marie's grasp, I reach beneath my pillow. It's still there, my most treasured possession, gleaming with the promise of magic. Cool beauty against the heat of my palm. Giving it up feels like surrendering the last part of myself. Yet I must.

'Marie, this will sound strange, but I need you to do one final favour for me. After this, there's nothing else, I promise.'

'I'm not fetching you any more herbs!'

'No, it's not herbs. Please indulge me. You're the only person I trust.'

Confusion flickers across her face. She's always tried so hard to understand my ways. Love for my sister swells inside until it's almost painful. I am glad she's marrying Mr Ibbotson. She deserves to be happy, to have someone to care for her, after all this is over.

'What do you want me to do?'

I pass over the necklace. 'I need you to hang my moonstone over baby Jean's crib. It must show; it must catch the light. Whatever happens, don't let the nursery maid take it down. Please. Promise me you'll do this.'

'I don't understand.'

'Neither do I. Not entirely,' I admit. 'But men far across the sea say this stone is holy. That it calms the lunatic. It's calmed me, and I've seen it calm others.'

Marie's chin wobbles. 'You are *not* a lunatic. And if this necklace soothes you, surely you should keep it by your side?'

I shake my head. 'It needs to protect Jean. Believe me.'

'Protect him from *what*?'

'Please, Marie. Do as I ask, now, before it's too late.'

She sighs. I can see it in her expression: she's starting to question whether I have indeed lost my wits. It happened to the old king, after all, and here I am, talking of circling evil and magic stones. Well, I'd rather have her believe I am out of my mind than know the truth.

'Must I do it right this moment?'

'Yes, please. I'll rest more easily once it's there.'

Wearily, she takes the stone and rises to her feet. She wobbles slightly, as if she's so tired that she can barely stand. 'All right.'

Marie steals softly from the room. The door closes with a

click that goes right through me. It feels as though she has taken the last ray of light and hope with her, leaving me alone with my demons in the dark.

I was sent to my room in disgrace. The banishment didn't bother me, for when I changed my wet clothes and pressed my ear against the door I could still hear every word that passed between my godmother and Bridget downstairs.

'It must have been an accident,' Rowena insisted. 'You've seen how the poor child blunders about. She can't even rinse a fleece without falling head over heels.'

'This was no accident! Camille knew exactly what was in that sack; she accused me of using it to hurt Lucy.'

Rowena clicked her tongue. 'I'll . . . speak to her in the morning. Try to make her understand.'

'You'll tell her the truth?' Incredulity sharpened Bridget's question to a point.

The silence stretched. I leaned so hard against the door that it creaked.

'No,' Rowena said at last. 'I won't lay that burden upon Camille. I never inflicted it on her parents. It's best they know as little as possible.'

Bridget grunted. 'Well, *she's* laid a burden upon *us*. What'll I do now? I won't have enough money to buy any more wolfsbane until I've taken the lambs to market. But even if I had the coins in my hand right now . . . the apothecary wouldn't sell me another sack. He's suspicious enough already.'

'Maybe . . . maybe Lucy won't need wolfsbane any more?' Rowena tried hopefully. 'She's much better than she was. Let's see how she goes with the regular sedating herbs, as she always used to. Maybe we've done enough to help her over this hurdle. We'll prioritize the distribution of what little wolfsbane we have left. I wish now we hadn't used it on the traps . . .'

I heard a scraping sound, Bridget drawing back a chair. 'There's more news,' she said, weary. 'I haven't even told you the worst of it. The mail coach was attacked, Rowena. People are saying it was a wolf.'

My godmother released a tiny hiccup, or perhaps it was a sob. 'No.'

'They could be wrong . . .'

Of course they were wrong. I wondered why my godmother, who was so learned, didn't question the statement immediately. Instead I heard her tread, going back and forth across the dining-room. When she spoke, her voice had altered. 'That's not a risk I'm willing to take. We delayed too long last time, and look what happened . . . Oh, God!' Suddenly Rowena was shouting. 'It's all over! We must leave as soon as possible.'

'Leave!' Bridget repeated. 'And go where?'

'I don't know! Anywhere! To – to the Garniers, at Martingale Hall!' Her step quickened. 'Yes. Yes, that's what we'll do. We'll take Camille home and . . . travel on from there. Susannah and Emmanuel will help me. They'll lend us whatever we need without asking any awkward questions.'

Relief loosened the tight muscles in my shoulders. Home! My parents' advice! It was everything I'd yearned for. Who cared if Rowena's reason for taking us there was flawed?

Outside, the rain sputtered like a candle. I tried to shut it out and paint a picture in my mind: a warm hearth at Martingale Hall, where Lucy and I could sit side by side, toasting muffins upon forks, safe. But I couldn't conjure the scene. I knew Rowena wouldn't let her stay there with us. Instead, Lucy would be packed into a carriage, staring abjectly out of the back window as it pulled further and further away down the gravel drive. I'd never see her again.

'We can hardly travel with Lucy in this state,' Bridget objected. 'There are no guarantees without the wolfsbane. Think of all the commotion, all of the new sights and smells! She could take a turn. Would you really risk the passengers on the stagecoach? Or your own dearest friends?'

Rowena slammed her hand upon the table. I jumped. 'Lucy is *better*,' she persisted. 'I told you. She can do this. She *has* to. We all knew this day must come eventually. I'll – I'll give her a trial tomorrow. Let her out around the house and the farm. You'll see. She'll be much better.'

Her words lingered in the air. The longer they went without answer, the more foolish they sounded.

Finally, Bridget spoke. 'And what about the cellar? That's what they're after, isn't it?'

'Our . . . our duty is obvious.' Rowena's voice wavered. She cleared her throat, and when she recommenced, it was threaded with steel. 'We must . . . destroy it before we leave.'

'And how, exactly, do you propose to do that?'

'It will be simple if we act fast. There's a small amount of wolfsbane left, isn't there? We'll use that, make sure there are no . . . surprises.' A pause. 'In that state, it will be the same as killing any other creature.'

'Pah! "In that state", there's a world of difference and you know it! I can't cast that weight upon my conscience. I won't. You'll have to strike the blow.'

'Of course it must be me!' Rowena returned hotly. 'I prayed to God it would never come to this, but it was always, always written for me.'

'Can you really do it?' Bridget sounded strangely curious now.

'Why would you ask that?' Rowena snapped.

'Because I reckon there's still some feeling there . . . despite everything.'

Rowena snatched in a breath. 'Not *feeling*, Bridget. There was hope. A belief in redemption and a cure . . .' Tears clogged her throat. 'We tried so hard to be merciful but nothing could prevent this. We all understand what must be done. I won't shirk my responsibility. May Heaven grant me strength!'

Her footsteps moved rapidly across the boards. The staircase wailed its complaint as she stamped upwards, heading in my direction. I scurried towards my bed, but Rowena didn't enter my room. She slammed the door upon her own chamber and started pacing again, her feet beating a regular tattoo as she whispered to herself. Praying.

I was more confounded than ever before. Eavesdropping hadn't given me answers, only more questions. There *was* an explanation . . . but Rowena had clearly said she didn't want to tell me the truth. I sat there on my narrow bed, listening to the sounds of her anguish, torn between pity and rage. I'd not been mistaken about the root-cellar: something suffered there in the dark. A living creature, and my godmother meant to destroy it.

I pressed a palm over my heart, trying to slow my pulse. Something shifted there; the outline of paper. My letters. In my haste to change out of my wet over-clothes, I'd not noticed them still nestled in my stays. What had Colin written to tell me?

Unlacing myself, I hurriedly plucked out each missive. They were crumpled but not torn. I lit a candle, all fingers and thumbs, and by its light I saw that the writing was thankfully still legible.

Even now I couldn't understand why Papa hadn't written back. My message, sent by express, clearly begged an urgent response. I couldn't imagine he'd deputise Marie to answer on his behalf, but maybe he had? Picking up her letter, I cracked open the seal and let the paper unfold.

My eyes skipped over the words. There was no mention of Rowena or poison; my sister had written her promised account of the local ball.

Her cares, her very world, seemed a million miles away from me. Glasses of sweet ratafia rather than wolfsbane tea, the trill of violins in place of sheep-bells. Spangled gowns and absolutely no wool in sight. I continued only long enough to see that Adam

Ibbotson had asked Marie to dance – but once, not twice as he'd used to do. That was all I could endure. It all felt so trivial.

I swapped letters. There was no wax seal bearing the Randall family crest, only a featureless wafer holding together the pages the postmistress had given me. I ripped it open.

My dear Miss Garnier,

I beg you will excuse the liberty I take in addressing you directly. The urgent nature of the matter I have to communicate must pardon me. When I last had the honour of meeting you, I promised to serve as your investigator in the village. It pains me to report that the results of that enquiry have been most alarming.

Imagine my surprise upon learning that I was not the first to ask questions; that in fact, a gentleman of forty or fifty years of age appeared in Deepbeck only twelve months ago, seeking information about Mrs Talbot. They tell me he vanished abruptly, without trace. Some gossips attribute his disappearance to murder; others believe that Mrs Talbot is holding him captive. Yet none of them ever took the trouble to notify the authorities! They argue that they did not even know his name, and they did not wish to run afoul of 'the Talbot witch' them-selves – in short, they are full of excuses. But I do not mean to act in so cowardly a manner. I wait only for you to apprise me of Mrs Talbot's exact location before sending out the magistrate.

I am more uneasy than ever on your behalf, my dearest Miss Garnier. My torture is more acute, since I have no way of immediately establishing your safety! Where are you? Pray, come to The Grey Lady the moment you receive this. My carriage, my very person shall be at your disposal. We will go directly to Martingale Hall, where surely even your brother Pierre

will look upon us with a forgiving eye when he compre-
hends what you have escaped from. Indeed, I entreat
you to come at once and believe me to be, as always,
your most devoted servant and earnest well-wisher,
  C.R.

CHAPTER TWENTY

For once I had no appetite. The silver tureen stood open at the centre of the dining table, spewing acrid steam. Bridget had burnt the porridge. Its caustic smell spoke of brimstone, of the infernal regions – very apt, for breakfast in the house of the village witch.

I took a sip of my herbal tea, knowing I could trust it, for I'd mixed it with my own hands. Lucy raised a pair of filmy eyes to watch me. I wanted to scream and flip the table over. She'd been so strong, so sharp, but they'd blunted her, turned her from a blade into a spoon.

The meal passed in agonized silence. Bridget had delayed too long in changing out of her wet clothes yesterday, and now her nose had swollen red. Rowena sat stiff as a ramrod, mechanically spooning burnt porridge into her mouth. It must have tasted foul, but she didn't complain, didn't even pucker her lips. Only the sweat beading her forehead hinted at the turmoil within.

Although no one spoke, my head was full of noise. The conversation I'd overheard repeated like a catchpenny tune, shot through with lines from Mr Randall's letter. I'd reached a conclusion: either the rabid dog of last year or the man who came looking for Mrs Talbot was trapped in the root-cellar.

Maybe both? And Bridget was testing poisonous medicines on her unfortunate prisoners before giving them to Lucy.

But she hadn't tested them thoroughly enough. She was snuffing out Lucy like a candle. I remembered her racing after a hare, her capable hands pulling my head up from underneath the water. Where was that powerful girl now? I prayed to God that she was still inside the waif slumped at the end of the table.

Bridget sneezed.

'I did warn you about catching a chill yesterday,' I said tartly.

She wiped her nose with her napkin. 'And whose fault was it that I ended up in the river?'

'Your own, I believe. No one forced you to run after the cart when it was clearly lost.'

'If *you'd* chased after it yourself and not just stood there gawking, you might have caught it. Lucy would have her medicine, and there'd be enough left over to—'

'Stop this.' My godmother did not raise her voice, but it carried authority. Bridget grumbled and snuffled into her napkin. 'What's done is done. You see Lucy is recovered now.'

We all looked doubtfully to Lucy's end of the table. She gave a yawn. 'Did . . . did Camille fall in the river again?' she asked.

'No, love, it was the handcart that went this time. But it doesn't matter. You'd had enough of that purple tea, hadn't you? You're well enough to see your animals in the barn today. And when you come back, I must have a serious talk with both you girls.' Rowena swallowed, and it seemed as though her words tasted worse in her mouth than burnt porridge ever could. 'There is much to discuss.'

How would Lucy process a 'serious talk'? Her glazed face proclaimed she was still lost among the stars. 'My animals,' she repeated, a smile tugging at the corners of her mouth. The sight of that smile, so diluted, made my chest feel like it was going to crack open.

Bridget coughed. 'I feel like nothing on earth. I need another brew before I can face what must be done.'

Rowena reached for the pot and poured her another cup. 'Of course. Sit with me for a while. Heaven knows we have enough to arrange between us.'

I scowled. This woman with her tight-braided hair and the scars that reached for her ear was almost a stranger to me now. She was going to sit here, finalizing the details of how to kill the captive in the cellar. Bad enough if it was simply a tortured animal, but if it was really the man Mr Randall wrote of . . . I couldn't bring myself to believe it. Surely my own parents couldn't have been so utterly mistaken in Rowena's character? They would not give me a murderer for a godmother!

But it didn't matter either way. I wasn't going to stay and find out. This was the perfect opportunity to get Lucy away to The Grey Lady inn. By the time Rowena and Bridget finished their tea, we'd be on the road travelling back towards Martingale Hall as Mr Randall had promised. If my godmother was able to explain her conduct, let her follow us and do it there, in front of my whole family. I wouldn't delay getting Lucy to safety any longer.

I pushed back my chair, having eaten nothing. 'We'll leave you to it. Lucy and I have lots to do in the barn.' I turned and offered Lucy my hand. She studied it for a moment before placing the tips of her fingers softly in my palm. It looked as though I were about to lead her into a dance. She rose unsteadily, rattling the cutlery as she gripped the edge of the table for support.

If glares carried heat, I believe mine would have set Bridget ablaze.

We shuffled out of the dining room, across the corridor and into the kitchen. 'Lean on me,' I urged Lucy, and she threaded her arm through mine. Once, I'd struggled to carry her with Bridget's help; now she was as light as a dandelion seed.

A thin, sour chill moved through the forest outside. All the blossom on the ivy that stretched over the house had died. The leaves were tinting red, as though a flame were slowly consuming the lodge. The year was spent, the beauty spoiling, and everything except Lucy smelt of rot. I clung to her.

We shuffled a few steps away from the house, leaving footprints on the damp grass. Then I stopped.

'Listen to me, Lucy. This is important. Can you focus on what I'm saying?'

No response. Lucy's nostrils inflated and subsided. Her expression reminded me of my mother when the pains of childbed were about to fall upon her: intent upon an internal voice.

'Lucy?' I spun her round to face me, placed my hands on her shoulders.

'You smell . . . frightened.'

'I am!' I cried. 'You were right from the very beginning: it isn't safe here. We're not going to the barn today. I need to get you away from this place, away from Bridget.'

'Bridget?' A crimson leaf spiralled down and rested on the top of her cap. She didn't reach up to brush it off. 'Why?'

'Because she's giving you poison and sedatives! She asked me to grind the ingredients and I looked them all up in a book. Do you hear?' Lucy only frowned into my face. She was as beautiful and motionless as a marble carving. 'Do you understand what I'm saying? She could have killed you!'

'The tea is my medicine,' Lucy answered softly. Her breath still carried its woody scent. 'I need it.'

'No, you don't!' I gave her a little shake. Her eyes came into focus, no longer blurred. 'You don't need wolfsbane! That could be what's *making* you ill. Don't you feel worse, after you drink it?'

'No. Not worse. I feel . . . numb.' She swallowed. 'And sometimes that's a good thing. Sometimes my heart beats so fast.' She fixed me with a look of such intensity that the breath was crushed in my chest. 'It's beating fast now.'

So was mine. 'Lucy, you're not listening—'

'I am! I hear every word that you say, each breath that you take, even when you turn over in your bed during the night. I'm not a fool, Camille. I know exactly what Bridget's giving me. And she needs to. She *needs* to!' With a wrench, she pulled herself from my grip and made for the meadow. Her gait remained unsteady, zigzagging left and right, but she was determined.

I chased after her. The path was cratered with puddles from yesterday's rain. Cobwebs stretched between the bushes, glimmering with captured droplets. 'Stop! Lucy, stop; you can barely walk. You're too ill to work. Come with me and see a real physician. Someone who can help you. I have a friend. He's not far away, just at The Grey Lady inn—'

She made a choking sound. 'So that's who you smell of, when you come home. What have you been telling this *friend*? You were supposed to keep our secrets.'

'I have!' I protested. 'I've barely said a word to him. All he knows is that one of Mrs Talbot's supposed sisters is ill, and he's offered to take us both to my home, to Martingale Hall.'

Lucy struggled on without looking back at me, walking as if her feet didn't quite belong to her. Once or twice I thought she was going to slip and turn her ankle, but she managed to right herself.

'Please, Lucy. We're wasting time. We need to go the other way, to the inn. I'll look after you. You'll be well again. My mother will nurse you, if only you'll let her!'

We emerged into the meadow. The grass was damp and boggy, quickly wetting the hem of Lucy's skirt to a deeper grey as she strode on.

'Can you trust this friend?' she demanded, not even turning her head.

'Yes! He went to university with my brother. He's visited our house, he's met my parents; he'll take us back, just as he has promised.'

Lucy drew up beside the barn doors. A single bleat sounded from within, more of an alarm than a greeting. She was breathing so quickly. I could see her pulse, flicking at her throat. 'Then you must go to him.' She balled her hands into fists. 'Get away now, while you have the chance.'

'I'm not going anywhere without you!'

She backed towards the barn, refusing to look at me. 'Yes, you are. I can't come along, Camille. I won't.'

'Why?' I matched her step for step, not letting her put distance between us. 'Stop avoiding me! Stay still, look me in the eye, and tell me why you won't come away to save your own life!'

Suddenly she did. Her eyes had completely lost their drugged gaze, and now they held questions no one had ever asked of me before. 'Don't you know?' she whispered.

Wordlessly, I shook my head.

'How can you be so blind?' She'd already stopped moving away. Now she took a step closer instead. 'My own life means nothing to me. All that matters is saving yours.'

We trembled, tête-à-tête, her breath hot against my cheek. For a moment, time stood absolutely still. Then our lips met.

Warmth flooded every inch of me. My mouth tingled, alive with nerves I hadn't even realized were there. Lucy tasted coppery, bittersweet, and now I knew the truth. I hadn't wanted to be like her. I'd simply *wanted* her.

Instinctively, I reached up to cup her face, but Lucy jerked back. 'What—' I began, opening my eyes to see that she'd already turned away and was crunching across the yard. 'Lucy?' She threw wide the doors to the barn. A few of the hens flapped out. 'Wait!'

Still giddy from her kiss, I moved forward, but I wasn't quick enough. The doors thudded shut in my face. There were bumps from within, the terrified blare of the sheep, and it sounded as though Lucy was actually trying to bar the entrance against me.

'Lucy!' I cried. My hands thudded uselessly against the wood. 'What's wrong?' Only her rasping cough answered me. 'Lucy, are you ill?'

'For God's sake, go!' she growled. Something heavy thumped to the floor. For a second I stood there, stunned, but then she roared again. 'Go home!'

My feet moved without my volition, taking me towards the river. What on earth had just happened? Lucy had kissed me. She'd kissed me, just as Colin Randall had . . . And then she'd pushed me away.

Images of Vauxhall Gardens flashed inside my head. I pictured Colin, his disarming smile. But Lucy's kiss . . . It could only have lasted a few seconds, and yet I knew it would never leave me.

My ears were humming like the great pipe organ at Lincoln Cathedral. I couldn't articulate what I felt, even to myself. It was Iphis and Ianthe from Ovid: a girl on fire for another girl.

Thudding across the wooden bridge, I stopped, bracing my hands upon my knees, and whooped for breath. A light wind wove its way through the trees, rustling in the undergrowth and cooling my hot forehead.

I hated myself for running. There was nothing to be gained; I couldn't outstrip my feelings. Nor would Lucy stop them by shouting at me and locking herself away. The kiss had happened. Nothing would undo it now. That moment was ours forever.

I touched my lips, feeling the warmth that still lingered. I had to go back. To force Lucy to leave with me.

'Help!'

The voice made my head snap up. I scanned the treeline. Nothing moved or clattered. There was no one to be seen.

'Hello?' I called.

The answer came in a weak, frayed thread of a male voice. 'Please, help me.'

I pivoted on the spot, the foliage and the berries a blur. 'Where – where are you?'

Then my eyes settled on the deadfall of vines and branches that made a screen across the root-cellar door.

I swallowed. Colin's letter. The man who had gone missing, looking for Mrs Talbot. Time seemed to stretch, weightless and silent.

'Are you . . . underground?' I breathed.

Suddenly, a cry. A crow started from the vegetable patch in fright.

'Are you in the cellar?'

Keening answered. This was the sound I'd heard so often, the darkling plea that took root, deep within my ear. Whatever wailed like that had lost all hope.

The shade of the trees fell over me as I approached the cellar. There seemed to be a pulse; an eldritch thrumming through the soles of my feet. It was a cool, dark place where only insects could thrive. A spider scurried across the clawed panels of the door and disappeared through the keyhole.

Placing my palm on the handle, I rattled the door. Of course it was locked. But weather had warped the wood, and surely, with enough force, it would open a crack . . .

A tortured splutter from within. I could bear the suspense no longer. Someone was suffering in there, someone Rowena meant to kill.

Using both hands, I pulled with all my might.

Whatever lay within heard me. It howled, drenching the whole meadow in despair. I tugged and tugged, leaning back so my whole weight dragged against the door. It was working. The wood around the lock was splintering, giving way . . .

'Camille! Stop!'

Bridget, in the distance. She wouldn't prevent me now. She'd never make it across the river before I freed what she was hiding here . . .

'No, Camille—'

Snap. A metal bite, somehow louder than the scream that followed high in its wake.

I flinched. The handle slipped from my grasp and I fell heavily back. The howling ceased abruptly.

I sat, winded, unable to comprehend what had happened. The door to the cellar wasn't open, though it had loosened. Now, fresh noises of pain were coming from behind me. An awful, liquid moan carried over the water.

Slowly, slowly I turned. On the other side of the river, Bridget lay sprawled, her skirts nearly over her head as blood washed the grass around her. Her left foot was bent at an angle, its tender flesh caught firm between the metal teeth of a trap.

CHAPTER TWENTY-ONE

There was so much blood. Even as I ran across the bridge, I was conscious of a taint in the air, vinegar and rust. Hot jets pumped from Bridget's calf and melted the morning dew. Maybe she didn't deserve my help, maybe I'd do better to release the captive in the cellar, but I didn't have the heart to leave her bleeding. The wet moans coming from her lips were awful.

'Help.' She clawed a hand into the mud, attempting to pull herself forward. 'Get me . . . away.'

Black spots intruded on my vision as I reached her side. The caught foot no longer resembled an extremity, it was something from the butcher's shop. Was I supposed to touch all that gore? The trap would be slippery with blood, impossible to remove. I yanked Bridget's skirts down instead. Her face and neck were deathly pale beneath. The force of the fall had cracked her moonstone pendant clean in half; the broken part pressed deep into the dirt.

'Lucy!' I cried. 'Come out and help me! Lucy, I need you!'

Banging and scratching inside the barn.

'No!' Bridget pleaded, frantic. 'Not . . . Lucy. Blood.'

Was Lucy in the throes of a fit too? Should I go to help her first? Oh, God, I didn't know what to do . . .

My anguished gaze fell upon the wheelbarrow, propped against the paddock fence. It would be my only hope of getting Bridget back to the lodge. As the chickens squawked in terror, I grabbed the handles and steered my way to Bridget. Somehow, I found the strength to heave her up into the barrow. Her eyelids fluttered and she lost consciousness. My trembling hands managed to unpeg the trap from its slick red chain.

'Lucy!' I cried again. I could only hear the hens babbling. For a second I wavered, torn. Something was wrong with Lucy, something more than just being frightened by the strength of our kiss. She might need my help in there . . . But Bridget was losing blood fast. There was no time; I had to get her to Rowena before she died.

As I pushed the barrow unsteadily forward, the second half of Bridget's moonstone dropped from the pendant to land in the gore. Its dancing sheen looked wildly out of place. I turned my face away, put my back into heaving the load onwards.

We made it into the tunnel of trees. All of my old enemies, the twigs and roots, came out in force to block my path. Bridget lolled limply from side to side each time the wheels hit a rut. Odd details stood out to me: dock bugs creeping over brambles, berries shrivelled on the bush; all the signs of nature's waste and decay.

Just as I felt my arms would snap off at the elbows, I glanced up and there was Rowena, skirts hitched, sprinting towards me.

'Godmother!' I gasped. I nearly wept with relief as she drew closer. She'd take over wheeling the cumbrous barrow; she could unhinge the trap and bandage Bridget's foot while I went back for Lucy.

But Rowena sped past me, the dead leaves whipping around her, and ran as though the hounds of hell were at her heels.

Bridget was right about one thing: I would have made her a terrible apprentice. All the physic she'd tried to teach me flew from my head. There was a herb to help staunch wounds, but I couldn't remember its name. After I'd dragged her through the house, leaving crimson smeared across the floorboards, and propped her on the parlour sofa, I was fit to vomit or swoon myself. Surely the blood ought to have stopped by now? I took one look at her mangled ankle, still glugging out scarlet, and knew there was nothing I could do. I didn't dare touch the trap. We needed help: real help. Secrecy be hanged. I was going to get Colin Randall and a surgeon.

'I'll be back soon,' I whispered, though Bridget showed no signs of hearing me. Her lips were tinged a worrying shade of blue.

The morning was sublime, a mockery of the suffering I'd left behind: low-hanging mist, birds trilling, and a fledgling citrine sun softening the landscape into smiles. I didn't have the energy left to run, but the wind remained at my back, pushing me along. I drank it in like cool water. There were notes of heather, of heath.

Everything felt surreal. So much had happened in a short space of time. I should be fretting over Bridget, and the man I now knew was trapped inside the root-cellar, but honestly all I could think about was that kiss. Who would have supposed one brief moment could hold such detail, such nuance? It replayed over and over in my mind, and I made no effort to halt its dance. I'd been such a blockhead. I never wanted Lucy for a friend. And she'd only kept pulling away because she was afraid of feeling too much for me.

Just a few hours earlier, I'd lain in my bed and planned out the future. I'd imagined marrying Mr Randall and offering Lucy a retreat in our home. Now that could never be. There wasn't room for them both inside my head – or my heart.

But that was a problem for later on. There'd be time to untangle my affections back at Martingale Hall.

Presently the breeze carried sounds: the clop of hooves and

harnesses jingling. I was getting close to the inn. Hastening forward, I burst through the oak trees opposite the stable yard. Luck was smiling upon me. One of Colin's magnificent black mares stood tied at the mounting block, champing at her bit, and in another moment Colin himself emerged from the side of the inn, carrying his hat and a riding crop. If I'd arrived a minute later, I'd have missed him. Shining boots rose to his knees; he wore an exquisitely tailored hunter-green coat. He gave the impression of order and authority that I sorely craved.

'Mr Randall!' I cried.

Everyone in the stable yard stopped to stare. Colin turned and nearly dropped his hat. 'Miss Garnier! Good God!'

Too late, I realized what a state I was in. My bonnet had long since fallen off, my hair was straggling from its combs, and I wore an apron of Bridget's blood. But Mr Randall didn't hesitate. He ran towards me, took me into his arms in front of everyone. I burst into tears.

'There, now. You are safe, Miss Garnier. I have you. I won't let any harm come to you. Let me take you inside, get you a glass of wine—'

'No! No, I have not a moment to lose.' I drew in a ragged breath. 'I need your help, Mr Randall.'

'You have it, always.'

The wind ruffled his raven curls as he stared intently into my eyes. Guilt plunged. He loved me so well, and all I could think about was Lucy.

'Are you hurt?'

I shook my head vehemently. 'Not me. Bridget fell into a trap and Lucy's having a fit and . . . and . . .' It occurred to me he had no idea who these people were, but I ploughed on. 'We need a surgeon.'

'Of course. I'll send to Deepbeck for one immediately. But where are the injured?'

I gestured to the path behind, tried to ignore the deep red

splash upon my glove. 'I can take him. I'll show him. But Mr Randall, you were right. About the missing man. There's someone trapped in the root-cellar. He called to me for help.'

'Ha!' It wasn't a laugh; more an expulsion of breath. 'I knew it. I *knew* it must be so. Thank God you came to me first,' he said earnestly. 'Wait there.' Releasing me, he whistled for a lad and pressed some coins into his palm. I didn't hear what he was saying, but he gestured at the road towards the village.

The black mare's flank shivered. She danced nervously sideways, away from me and the taint of blood. I wished Colin would come back. The world was turning merry-go-round. Eyes were everywhere, whispers and voices fracturing. All the grooms and the travellers thought I'd been attacked by the wolf. Only now did it occur to me how reckless I'd been, striding along like bait in the open, alone.

I staggered, but suddenly Mr Randall returned and his arms came up to catch me fast. 'Don't worry. The boy's going to Deepbeck. He'll bring the surgeon and the constable back here to the inn.' Playing the hero suited him. He pulsed with purpose, as though he'd been waiting his whole life for a moment like this to prove himself. 'It might take some time. Tell me where your friends are, I'll ride out at once while you rest here.'

It was tempting. The idea of a wing-chair beside the fire and a sweet cup of Bohea tea beckoned to me with an inviting smile. Colin looked so strong, so alive; I could leave all of this in his capable hands. But then Lucy flashed across my mind, as vivid and sharp as her kiss had been.

I took a step back.

'I'll come with you. I'll help. I'll carry Lucy back here myself, so the physician can tend her the moment he arrives.'

A lift of his dark eyebrows. 'My dear Miss Garnier, I applaud your courage. But are you sure you are equal to such exertion?'

I wasn't. Yet the thought of Lucy gave me the strength I needed. I must stop being the helpless young lady who relied on other people to wait upon her. 'I can do it,' I gasped. 'I can show you the way to Felwood Lodge.'

CHAPTER TWENTY-TWO

Pain devours me as a dog devours a bone. Heat forks along my veins to my core where it squeezes and pushes organs aside. My body has done its best to contain the plague, but a besieged castle cannot stand forever. Muscles spasm beyond my control. There's a crunch, a howl of pain rips from my throat and I hear Mama, speeding down the hallway. She always tries to reach me first, when I cry out. She doesn't like the servants to see my decline.

The door creaks open and she steps over the threshold, her nightcap askew. 'Camille?' Her breath catches as she sees me. 'No. This is not possible.'

What now? What new and frightful symptom?

The moment I pull myself up against the bolster, I realize something's changed. There's softness against my cheek and weight, draped like a cloak across my shoulders. My hair. They cropped it short, but, as I pull a strand out in front of me to examine, I see it's longer and thicker than ever.

Mama comes forward to sit on the edge of my bed. I didn't believe anything could equal my pain, but the agony in her eyes comes very close. She pulls my head into her lap and strokes my newly grown locks.

'You are too young for grey hair, my Camille.'

So my hair has turned grey, like the world around me. I never expected that. The disease is taking unexpected turns. I can't predict its path.

I try to focus on the sweep of Mama's hands, the comfort it spreads. My mother's scent, the smell of childhood tears and consolation, feels antiquated. Something from another lifetime. I suppose it was. I must face the fact that my life, as I have known it, is drawing to an end.

'I never dreamed Rowena would allow harm to come to you.' Mama's voice rumbles through her body straight into my head. 'If I had thought for a single moment . . .' Her voice cracks. 'I trusted her. I trusted her to care for you as her own.'

Mama waits, as if I might reply. But how can I speak of Rowena; how can I even bear to think of her?

'You still have nothing to tell me, my dear? Please, confide in me! Perhaps if the physician had a hint of what happened to you, he might be able to help us?' Her breath quakes. 'I know I was unkind to you after Vauxhall. I regret that most bitterly. Let me make it up to you now. Please, Camille, say something to me. I cannot keep living in this suspense. Must I really believe my old companion Rowena cares nothing for me and my children now?'

I suck in air. It's selfish of me to edge around the topic of Rowena. Poor Mama will suffer dreadfully thinking her childhood friend has turned tyrant and poisoner. If nothing else, it behoves me to clear Rowena's name by retracting what I wrote in my express – while I'm still able to do it.

'The letter,' I grind out.

'Which letter, dearest?'

'The . . . express. I was wrong. Rowena never meant to hurt anyone. She wanted to help. To help Lucy, even to help the person who'd wronged her most in all the world. And Bridget tried so hard! She stayed, she made it her life's work.'

Mama's hands grow still. 'Who is Bridget?'

Her words sound an internal alarm. I feel my hackles raise. 'Bridget. Rowena's friend. I told you about her. And I wrote to Papa that—'

'My darling, we never received a single letter from you! I thought you were sulking, punishing us with your silence.' She must sense me stiffen in her lap. 'Camille? Is it another pang?'

You could call it that. But this is a different kind of torture from the one that torments me physically; it's the swooping, falling sensation of dread. 'No. The mail coach was attacked, but I thought . . . Then you know nothing? Nothing at all?' No wonder they've been badgering me with endless questions. 'I . . . I need to talk with Pierre. I tried to before, but he ran away.'

'You cannot, just now—'

'Then where is Papa?' I demand. The ground is slipping beneath me, the darkness rising up. I burrow my fingernails into my palms to keep steady. Dear God, I haven't seen my father since I first arrived home. That never struck me as odd, for a gentleman's place is not in the sickroom; he leaves nursing to the ladies of his family. But now I realize that I can't detect his scent: brandy, starched linen, a hint of bergamot. He's nowhere to be found. Only the ghost of him lingers over his belongings. I struggle up from Mama's lap. 'Where are they both?'

My mother rocks me. 'Hush, dearest. They are miles away. But speaking of post, I expect to hear from them any day now. We'll get to the bottom of this.'

I shrug her off. 'Where have they gone? *Where* have they *gone?*' It comes as a husky roar.

She edges back on the bed, eyes wide and frightened. 'Calm yourself, Camille. Where do you imagine they've travelled to? The gentlemen are in Felwood. They've gone to confront Rowena.'

*

I'd thought along similar lines to Papa and Pierre. I'd planned to arrive like the cavalry charge and win the day, freeing the captive from his cellar and snatching Lucy from her poisoner.

231

I even summoned the courage to ride on horseback for the first time. Sitting behind Colin, I wrapped my arms tight around his waist as his black mare jolted beneath us.

The woodland looked different from a height. All of the silver birch trunks were peeling and tatty. Holly bushes prickled in between. I thought of the many times I'd taken this path and dreamt of Mr Randall by my side. I had him now, his heartbeat in my ear. Yet as I closed my eyes I imagined how it would be if Lucy sat in front of me instead. A smaller waist, wool against my cheek, her natural scent in place of his sandalwood cologne. Maybe her hair would tumble down her back and tickle gently at my nose as we rode. I wanted that. I didn't realize how badly until I pictured it in detail.

What was I to do?

Mr Randall gazed out into the distance, his chin held high, scanning for danger. He was everything the old me had ever dreamed of: handsome, dedicated, rich and brave. Marie and I had whispered about his fine looks when he'd visited Martingale Hall, but back then neither of us had dared to hope he'd ever form intentions.

Yet he had. An eligible gentleman desired me for his own. Pierre's objections amounted to nothing in the grand scheme of things. When we finally arrived home, and he realized how Mr Randall had aided me in my time of need, all would be forgiven. My parents would be glad to grant Colin my hand. They'd urge me to take my place in a life of comfort, wealth and consequence, and I could have done it happily, once. If I'd never kissed Lucy.

She wouldn't let me go – which was funny, considering she was always telling me to flee. Yet she'd done that out of kindness. She'd known that her life in Felwood was fraught with danger, and that she could offer me nothing. Even with my vivid imagination, I couldn't picture a future for us two. There was no money, no estate, no legal ceremony to bind us to one another. Before others, we'd have to claim we were dearest friends – for society would never accept a romance between two girls. It made so much more *sense* to choose Colin. But my heart had chosen already, and it told me that while I had Lucy's company I could survive. I might forgo food, or shelter, or air, but Lucy was essential.

As I watched the breeze knock the last sycamore seeds from their branches, sending them twirling down, I knew I'd have to reject Mr Randall. All I'd done was use the poor gentleman for my own ends, and I felt like a brute.

'Whoa, Shadow!'

I tightened my grip on Colin as the horse tossed her head and gave a violent swish of her tail. 'There, now,' he said.

'It's a right turn here,' I murmured into the back of his coat. Even the directions I gave were selfish. I was taking him straight to the barn and the cellar instead of the lodge. Bridget might have bled to death by now, yet all I cared about was Lucy.

We took the narrow track. No birds called, no squirrels loped across our path; there were only the twigs chattering in the wind and the dead leaves, gusting in our path.

Shadow snorted. She danced a few more steps and then her ears flattened back. I nearly lost my balance. It was like being on a teeter-totter that stamped and huffed. Shadow wouldn't go on.

'Easy! Easy,' Colin soothed. 'What is it, girl?'

Peering around, I saw nothing that might spook a horse, only a vault of branches above and softly dropping leaves. But I could feel something. A tension, a pulse.

With a little buck, Shadow cavorted forward. I didn't feel myself fall. One moment I was on her back, the next spluttering through a pile of yellow leaves.

'Miss Garnier!' Colin's voice from up ahead. The pounding of hooves stopped. I heard him slithering to the ground, looping the reins over a tree.

I tried to call out to him, but I didn't quite have the breath. Twigs scratched against my cheeks as I struggled to sit up. Thankfully I hadn't hit my head or broken any limbs, just grazed myself. A fly hovered before my face. I brushed it away. Then another flickered in the corner of my eye.

Colin's steps crunched towards me. 'Are you injured? Shadow's too jittery; we'll have to continue on foot . . .' He extended a hand to help me up, but his speech juddered to a halt.

'What is it?'

His gaze was over my shoulder, his face frozen. I caught a whiff of something feral, earth and meat. Painfully, I swivelled around.

Suspended on the fringed leaves of the bracken was Firetail the rooster. I recognized the buff and teal body, but his neck was broken. Flies swarmed over the wet stump where his head had once sat. Crying out, I grabbed for Colin's hand and pulled myself up.

'How did Firetail get here? He was in the barn . . .' And suddenly it felt as if the sky was falling along with the leaves overhead. 'Oh, God. Lucy was in the barn!'

'Wait—' Colin began, but I couldn't. I pulled him on with me.

My legs were unsteady from my fall. A hot, sick trembling had taken hold of me, yet still I ran, past Shadow stamping on the buttery leaves, dragging Mr Randall in my wake. He didn't try to stop me and I was grateful for that. No matter how terrible the catastrophe, I needed to see it with my own eyes.

A metallic scent sliced through the air as we broke through the arch of trees into the meadow. I halted in my tracks. Opened my mouth to scream, but no sound came out.

The fences were snapped into matchsticks. The paddock itself resembled a battlefield, gore splattered everywhere, the rusty patches of grass broken up by feathers and lumps of offal. Our dear animals! Friendly sheep, hens that squabbled and clucked: massacred, scattered around like discarded playthings. Silent tears poured down my cheeks, yet I could barely acknowledge my grief. One thought occupied my head. Lucy. Where was Lucy?

'Good God!' Colin exclaimed. A quiver ran through our joint hands. His voice sounded hoarse, choked. 'Is that – over there – is that the root-cellar you told me about? The door's wide open.'

My gaze flew across the river. So it was. The captive was free, maybe helped by my efforts to loosen the lock earlier. But I could no longer find it within myself to care about that.

'The mad dog. The mad dog must have attacked the farm after I left to fetch you.' My tears flowed fast and hot, quicker than I could scrub them away. Lucy couldn't be dead. She *couldn't*. She was fast and smart – she would have found a way to evade the attack, maybe even climbed up to the hayloft. I forced myself to push on. 'We have to find Lucy!'

Colin coughed on the cloying stench. 'Miss Garnier! Stop – do not—'

Ignoring his protest, I moved rapidly towards the broken fence. Steam billowed from the open hatch in the barn, which we used to release the sheep into the paddock. More flies hovered there, attracted by the heat. I steeled myself for the hideous scene that must be awaiting me, a pit of gore equal to anything in *The Monk*.

It was then that the growl pinned us to the spot. A shaggy bulk emerged through the hatch, accompanied by a waft of foul-smelling mist. Muscles rippled beneath its gunmetal pelt. The gossip had been right: it wasn't a dog. This was something larger and leaner than I'd ever imagined.

Colin cried out, pushing me behind him. The wolf's hackles rose and its lips curled back, showing wine-stained fangs.

'Run,' Colin said in a strangled voice. 'Run for your life.'

Without warning, the wolf gathered itself and sprang, clearing the remains of the fence in one easy leap. I turned on my heel and fled, Colin fast at my heels.

We flew back into the tunnel of trees. Up ahead, Shadow reared, emitting chilling screams. Her reins were knotted to a trunk, pulling taut. She was Colin's fastest horse. If we could mount her quickly, she might be able to outrun the beast . . . But suddenly, the leather snapped and Shadow charged to freedom, clods of dirt flying from her hooves.

'No!' I screamed. She'd been our only hope. Without her, we were too slow.

Already I could hear the wolf panting, smell its foetid breath. I pushed myself with every ounce of strength I possessed, but it wasn't enough.

Crack. It sounded like the trap closing on Bridget's leg. Something jerked me back and my skirts ripped with a scream of their own. Colin and I fell down in a tumble of limbs, skidding through mud and leaves. The scent of rot filled my nostrils.

I couldn't see any blood. I couldn't feel any pain. Pulling myself roughly to my feet, I realized the wolf had only managed to get hold of my gown, not my flesh. But Colin was still on the ground. The wolf glowered over him, an enormous shadow. Saliva hung in strings between its filthy teeth.

Colin's handsome face turned upwards, red oozing from the side of his mouth. His eyes grabbed mine. 'Go!' he choked. 'For God's sake save yourself!'

The wolf pounced.

Blind with tears, I dragged myself away before I could see the carnage: my lovely beau reduced to meat. The world seemed to flash then darken. Growls and terrible wet squelches followed cruelly in my wake. I knew, rather than felt, my sorrow. All emotion suddenly evacuated, leaving me numb. Instinct took over and forced me to keep going despite the cramp in my side, despite the fire in my lungs.

I'd never been so grateful to see the turret rearing from the trees and piercing the clouds. My only hope was to reach the lodge. My steps crunched, my breath heaved, and my heart hammered like an anvil. I was running for all I was worth, yet still I thought I could hear paws, gaining upon me . . .

There it was, the ivy drooping over the lodge's entrance, as welcome as the sight of home. I just had to get inside. Reaching out, I yanked the door open and fell across the threshold into the kitchen. I only managed to shut the door halfway behind me before the wolf leapt again, thrusting its huge, snarling snout through the gap.

'Go away!' I shrieked.

The stench of its breath was unbearable. I leant my entire weight against the door, but I couldn't stop it; I couldn't shut it out. The wolf pushed back, impossibly strong.

'You foul mongrel, you mangy, stinking mutt!'

My muscles were falling slack. The door gave a little in my direction. The wolf gnashed at the air, mere inches from me. I couldn't die now; I couldn't let Colin's sacrifice be for nothing. Desperately, I pulled the penknife from my pocket and flipped it open.

'Go . . . away!'

Squeezing my eyes shut, I slashed. There seemed no resistance, no ligament or bone. The wolf's flesh hissed and parted like butter. There was a cry of agony and suddenly I fell forward, slamming into the door as it finally, finally closed.

CHAPTER TWENTY-THREE

My breath came in shivering gasps. With the door shut, it was too dark to see clearly. Felwood Lodge sat strangely silent. The chattering of my teeth, the shaking of my body against the wooden panels, filled up the void. All the energy that had driven me on now drained away. Only shock remained.

Gradually, I was able to focus on the space around me. The fire had blown out in the commotion, which accounted for the darkness. But it didn't explain the chaos. Stools were overturned, the cupboards dented, the floor littered with broken glass. Violence had taken place here.

Thoughts jostled for attention. Would the wolf try to break down the door now? Had Rowena been in the barn with Lucy? I could no more answer these questions than the Sphinx's riddles; my mind felt paralyzed.

Somehow I climbed to my feet and limped, trembling, towards the hallway. It was a mess of dirty floorboards and scuff marks on the walls. Feathers drifted, disturbed by my footsteps. The trail of blood from where I'd dragged Bridget to the parlour earlier had darkened to resemble mud. Swallowing, I nerved myself to go and check on her. But then I noticed the prints leading upstairs.

I grabbed the banister to steady myself. The tracks weren't quite paws – but they weren't footprints either. Fighting every instinct in my body, I followed them. The steps screamed each time I placed one of my feet down.

I'd nearly gained the landing when Rowena appeared there. The sight of her punched the air from my lungs. Her skirt had ripped up to the knees and one sleeve was missing from her gown. The steely tresses covering her left ear were matted with blood. She looked at me, leant back against the wall and slowly slid to the ground.

'Godmother!' I took the last few steps. 'Are you hurt?'

It was the stupidest question I could have asked. But Rowena held out her bare arm as if seeing it for the first time. 'Just scratches,' she breathed. Then, inexplicably, she began to laugh. I hoped I never lived to hear another laugh like that, so utterly devoid of mirth. 'I have the devil's own luck.'

'Where's Lucy?' I demanded.

She blinked her one good eye. 'In her room, at last.'

A sob of relief burst out. Part of me flickered back to life. 'You managed to get her safely out of the barn? You both escaped?'

'Yes. But I've never seen her so ill. And bringing her back here, with Bridget's blood everywhere . . .'

'How is Bridget? Did you manage to bandage her wound?'

Rowena swallowed. 'My dear, Bridget is dead. I knew the moment I saw you with her in the barrow that she didn't stand a chance. She'd tipped the teeth of those traps with poison . . .' She trailed off and my own horror was reflected on her face.

I slumped down to my knees. Was this all my fault? Had I just inadvertently caused the deaths of Bridget and Mr Randall with my desperation to get inside the root-cellar?

I couldn't think straight. I needed to see Lucy, safe. Only her presence would dull the pain.

I was about to rise when Rowena spoke.

'It was the same day, you know.' Her tone was limp and dead. 'We baptized you and Lucy together, just before I left Lincolnshire. A shared christening. I stood godmother for you, and Susannah for Lucy.' Her blue eye sought mine. 'I was selfish. When I saw you, so lusty and bonny a babe, I hoped, somehow, with that ceremony, to twine your fates together. Then I allowed you to come here, against my better judgement, hoping you could bless Lucy's future. I had it in my mind to present you as a gift, a friend for her to keep after I'm gone. But I no longer wish for that.' She shook her head. 'No, it was a fantasy. You must go, Camille. Never mind your belongings; they can be replaced. Take my purse by the door, run straight to The Grey Lady and catch the first coach home. Don't stop to look back. Go now . . . and tell your mother I am so sorry.'

'I'm not leaving—'

'Go!' she hollered.

'I can't!' I gestured helplessly down the stairs. 'The wolf is still out there!'

Every vestige of colour drained from her skin. 'What do you mean?'

'Outside! It – it killed the sheep!' I knew she must be stunned, but her face looked utterly bewildered. 'Didn't it chase you from the barn too? I thought . . . your injuries . . .'

'He got out,' she breathed.

The front door opened and closed again. I sprang up, grab-bing for my knife. Unsteady footsteps approached – not the click of claws against wood. It was a person. As I reached the head of the stairs, Colin Randall emerged from the kitchen, bedraggled but miraculously unharmed.

The knife dropped from my hand. 'Oh, thank God! Mr Randall! You're alive!'

I started forward, scarcely able to believe it. But although he wasn't hurt, he was altered. His wide smile, which used to make my heart skip a beat, looked wrong, even menacing.

Before I'd descended more than two steps, another, shorter man limped out from behind him. I stopped, gripped the banister. 'Who . . .' I began, but answered my own question. 'Merciful heaven. This is who they were keeping in the root-cellar!'

The man resembled a convict escaped from the deepest recess of Newgate. His hair had been cropped close to his skull, accentuating the hollow cheeks of near starvation. He wore the tattered remains of a shirt and knee breeches. Not an inch of his skin was free from bruises or scars. Blood crusted at the corners of his mouth. A diagonal gash crossed the bridge of his nose, weeping and bleeding at the same time, a wound that seemed like both cut and burn.

Colin mounted the stairs and bounded up on to the landing. 'Yes. Look what your godmother did! She trapped and drugged him for a whole year. But he's free now, thanks to you.'

Was that where Bridget and Rowena had crept, night after night – to wrestle with this poor wreck? Had they pushed their poisons upon him, threatened him with the sword of Bridget's soldier? Why?

The man remained below, glowering, and suddenly I knew why he unnerved me. It wasn't the filth or the emaciation; it was his eyes, almost as familiar as my own in the glass. Golden. This was Lucy's father, Sir Marcus Alaunt.

He'd been the man asking questions in Deepbeck, last year. He must have found the lodge. But he didn't manage to take Lucy away. Instead he'd been kept as their prisoner all that time.

Behind me, Rowena scrabbled to her feet. A vein pulsed in her temple. Colin smirked and swept her an elaborate bow. 'Your servant, madam. Why, you look as though you've seen a ghost! Don't you remember me, Aunt Rowena?'

'Colin?' The name seemed to crack in the air like a whip. Rowena swallowed. 'That tiny boy . . . Yes, of course they'd send you to find Marcus. A face so changed I wouldn't recognize it.'

I wasn't sure I recognized him, either. The way his gaze licked at both of us, his full-toothed grin; it was as though a beautiful mask had slipped.

'Oh, I was playing this game long before Uncle Marcus disappeared,' he tittered. 'Back when we were seeking only you. We knew of your connection to the Garniers, of course. It was just a matter of insinuating myself into the children's lives and waiting for the right opportunity. Getting the son in trouble did nothing.' He shrugged. 'But the girl . . . in the end, she led us straight to you.'

'You're one of them,' I gasped, my mouth finally catching up with my brain. 'One of the Alaunts. All these weeks you were just using me to—'

His dark brows lowered as a shadow passed across his face. 'Hush, Miss Garnier. I did you no wrong. Everything I said, I meant in honour. We *shall* be married. But first I had to find my uncle and free him from his wicked imprisonment. Don't you see? To think your godmother had the effrontery to call *him* cruel!'

Slow, laboured footsteps on the stairs. The man with Lucy's fiery eyes shambled into view. His left foot twisted inwards, reminding me of Bridget's caught in the trap. It'd been broken and reset without splints. Starved as he was, Sir Marcus carried a presence, a sense of power and malice. The look he turned on Rowena I would never forget. Pure, dark loathing.

Rowena pushed herself between me and Colin, spreading her arms on either side, shielding me. 'Spare the girls,' she said, her voice admirably even.

Sir Marcus's throaty chuckle sounded as if it had emerged from the depths of the earth with him. 'As your friend Bridget spared me? All those tests, all those nights caged in my own filth after she forced down potion after potion? Keeping me in this weak form.' His eyes flicked upon me. 'At least this chit showed sympathy. She tried to get me out of that cellar, which is more than I can say for my dear daughter.'

'Lucy will *never* be your daughter,' Rowena flared with sudden vehemence. 'My blood still runs in her veins, no matter how yours pollutes it.'

Sir Marcus skulked forward, head tilted. Somehow his face seemed to be longer, his nose broader than before. Colin flexed his hands at his sides.

Whose part was I supposed to take? Husband and wife each wore scars inflicted by the other. The abuse was mutual. But Colin showed no injury. His shirt had ripped open, sweat plastered the curls to his forehead, yet there was barely a scratch upon him.

'I don't understand,' I bleated. 'How did you escape the wolf? And where is the dog, who made noises in the cellar—'

'Marcus *is* the wolf!' Rowena cried. '*He* is the mad dog we caught last year. Run and lock yourself in the turret, now!' She pushed me so hard that I flew, nearly hitting the door at the end of the hallway.

I did exactly as she said. My heart thundered in time with my feet, up the spiral staircase. It wasn't possible. This could only happen in a tale: Daphne turned to a laurel tree, Io into a cow. But then I remembered cutting the wolf's muzzle with my knife, and the matching wound on Sir Marcus's nose. I thought of the noises I'd heard, both man and beast in turn. I knew Rowena's secret now and it was beyond poison, beyond human comprehension. The man she'd married wasn't just dangerous. He was a werewolf!

I found Lucy's bedchamber brighter than it had ever been before. Ragged patches of light flashed through slashes in the curtains. There were grooves raked into the wall, a dark patch on the floor beside a toppled candelabra. Lucy herself lay on the rumpled bed, her hair fanned over the pillows. Her gown was a patchwork of rusty brown stains and feathers, her throat so red from the silver choker that she looked like a hanged woman. Rowena had actually tied her wrists to the bedposts to prevent her moving.

Catching sight of me, she pulled at the restraints. 'Camille?' she cried, incredulous. 'No! What are you doing here? You're meant to be safe, on your way home!'

'I came back for you, of course!' I kicked the door closed and dashed to the head of the bed, where I began to pick at the knots. 'Are you better now? Why are you bound like a criminal?'

'Stop! I *need* to be restrained. Don't untie me! It's not safe; I might hurt you,' she protested. I didn't listen. I couldn't bear to see her trapped.

'You can't be tied up now. We need your strength . . . Something terrible has happened downstairs.'

'I know! Bridget is dead.' The second rope clattered to the floor. Lucy paused and then, as if she couldn't quite help herself, wrapped me in an embrace. My nose burrowed deep into her hair. Something inside unclenched.

'You're so stupid!' she sobbed on to my shoulder. 'Why did you come back? What's the matter with you? Why are you such a perfect, pretty little idiot?'

Another time I would have laughed. I pulled back and tried to dry her tears with my thumb, but that only made her angry.

'You need to go, Camille. You need to run far away and never return.' Yet, even as she said it, her hands were gripping me tight.

'I'm trapped in here with you. I let your father out of the root-cellar!'

The muscles in her face fell slack. 'You did *what*?'

'I didn't know! How could I possibly suspect he was a . . . a . . .' Even to speak the word felt absurd. And now the flood-gates burst open in my mind. The family illness. The moon.

Colin and Lucy, sharing Sir Marcus's Alaunt blood. The odd prints leading up the stairs . . . I looked at Lucy's wild beauty with fresh eyes and suddenly it was difficult to breathe. 'Oh, Lucy! Do *you* change too?'

She flinched away. 'Not fully. *He* didn't, before he built up a tolerance to the wolfsbane. It kept us both in our weaker form.' Fresh tears shimmered in her eyes. 'Do you finally understand? I *told* Mama. I told her having him near made me worse, I told her it wasn't safe for you to come.' She stopped abruptly. 'Camille. Where *is* my mama?'

As if in answer, the door splintered open and smacked back against the stone wall. Lucy pulled me instinctively on to the bed beside her. But not even the warmth of her protective arms could soften the sight of Colin prowling into the room, both hands gloved in scarlet. Sir Marcus limped behind, wearing a beard of gore. He bared his teeth at me and I saw that they were rimmed in blood.

'What have you done?' I screeched. 'What have you done to my godmother?'

Colin raised his bloody hand to his lips and sucked his index finger clean. 'I'm afraid she proved . . . uncooperative.'

A high-pitched tone whined in my ears. I felt sick. How had I ever found him attractive? How had I kissed those lips that now twisted in a diabolical smile?

Lucy choked, a throttled sound in her throat that I thought was pure grief. But then she bent forward and started to contort. One of her coughing fits had seized her. We were helpless, marooned on the island of the tester bed as the men slowly circled the turret room, Sir Marcus pacing one way, Colin the other.

'I trusted you!' I screamed at him. Lucy's cough stabbed at the air. 'I trusted you and—'

'And I kept you safe! I didn't let my uncle hurt you at the barn, did I? I never laid a finger upon you. I can control it, you know,' he said proudly. 'Turn whenever I want. That's how it should be.' He regarded Lucy, fighting for breath, her fingers tugging at her choker. 'I'll teach you, cousin.'

'We'll all live together at Moyset Chase,' Sir Marcus insisted. 'As we were *meant* to. I can't wait to tell the pack that you've been found at last! Your mother tried to turn you from your true nature, Lucy. She poisoned your mind as well as your body.'

Lucy whooped. I scuttled towards the pillows as she fell on to her back. 'Help her! She's sick!'

'She is *not* sick!' Sir Marcus roared back, a vein standing out in his neck. 'This is what she is!'

Lucy's back arched away from the mattress, an invisible string pulling her up, up towards the stars on the ceiling. I feared she'd snap in half, like my girlhood doll. The silver choker at her neck had tarnished black as midnight on a moonless night.

Colin stopped pacing. 'It's the necklace,' he said simply. 'Can't you see it's throttling her?'

A low hiss started. Something was burning, steaming. Lucy screamed. I couldn't believe it was the same voice that sounded so beautiful in church; it caught and tore as it ripped through her throat.

Colin was right: the choker was burning her, eating into her flesh like acid.

'Take it off,' he urged. 'I can't.'

Tears blurred my vision. Deep down, I knew what would happen. But I couldn't watch Lucy in such agony. Her head thrashed about wildly as I parted the mass of her hair and reached for the necklace's clasp. Flinched. It was hot to the touch.

Silver fights infection, Rowena had told me. *Pulls out impurities. Wards off evil.* But my nostrils filled with the terrible scent of Lucy's pale skin, cooking, and none of that mattered. Gritting my teeth, I opened the choker and tossed it off the bed.

Sir Marcus barked a terrible laugh.

'Lucy?' She fell limp. Her eyelids shut then started to flicker. 'Lucy!'

Giving a jerk, she rolled from the bed. My hands scrabbled on the sheets but I couldn't catch her. There came a crack as she hit the floor, then a sudden flash of white. A horrible wet popping filled my ears; the same sound I'd heard when Colin fell, what I'd thought was the wolf eating him.

As swiftly as it had come, the burst of light receded. Slowly, I blinked. Spots of colour quivered at the edge of my vision. Lucy had vanished. Lying in her place on the stone flags was a huge grey wolf.

Instinct shrieked at me to run, but I could only sit dumbfounded as she rose to her massive paws. A great barrel chest, eyes that blazed like hellfire.

'Now you see her truly,' Sir Marcus said with satisfaction. 'Just as you saw me in the barn. Isn't she beautiful?'

When she growled, I felt the vibration in every bone of my body. I shuffled back upon the bed, but Colin came up behind and gripped my shoulders, holding me in place. 'It won't hurt much,' he whispered, soft as a lover. 'Just a little bite. Then you can be like us.'

Turning my head, I bit *him* on the hand with all of my might. Colin exclaimed and I managed to twist free of his grasp at the same instant the wolf-Lucy pounced. I thumped to the floor, landing heavily upon my knees. Lucy was tangled in the bedsheets, snarling when I pulled myself up and lunged for the turret stairs.

It was like trying to run a gauntlet: first the spiral steps beneath my trembling legs and then the hallway, slippery with Rowena's blood. Her poor body lay crumpled at the bottom of the second staircase, a gaping orifice where her heart should be. Disgusted, I twisted my face away, and what I saw over my shoulder nearly made me lose my footing. Not one wolf in pursuit behind me, but three. One metal-coloured, one a cloud of smoke and another, black as Colin's ebony hair.

I'd never make it out of Felwood alive. It was futile even to try, yet still I charged on. The wolf I took for Sir Marcus leapt as I entered the kitchen, missing me by a hair's-breadth and slamming into the wall.

Powered by sheer terror, I made it out and into the labyrinth of the trees. Everything was spinning. Wind swirled leaves in a hurricane around me and the sky was a net of branches, holding me in. I couldn't single out the landmarks I used to guide myself on a normal day. Nothing was real.

I knew I couldn't last for long. Even in her human form Lucy always outran me. I didn't even reach the hedged pathway before she hit me from behind with the force of a stagecoach. I went down hard, burning the palms of my hands against the earth. There was that scent again, the too-sweet smell of mulch and decay. I felt the desiccated leaves beneath me, saw the ants that moved across them and heard the crows, shrieking from up high. All these things would feed upon my body when the wolf had taken its fill.

I twisted on to my back. Wolf-Lucy parted her jaws, scarlet stringing between her teeth, ready to bite. I closed my eyes, braced myself for death.

Suddenly, everything stopped. The breeze moved cold against my tear-streaked face. I heard the shifting of the trees, tentative birdsong. When I opened my eyes, the wolf was sitting down, whimpering, her rueful gaze on the moonstone necklace hanging on my bodice.

'Lucy?' I whispered.

Something of her dwelt in those burning eyes. Something contained, seeking its freedom. And Sir Marcus had spoken truly. Even like this, she was strangely beautiful. That soft, grey pelt. Tentatively, I reached out a hand. 'Is it . . . still you?'

Neither of us saw the movement in the undergrowth as Colin snuck towards me, camouflaged and silent as the grave. Before I could pull myself into a sitting position, he emerged in a stormcloud of black fur. I screamed. Fangs sank into the soft flesh of my waist. Pain bloomed and radiated out. I could feel my own blood, spurting in hot streams.

Lucy pounced, hitting him from the side and knocking him clear. The two wolves sprawled into the bushes, a mass of flailing claws and teeth.

Oh God, the pain. I struggled to my feet, nearly dropping straight back down again from sheer weakness. If my injury was even half as bad as it felt, I was surely done for. There must be pints of blood lost. I needed help; I couldn't wait for Lucy to turn back to herself. If she ever would. The moonstone may have stopped her once, but now my blood had been spilt I dare not hope she could keep control. For a second, I watched her tussle with the black wolf: enraged, deadly.

She was fighting for me; but whether as a lover or a meal, I couldn't say for sure. Weeping, I turned my back on both of them and ran.

It was a shambling run, weaving from side to side as pain tore me apart. I clutched a hand to my hot, sticky side. Black patches spread like damp across my vision and behind them images swam: sprawling branches, winding ivy, a tree fallen and consumed by moss. I toiled on, growing fainter and fainter with each step. When I exhaled, there was no longer a great plume of smoke on the cold air but a thin stream, like a snuffed candle.

For the second time that day, I headed for The Grey Lady inn. But I'd gone astray. I was much further down the road; I couldn't see the chimneystacks rising above the trees. With what felt like the last ounce of my strength, I ducked under the oak branches and into the road.

A volley of shouts bounced around. Someone called, 'Stop!

Stop!' A horse whinnied and metal clanked. I turned to see a travelling chaise hurtling towards the spot where I stood. It skidded to a halt, mere inches from mowing me down.

'God's blood, lass! What's tha doing?'

I gaped up at the startled driver, a man with large red cheeks. 'Please, sir . . . I need help.'

Warily, I withdrew the hand from my side and inspected the wound. The bleeding had stopped, leaving a hard crust on my bodice. There was no torn skin, no gaping hole, only ghostly silver scars. I blinked. How could that be?

But the driver saw the stains, the tears in my clothes, and called for his master.

A door opened; the head of an elderly gentleman poked out of the carriage. His watery eyes seemed to bulge at the sight of me. 'What's all this?'

'Please, sir,' I repeated. I was running short of breath. 'My name is . . . Camille Garnier of Martingale Hall, near Stamford. I'm injured. Please . . . take me home? I know it is a long way but . . . my father . . . my father will pay you handsomely.'

'Upon my honour!' the man blustered. 'Sophia, did you—'

'The poor child!' The man's ancient wife appeared on the other side of the chaise, muffled in furs. She waved a hand at her footmen. 'Make haste, get this girl inside the carriage at once.'

Before I knew what was happening, the footmen had jumped down from their perches. A servant scooped me up in his arms and deposited me inside the chaise, on satin squabs with a hot brick at my feet. My aged rescuers stared intently at me from across the carriage. They looked well-to-do, with fine-cut clothes and plenty of fur blankets. Just like that, I'd tumbled out of a world of terror, of werewolves and gore, back into the life I'd always known.

'Thank you,' I gasped.

The man said something. I nodded weakly, but I didn't hear.

My adventure was over, my tale of horror finished. My consciousness slammed shut like a book, and I was naïve enough to think I could end the story there: fast asleep and rattling towards home.

CHAPTER TWENTY-FOUR

Cautiously, I lift the corner of the curtain. The moon sails majestic tonight, her gravid belly almost at full swell. Not a cloud dares to touch her. The light tingles on my skin in a painful but enjoyable way, like placing a finger upon ice or cupping my palm a little too close to a flame. Everything looks so beautiful. At times like this, I almost convince myself that turning won't hurt at all.

It can't be long before I find out for certain.

My eyes sweep over the silvered landscape outside, and my mind carries on beyond their vision. Along the toll roads, miles and miles across the fells, bobbing at last downriver to Felwood Lodge. Are Lucy, Colin and Sir Marcus still there where I left them? If my father arrives to find three wolves at their most powerful time of the month . . .

I drop the curtain back into place. Maybe Lucy will protect him for my sake. Or maybe the girl I knew and loved has been devoured entirely by this curse.

Muscles shift; my spine gives a crack. I groan. There's nothing I can do for Papa and Pierre from here. But I can still help Mama, Marie and Jean: I can leave. Go anywhere, far from the eyes of society. I was stupid to think I could carry on as before.

Girl or wolf, I was never going to return to Martingale Hall and slot neatly back inside my family. I'm corked wine, soured milk, irrevocably changed. Lucy managed to control her condition for a long time, but there's no Rowena to wrestle with me, no Bridget serving wolfsbane tea to keep my human form. No; leaving is my only option now. I won't stay to let Martingale Hall become a crypt. I won't be the reason its fine carpets are awash with blood, its portraits slashed, its servants piled in a grisly heap.

The broken doll of my childhood gazes forlornly down at me from her shelf as I creep towards the door. She knows what it is to be torn in two like this, snapped beyond repair.

I need no candle to guide my steps. With perfect night vision, I slip through the darkened house. Not a servant, not a single member of the family hears me stir, but I listen to them. One of the scullery girls mutters in her sleep. Baby Jean has a cold; his little nose sounds blocked. I jerk away from his tantalizing scent. Instead I inhale Marie's sweetness, Mama's floral notes. It's the only way for me to say goodbye. Crossing the deserted kitchens to the ignoble trade door, I quit Martingale Hall for the last time.

All of nature feels primed. Power hums through the obsidian sky. At last, at last, I can surrender to the pull of the night. Martingale Hall grows smaller behind me and my sense of self dwindles with it. Maybe after I change there will be nothing left of me inside – but at least the pain will be gone, too.

The chestnut trees stir, softly bristling, as rabbits flee my path. I can sense the moon growing; myself growing. It's too soon. I have to get off my family's land, away from the people I love.

I try to run. The heat builds, my skin prickles and my bones are turning to glass. I taste blood, feel it on my palms. This is it: the moment I dreaded.

There's a glow, white as moonlight – the flash I saw when

Lucy changed. Agony forces me to my knees. My vision tunnels. I don't see the brightness any more; only a chasm into which I'm falling, falling . . .

'Camille!' Something clamps on my arm, catches me. 'Camille. Come back.'

My eyes are wide open, but there's nothing, only a black wall in each direction I spin.

'Find the light.' On the horizon, like the breaking of the sun, rises an unearthly, bluish sheen. The hand on my arm squeezes. 'Follow it!'

The ghostly blue light wavers and quivers in the dark. If I could only reach it, touch it . . . Even as the thought crosses my mind, the light turns and rushes back in my direction, roaring like the tide. There's a swell of cool air as we collide and I break through the wave, gasping for breath. Vision floods back.

I'm kneeling on the grass where I fell. A hand hovers in front of me. There, nestled in its palm, is a moonstone necklace identical to the one I wore. Turning my head, I see two more gems: topaz gleaming bright.

'Are you with me?' the voice asks, and I know it now. But I still can't believe my senses. Lucy crouches by my side. Twigs are tangled through her unbound hair. Dirt is smeared across her cheeks. The glorious eyes, which I took for gems, have sunk deeper into her skull.

'Are you a dream?'

'No.' Lucy coughs and pulls me to my feet beneath the chestnut trees. Everything reels except for her. I'm anchored by her touch, her sweet musk, the moonstone she clutches. 'Not a dream. More of a nightmare, I suppose.' She grinds her teeth. 'Hurry, Camille! Come out of the moonlight.'

My wits aren't fully restored. 'Why . . .' I falter. 'How are you here?'

'I escaped them. My *family*,' she spits the words with contempt.

'They're damnable, worse than I ever imagined. And now they're hunting for both of us.'

We sit in the shadowed kitchen. The staff have retreated to their attic above, leaving the grates powdery with ashes. Our facilities here are at least three times the size of that cramped and smoky room in Felwood Lodge where I helped Bridget grind her herbs. Copper pans hang from the wall in all shapes and sizes. There's a sideboard with a fine porcelain dinner service, the latest cooking range, and a pantry stocked full of food. Perhaps I should have dwelt here all through my sickness; the variety of scents distract from other, more human odours.

The moonstone necklace Lucy brought with her glints between us on the knife-scarred table. It's a help, not a cure. My two warring sides are balanced precariously on a tightrope, like the performers I once saw at Vauxhall Gardens.

'Look at you,' she says miserably, her gaze tender. She appears older and her glorious eyes are threaded with red veins. 'Look what he's done to you, my pretty Camille. Your hair . . . your eyes. This is what I always dreaded. I wanted so badly to keep your brightness alive. I'm so, so sorry.'

I flinch against the memory of Colin in wolf form, his teeth ravening at my flesh. 'Why *do* I have this grey hair? Why am I different from you and . . . *him?*'

Her fingertips drum on the table, ever playing their silent tunes. 'I guess the curse was always a part of us. Your body's had to . . . make way, make changes to accommodate it. Did your wound heal?'

I nod.

'My mother said it's a bite that turns a person. Scratches don't. Some people just die outright. But a well-placed bite, where the victim survives . . . that's where it creeps in.' Her fingertips still. 'I'm so sorry, Camille,' she says again. 'I should have seen him. I should have protected you.'

My heart pleads for her. She didn't mean for any of this to happen. I want to kiss her, but I also want to shake her until her teeth rattle.

'No - you should have *told* me from the start,' I grind out. 'You should have told me what you and your family are. Maybe most people wouldn't have believed it. But you know me! I spent every day at Felwood Lodge reading about magical transformations: gods into animals, people into stars. Of all the girls in the world, I'm the one who would have listened to you.'

She winces, her face pained in the shadows. 'That was Mama's instruction. She insisted such knowledge would haunt you, change your life. I know I teased you for being ignorant and carefree but . . . honestly, Camille, I loved to see that in you. I wanted to keep your light.'

I trace a finger over the moonstone's sheen. 'Is this one hers? Rowena's?'

'Yes.' She lowers her eyes. 'I pulled it from her body.'

My skin chills. It's as though Rowena has entered the kitchen and stands with us. There are so many words left unsaid. An apology burns a hole inside my chest. I was such an idiot. I fell for Colin's tricks and led him straight to her house, loosened the door to the root-cellar so that Sir Marcus broke free. I brought Rowena's whole world crashing down. Yet my godmother's last actions were to push herself in front of me and beg her husband to spare me. I don't realize I'm crying until I taste the salt on my lips.

'She was wearing her moonstone . . . but your father still killed her!'

Lucy glowers. 'The moonstone helps you to find the light, but only if you want to see it. I told you before – my father has no desire for holy gems and goodness. He loves the darkness. He embraces it.'

'And your cousin Colin . . .' Blood rushes to my cheeks as

her gaze on me sharpens. 'He said he can change to a wolf and back at will?'

'Yes,' she says bitterly. 'And what fun he had, attacking the stagecoach, digging up graveyards, terrifying the village. You have to understand, Camille, that for my family there is no divide between the human and the wolf. There's no battle within, as there is for us. Evil has consumed them and both parts work in league.' Her hand seeks her silver choker. She must have found it on her bedroom floor. 'Maybe they're smarter than me. Maybe I'm doomed and it's useless to struggle on. But I *will* keep fighting the darkness. As long as I still have breath.' She holds out a trembling hand. 'Will you fight with me, Camille?'

Gingerly, I take her hand. It feels like the only solid thing left in the world.

'Are we fighting against the wolves in us . . . or against the Alaunts?'

'Both,' she says decidedly. 'They're coming for you. All of you here at Martingale Hall. That's why I came ahead to raise the alarm, even though the moonlight was agony. No one, *no one* can learn the Alaunts' secrets. You're either part of the pack, or you're killed.'

The tightrope judders beneath my feet. She said this before, but I could hardly take it in. 'What?'

'Colin *did* want to marry you.' She grips my hand, just as hard as she squeezed to keep me from transforming. 'Our family are so inbred, they're always after fresh blood for their lineage . . . like my poor mama. She didn't learn the truth about her husband until it was already too late. But Colin thought you were different. That you would come around to the idea of being a werewolf, take his side. The last thing he expected was for you to run home and tell your family what he is.'

'They don't know!' I blaze. 'Not one of them realizes what's happening to me. I tried to warn Pierre about Mr Randall, in

257

case he tried to reach us, but I couldn't get him alone. I didn't say a word about the bite, or your father, or any of it.'

'It doesn't matter. They've decided now: your family must die. They bundled me into their carriage and set out for their estate, Moyset Chase. My father was to return home in triumph and gather the rest of the pack for a hunt. I managed to escape at one of the stages and find my way here . . . I didn't even stop to look at the stars. They'll guess where I've gone,' she says with certainty. 'I only pray they abandon their journey and come to fetch me back at once. If it's just two of them, we might stand a chance. But I can't protect your family against a whole pack of werewolves.'

Dear God. Suddenly I'm relieved that Papa and Pierre are far from here. 'You all left Felwood Lodge before our chaise arrived?' I ask to make absolutely sure. 'You didn't see my father or brother?'

Her eyes grow round. 'They've gone to Felwood Lodge? Why on earth would you allow them to do that?'

'They left without my knowing!' I bleat, but it's not a good defence. I've let shock, fear and trauma silence me for too long. I ought to have told my family more; I should have realized that Colin never posted any of my letters to them. 'My father wanted answers. To . . . discover what had happened to Rowena.'

A muscle twitches in Lucy's cheek. 'He'll wish he never went looking. The carnage left behind isn't for the faint of heart. But at least that's two members of your family out of harm's way – for the time being.'

Her tears remain suspended in her eyes, but mine won't stop. I grip the moonstone. 'Lucy . . . are you all right? I can't imagine what you must have been through since I left. I shouldn't have abandoned you there, with them. I was just so afraid.'

She drops my hand and quits her chair. 'No. Please don't start that. We can't let grief take over.'

I know what she means. Sorrow is a kind of darkness in itself; I can feel it, teasing at the edges of my mind, ready to seize control. But this is her mother's murder we're talking about. If Lucy doesn't mourn for her, the wound will fester. 'You can't repress *everything*.'

'Believe me, I'll cry enough when this is all finished. But first Mama must be avenged. I couldn't do it alone, at home. They're too strong, and I didn't have what I needed . . .' Suddenly she's opening cupboards, pulling out jars. 'What do you use to poison vermin here? Arsenic?'

It's useless to ask me. Servants do these tasks, I never have. 'I suppose . . .'

'Arsenic would be perfect. Where is it? I need you to show me everything you keep in here, Camille.' She sniffs the air. 'There's meat in the larder, isn't there?'

There is: lamb. Its scent has been thrumming through our whole conversation. 'Yes, why?'

'Because I have a plan.' Turning back to me, she spills out her pockets on the table. 'There's some wolfsbane and other herbs salvaged from Bridget's physic patch. I saved what I could. But I need silver – not obvious like the dinner service at Felwood. Small bits. Like – earrings. Do you have anything in your dressing room? Pure silver studs?'

I blink, unable to keep up with her. 'I . . . yes, I think so.'

'Fetch them, please.'

'But you said your father and Colin are coming! How is my jewellery collection going to stop them? Surely we need a knife or—'

A wail cuts me off. The breath locks in my chest. Jean is crying, and now I'm alert to his presence his odour is like a thick mist before my eyes. Lucy reaches for the moonstone in my hand; we clasp it together.

'Do you trust me, Camille?' she whispers, her eyes trained upon the ceiling in the direction of the noise.

What a question to ask. But the truth is, I remember her kiss with more intensity than even Colin's bite to my side. My heart *does* trust her.

'What makes you ask that?'

Jean cries on.

'Because this is the part of my plan you're going to hate.' She shifts her weight, a dark figure against a dark table. 'It's not just the earrings. I need you to fetch your baby brother, too.'

CHAPTER TWENTY-FIVE

I've spent so long trying to avoid Jean. His velvet-soft head, his pudgy limbs with the little rolls of fat, the warm weight of him. Most of all the aroma. Mama always says there's no scent more delectable than that of a clean baby. 'Jean's scrumptious,' she'd tell me. 'I could eat him up.'

She'd be horrified if she saw me with him now. Drool strings down my chin on to the bundle I carry as I enter the darkened stable block. God only knows how I've made it this far. It feels as though I've been resisting Jean for miles. The moonstone necklace Marie put over his crib is now wrapped around his middle. His brown eyes watch it, fascinated. He doesn't grizzle; he's content, full of milk, and somehow that's worse. He feels safe with me, his sister, when the truth is far, far otherwise.

My feet click across the tile floor strewn with wisps of hay. Indistinct horses nicker from their stalls as I pass. At least here there are smells to dilute the temptation of Jean: dung, straw, horsehair and leather.

Hearing me approach, Lucy opens the door to the tack room and I hurry to join her. The twang of leather is even richer inside, leavened with metal and polish.

A lantern illuminates saddles on their racks, hanging bridles, halters and leading ropes. Lucy's pulled some of the saddle cloths down and practised tying them in various ways. Her nostrils flare as I bring Jean closer.

'You have his blankets? The cordial?'

He coos at her, all sweetness. 'As you see,' I reply.

Can she see? Her pupils have dwindled to points. My courage shrinks with them. Jean is in dire peril. I've lost two baby siblings already, I couldn't bear to add another tiny skeleton to the graveyard.

'What are you going to do to him?' I whisper.

Lucy glances at the second moonstone, Rowena's moonstone, where it hangs alongside a snaffle bit. 'He'll be all right. It's us who'll have to hold our nerve. Luckily I'm used to that, I've spent years biting this back, but you might need a bit more help. Keep the moonstone on him. We'll each swallow a flower of wolfsbane too; that should stop us from turning.'

'The nursemaid checks on him every few hours,' I fret. 'When she sees he's gone, she'll raise the alarm.'

'By my reckoning we have less than an hour. I came on foot, remember. My family have a carriage.' She moves the various rags, polishes and bits of metal from the cleaning table. 'Lay Jean down here, on this surface.'

It's strange: I walked all the way from the nursery wishing Jean were far away, where he couldn't stir my hunger; now I'm reluctant to let him go. When his warmth leaves my chest, I feel bereft.

We gaze down upon him, lying on his back, kicking out his legs, and our grave, pinched faces are such a contrast to his gummy smile. He doesn't belong out here in the lantern light and dust.

'I never saw a baby before,' Lucy says softly. 'Not in the flesh.'

I don't like her choice of words. I wipe Jean's nose, brush some horsehair from the path of his reaching hand. Once, when we were milking in the barn, I told Lucy about Jean and she sent me outside, overcome. Her actions make more sense now.

'What is it?' I whisper. 'This . . . urge? Why does Jean tempt me so much more than anyone else?'

She runs her tongue over her lips. 'I think because he's everything we're not. Unpolluted. Natural. Blameless. The wolf wants to consume everything good and light.' She swallows. 'It even wanted to destroy how I feel about you. It nearly did, back at Felwood. But I stopped it in time. That has to count for something?'

A tremor runs through me. I clutch for her hand, but that's all. Right now I can't risk the emotion of responding; every ounce of concentration is needed to keep Jean safe.

Distantly, Pierre's hunter whinnies.

I clear my throat and let go of Lucy's hand. 'All the stable workers live in a building close by,' I tell her. 'They'll come looking, if we make too much noise. They'll think the horses are being stolen.'

'That's a chance we'll have to take. We *must* do it here. Somewhere with a muddle of sounds and smells, to confuse them. It will actually help if the horses are agitated.'

She doesn't understand a life spent cheek by jowl with others; she isn't used to servants coming up a separate staircase, lurking out of sight. 'Some of our staff are armed, though. Maybe I should just warn them in advance? Couldn't we let the game-keeper shoot the wolves with his gun?'

'Don't be a blockhead, Camille. You know that won't work!'

'But I *don't* know,' I point out. 'I don't understand any of this. I need you to teach me, as I always have.'

Softening, she reaches for the purple-blue flowers of wolfs-bane. Precious few are left and their petals are withered. 'Weapons can still hurt you in your human form. But when you're a wolf, you're tougher. And the wounds you do suffer as a wolf tend to heal pretty quickly.'

She plucks off a flower and passes it to me. I take it, feel the dryness crumbling on my fingertips.

'This is how we controlled my father. He fell into a trap laced with wolfsbane, just as Bridget did. It's deadly to a normal person. Not us. It holds us in our human form. We force-fed my father wolfsbane, kept him weak, at least until he built up the tolerance . . . But even so, eating some now will still confuse his system, impair him a little.'

Lucy takes another star-shaped flower and presses it between her lips. I follow suit, feel again the dizzy, melting sensation of the poison.

'This giddiness will pass,' Lucy's voice floats from somewhere nearby. 'It's only one flower. You won't swoon.'

Easy for her to say; she's more accustomed to taking large doses. I slouch backwards but a saddle stops me from leaning against the wall, pressing hard into my spine. Maybe if I keep talking, my wits won't drift apart. 'So . . . you want to turn Sir Marcus and Colin back to humans . . . and then the arsenic will be able to kill them?'

'Yes, but, as I said, the wolfsbane might not work well on my father, and we haven't got much of it left to use. If he stays as a wolf, the only thing that will really be able to hurt him is silver. Hence the earrings.'

Everything wobbles. My mouth feels horribly numb. 'Colin can't even touch silver in human form,' I remember. 'He made me take your necklace off for him; he said he couldn't do it himself.'

Lucy sniffs. 'So much the better. It will hurt him more. As I told you, the Alaunts are infected, through and through. Since there's not much divide between the man and the wolf, I'm designing a weapon that will target both sides.'

My surroundings swing back into focus. When I look for Lucy, she's on the boot-stained floor, going through her inventory. I swear she's brought half of our kitchen with her.

Jean coughs. The novelty of the small, musty room has worn off for him and now he wants his crib back. His lower lip starts to tremble.

'It's all right,' I hush, keeping my eyes on the moonstone. Between that and the wolfsbane we just took, the baby's presence is a little easier to bear. Everything is muted.

'Give him the medicine now,' Lucy instructs, head still down. 'Put him to sleep before he starts fussing. As large a dose as you can.'

I feel horribly like Bridget as I feed my brother a slug of Godfrey's Cordial. But he's used to this; he takes it often for colic. He gives a burp and then his tiny eyelids begin to droop.

'What now?' I ask.

Lucy's hand seizes on the work-basket I brought from my dressing-room. She takes a minute to select a needle before she answers. 'Now is the hardest part of all. Grab that other moonstone, put them both close to Jean.'

My stomach wallows. 'Why?'

'Because . . . we need to make him bleed.'

No, we can't do that. He's just a baby, he's so small. And the blood . . . He smells edible enough as it is. Is she out of her mind?

'You promised me!' I shout. Jean flinches, eyelids fluttering open and I lower my voice. 'You said you wouldn't hurt him!'

Lucy jabs the needle into the tip of her own thumb. 'Look. A pinprick. That's all. Hardly worse than the inoculation against smallpox.'

But I remember the way Lucy stared at me, after I scratched my arm with a pin. As if she'd swallow me whole. I stand in front of my brother, barring the way to him. He gives another little cough.

'I can't. He'll be irresistible.'

'That's the point!' she cries. 'It's the only way my plan will work. We can't fight two wolves without turning ourselves, and God only knows who we'd hurt in the process of doing that! The Alaunts are more powerful and they're in control of their changes; they'd win without a doubt. All we can do is try to outwit them. We *need* the baby's blood. My father and Colin need to be tempted to the point where they won't stop and think too much.'

'It's *you* who's not thinking! I won't risk it. I'm not strong enough. I couldn't live with myself if I hurt my own brother.'

Lucy sighs heavily. 'Camille, please. I understand how much you love Jean. And of course I understand that it's wicked to harm a baby in any way. I know better than anyone that you'll have to fight your terrible urges with everything you're worth. But you *are* strong enough. The wolfsbane and the moonstone will hold it in check. I trust you to do this.'

All at once I'm outside Felwood Lodge again, listening to Rowena and Lucy through the open parlour window. Lucy was so afraid that she'd fail the test of sleeping in the same room as me, that she'd hurt me . . . Now I'm in the same position.

'I don't trust myself, and you shouldn't either. I'm not competent like you are; you've seen how I bungle everything.'

She casts up her hands, needle flashing, and as the shadows scurry over her face I see she's as desperate as I am. 'Not something important like this. I believe in you.'

After all her sniping and mocking of my clumsiness, this should mean the world. It does. Yet still my heart is a coward. 'But Lucy—'

'The Alaunts are coming here expressly to kill your family,' she stresses. 'This is my mess. I need to fix it, and this is the only plan I have.' Her breath judders. She adjusts her choker, wincing. 'I'm terrified too! Of course I am. But what else can we do? I have to be blunt. It's either a pinprick for Jean now, or my father devours that poor child alive when he arrives. Tell me honestly which option you'd prefer?'

*

After all, there was never really a choice. I was always going to end up sitting here, huddled on the cold tiles of the corridor that runs between the stalls, the lamps all lit and the door wide open to the night. I've cast the die and gambled everything I have on Lucy: her judgement, her self-control. And, just like a high-stakes bet, if it doesn't pay off it will prove the ruin of my entire family. But the truth is, if I were sitting at a Faro table, I'd never be foolish enough to lay down money on these odds.

Moths hover by the lamps. A breeze ripples in, scattering hay. Pierre's hunter starts to kick at his stall, the way Shadow once did at The Grey Lady inn. The wolves must be close now . . . but how many? Just the two, as Lucy hopes? If it's a whole pack, we're lost.

Raw, animal fear burns like acid in my nostrils. I try to focus on that, but it's like trying to make out the notes of a single flute amid an orchestra. Still the smell of Jean's blood booms louder than all. Inescapable.

I squeeze my eyes shut, adjust the bundle in my lap. *Resist, resist.* It sounds so easy in principle. But my hunger gnaws, equal to any of the poor starved beggars in St Giles' rookery, and I'm clutching an exquisite feast. All I have to do is stoop my head, open my mouth . . . My jaw drops without my permission and I have to clamp it shut again.

A horse snorts. My ears prick. I can't hear Jean at all. Lucy promised me he wouldn't be hurt, but what if, what if . . .? As I wrap his blanket tighter, doubt nibbles alongside the hunger. I trusted Colin Randall once, because he'd kissed me, because he was comely and I desired him. Haven't I just placed my confidence in Lucy for all the same reasons?

No; I shake the thought away. She wouldn't fool me. Not the girl who sought fossils as monstrous as herself for friends, the girl who painted stars. I know her. I've seen the best of her, the worst of her, and I love her still.

Wind soughs through the trees, ominous. I clutch the blanket tighter to my chest, making the scent even more maddening. My arms shake. A tear slips down my cheek. I open my eyes, seeking the moonstone's comforting glow, but, as I do, the horses whinny in alarm. Hooves shift and click. The lamps flicker. A sour taste is tainting the air; a graveyard tang.

They're coming. But here's another hurdle. Will they arrive as gentlemen, presenting themselves at the front entrance to Martingale Hall, or leave the carriage at the gates and cross the park as wolves, the way Lucy expects?

I turn my head towards the door. Freeze. Floating in the sea of darkness outside are four reflective discs. Two pairs of eyes, down low, sloping nearer.

Whimpering, I hug the bundle close.

Lucy guessed right; there's only the two of them, but they're so much bigger than I remembered. Shaggy bulks with a soulless gaze, wicked smiling mouths and tongues that drip saliva. Even the wolf in me cowers, sensing their dominance. The grey one, Sir Marcus, has filled out, no longer flea-bitten and mangy. Out of the cellar, without regular wolfsbane, he must have grown in strength.

The horses stamp and snort. Vibrations travel across the tiles, up through my hip bones. The black wolf-Colin skulks forward into the stable, his blood-tipped claws clicking on the tiles. His matted fur is dark as an abyss. I can't breathe.

He sniffs appreciatively at the precious burden I hold, drool slithering warm across my hands.

'Don't,' I gasp.

A sudden burst of light stabs at my eyes. When it fades, Colin is crouched beside me, changed back to his human form. 'Oh, Miss Garnier.' It sounds like the admonishment of a schoolmaster. He smooths the dark hair back from his brow, revealing a face that is sweaty, bruised, and yet still utterly captivating. 'How has it come to this? Such foolishness, to run back home. And where did you get this tasty morsel? The scent of it drew me across the park. It smells . . .'

He smacks his lips. The hunger shivers through him into me. I grit my teeth.

'But we're not a full party, are we? Where is my cousin Lucy? I thought she'd come to rescue you from us *monsters*.'

'She's in–inside the house,' I sob. 'She couldn't control herself! She turned, and my family . . .' I don't need to force the tears or pretend that terror is choking my voice. 'I managed to escape with my baby brother.' Bending forward, I start to rock what I hold. 'I wanted to save him! But Colin . . .' I meet the melting brown eyes that peer down at me with indulgence. 'I want to eat him, too. So badly,' I whisper. 'Oh, God, Colin, won't you help me?'

He looks exhilarated; he even smiles to show his bloodstained teeth. 'Hush. Don't cry, my dear. Your instincts are natural. Stop fighting them, Camille. Be as you were in Vauxhall Gardens: free to take your pleasure without scruple. I've set you at liberty with that bite. You were never dull like the other Garniers. You are one of *us* now.'

Wordlessly, I shake my head. Fresh tears flow.

'You know it does not need to be this way,' he goes on, his voice like velvet.

As if on some unspoken cue, the grey wolf slinks in through the door, making Pierre's hunter cry out.

'See? My uncle is gracious. He hasn't come in here ripping and tearing as he could . . . despite that *smell*.' He sniffs again. 'Uncle Marcus remembers you tried to help him in the cellar. He could be persuaded to forget this . . . unfortunate business.'

'But – but my family . . .'

The grey wolf snuffles. Shadows swarm over his pewter fur as he runs a tongue across black lips. I'm hugging the blanket too tight, trying to protect it.

'It sounds as if Lucy has dealt with them already,' Colin says with only a touch of regret. 'It's just as well. They knew too much. But *you* can live. You can still join us.' He lowers his eyelashes, peeps up at me with a hint of coyness. 'Didn't you want to be my bride, Miss Garnier?'

My ribs feel as though they're caving in. I shuffle to the side, putting a little distance between us. 'Of course I did!'

The grey wolf approaches with a soft patter of paws. The same paws that scraped across Rowena's face, blinded her eye. The scent of Jean is making him tremble like a racehorse. Colin nods to the blanket, his own lips twitching. 'Then you must submit. Give your alpha, Sir Marcus, the choicest part of the meal, and we'll forget this ever happened.'

A choking sound escapes me. Before I know it I am coughing, the way Lucy did. The moonstone . . .

Colin sees me grab for it and swats it from my hand. 'Stop this pointless struggle!' he hisses. 'I changed you! You belong to the night now.'

Perhaps he's right. My skin itches at the thought of the contamination within. I hate it, but it's stronger than me. I might as well try to pit one of Papa's spaniels against this huge grey wolf.

The world swirls in a painful cacophony: the horses fretting, Sir Marcus growling, the lights dipping in the night-time breeze. Outside the moon is calling, calling . . . How good it would feel to surrender.

I squirm away from Colin, rise to my feet and rock the blanket in agony. 'Oh, God,' I say again and again, 'Oh, God.'

A chestnut horse stares at me from the back of its stall, its eyes rolling white in the gloom.

'You try our patience, Miss Garnier,' Colin says, an edge creeping into his voice. 'This offer will not remain upon the table. If you don't submit, we'll be forced to kill you.'

'Just . . . give me a moment. To say goodbye to my brother.'

But Sir Marcus is unwilling to wait. That sweetest of all

nectars, the blood of an innocent, sings to him. He noses at my legs, around my skirts, muttering in the depths of his throat.

Anguished, I stop. Swallow. Bend slowly, slowly down towards him. I know there is a man in there, but all I can see are his fangs, his ravenous eyes and the wads of saliva that fall to the floor. I go as if to lower the bundle . . .

'No!' I cry, snatching it back. 'I can't do it!'

Another flash as Colin resumes his beastly form. I've forfeited my only chance of clemency.

My legs move, but they're too slow. Sir Marcus leaps, wrenches the blanket from my grasp and falls upon it in a wild frenzy. Colin follows suit in an instant, tearing without mercy. The two of them are nothing but a fury of teeth.

I don't stop, don't wait for them to finish eating. I sprint for all I am worth, out of the stable block and across the dewy lawns until I am safe beneath the wavering cover of the chestnut trees.

CHAPTER TWENTY-SIX

Here under the canopy it's dark and damp, pungent with decomposition. Sobs convulse me; threaten to split me in half. The groundsmen have raked the rusty, serrated leaves into piles, ready to burn. I weave between the stacks, crying my brother's name.

One of them shifts. There's a sifting; leaves slide in an avalanche, and suddenly Lucy emerges, holding the baby in the crook of one arm. Her other hand is balled into a fist, dribbling blood where she's driven her fingernails into her palm.

'Jean!' I snatch him from her. His little eyes are filmy and confused. The moonstone sparkles gaily on his chest, wrapped around the saddle cloths we've swaddled him in. He's stringent with horse sweat and the little bit of dung we smeared over the blankets, doing everything possible to mask his scent.

'He's fine,' Lucy gasps. 'I didn't touch him. I – I kept it in. He's only just woken up from the cordial.'

Seeing my tears, Jean starts to blubber too. I want to pull him close and let myself weep on to his hair, thin as dandelion seeds. But I keep him at arm's length.

'We did it, Jean,' I croon, jiggling him gently. 'They took the bait. They believed my act.'

'They did?' Lucy cries. She's peering behind me, avid as a sight hound. I catch that scurrying smile before her face becomes grave once more. 'Look, Camille. I think it's working.'

I turn. Beyond the columns of trunks, across the lawns, Martingale Hall is starting to wake. Windows light up, doors open and one of the grooms emerges from the staff lodging carrying a torch. There's a volley of shouts, but no words ring clear over the barking of the dogs and the shrieking of the horses.

Or *is* it the horses? As Lucy grips my shoulder with her bloody hand, I hear again the sound that taunted me from the root-cellar, only now it's warped, strangled, off-key.

The wolves didn't hesitate. They smelt the lamb chops, the precious drops of Jean's blood, and they ate. How much did they swallow before they realized there was never a baby in that blanket but my doll, stuffed with a deadly feast? Wolfsbane and arsenic for seasoning, studs of silver in the meat. Poison for both the human and the beast in them.

As the groom approaches the stables, two yowling creatures stagger out on to the manicured lawns. He swears and pulls back. They're . . . steaming. Smoke wafts up from their shoulders with the scent of singed fur.

'They have silver on the inside now,' Lucy says, hot against my ear, 'and their hearts have more impurities than it can ever pull out.'

One of the figures collapses and twitches madly. I think it's Colin. Skin blisters and pops beneath a jet-black pelt. The other shambles into the light of the torch, neither man nor wolf. The groom screams. It's a hideous, monstrous hybrid, unsteady on two legs. Pointed ears, hands with claws, and a face melting like wax. The groom tries to ward it off with his torch. It approaches him, stretches its fanged mouth. But only a rush of foam pours out and then it drops, contorting beside its fellow.

I feel sick. I look to Lucy, unsure how she'll take the excruciating death of the man who was, despite everything, still her father. But her eyes are hard in the darkness.

'Lucy—' I start.

She squeezes my shoulder to quiet me. 'Mama is avenged now,' she whispers. 'Your family are safe. That's all that matters.'

She's wrong. Werewolf or not, Lucy isn't a monster, and I know this scene will return to haunt her conscience. We did what we had to do. I wouldn't take it back now. But if there ever comes a time I can look on such suffering as this with pleasure, the wolf will have won indeed.

Lucy shuts her eyes. 'I've seen enough. It's time for us to go.'

More stable-workers have come to gawp at the sizzling, dead beasts. A light burns in Marie's room and I expect the nursemaid will go to check that Jean hasn't been frightened by the noise. What a story he'd tell her if he could speak. But he won't remember this, or me.

'All right,' I say shakily. 'I'm ready to leave.'

Of course I'm not. But I never will be. The only thing I'm certain of is that I'm not afraid any more. I won't be the lone wolf; I have a pack, even if it's just a pack of two. Lucy and I have survived this night together. We can survive anything.

We slip quickly towards the servants' entrance, unseen, while pandemonium rages in the stable yard. There are other staff gathering now, horses being saddled, messages dispatched. People who have waited on me all my life and I'll never see again. It feels as though part of me is dying along with the werewolves. Maybe it is: the girl who desired Colin, who wanted his wealth and status.

I ease the wailing Jean down upon the steps, where he'll be found any moment now. I plant a kiss on his forehead. His face is red and blotchy, his nose wet, yet, for all this, he still smells delicious. My going away is the right thing to do for him. For all of them. My family couldn't handle me when I was just a girl who kissed soldiers – how would they cope with the wolf? Only Lucy can understand me, and I think perhaps she always did. For, when I imagine the days and weeks that will pass in this house without me – Marie's wedding, Jean's breeching, the endless rounds of tea and card parties – the sorrow is tinged with relief. That life would have smothered me in the end, just as she said.

Gently, I detach Rowena's moonstone pendant from Jean's curling fingers and hand it to Lucy. 'Always follow the light, brother,' I whisper. 'And look after everyone for me.'

Lucy fastens the chain bearing the moonstone around her neck. 'Camille, it's time. I'm sorry. We must run before they see us.'

With a painful wrench, I turn my back on my crying brother. Lucy reaches out to grab my hand and holds it tight. 'Fast as you can,' she urges. Then, with a wry lift of the eyebrows that reminds me of her old self, 'Maybe one day you'll manage to beat me in a race?'

We make for the treeline, Lucy tugging me on until we're swallowed by the forest. Where it'll take us, I don't know. Perhaps more danger awaits. Our lives won't be easy with this curse. But Lucy and I will be together, and that's enough to reconcile me to closing the book of my past. Where one story ends, another begins.

It's no dream now, the image of a serene woodland I saw from my bed. It's all around me: a taste of fresh earth and damp bracken, winter-brittle bushes, the quick dart of a crow. We can't return to Felwood, but we'll find somewhere better, a place that we can truly call our own. Fight together against the darkness, and run wild in the best possible way.

'Lucy, look up!' Dawn pushes insistent on the horizon, forcing the inky blackness into retreat. The night is ending and the stars are beginning to fade. Branches above us seem to reach out, trying to catch them before they go.

She stops. Her mouth hangs open. 'They're . . . they're beautiful.'

There's the faintest glint of what might be a meteor streaking across the changing sky.

Lucy smiles back at me, ecstatic. Her golden eyes are stars in their own constellation. Both the silver choker and the moonstone spark from around her neck, scattering light. Suddenly, I regret nothing.

I let out a whoop; part human, part animal, and we run on. The woods are calling back. Ballrooms and carriages, ostrich fans and scandal sheets, shrink until they are nothing but a memory – a vague, troubled dream I once had. But now I am awake. Alive.

I never knew there could be freedom like this.

Acknowledgements

The people closest to me will know that I've been desperate to write a werewolf novel since at least 2019. Chief amongst these is my friend and agent, Juliet Mushens, who never gave up on finding a publishing home for my 'wild' ideas. She secured the deal for this book just when my family needed it most. Thank you as always, Juliet.

I'd like to thank my brother Gavin for feeding my shapeshifter obsession with every film and book on the subject. A special mention for my husband, Kevin, who has endured more debates about how to kill a werewolf than any sane man should have to. Thank you to Charlotte and Louise for their sympathy as I struggled to find my feet in a new genre – they are the friends who would help me, no matter what.

I've been fortunate to work with many talented editors on this book, all of whom have been simply wonderful. Thank you to Vicky Leech and Natasha Bardon for having faith in my concepts, to Kimberley Atkins and Rachel Winterbottom for their brilliant insights, and to Editorial Assistant Chloe Gough for her organisational superpowers. What a team! Also thanks to my copy editor Linda McQueen, to Toby James for designing the cover of my dreams, to Maud Davies, Sian Richefond, Fleur

Clarke and everyone else at HarperVoyager and Magpie who have worked upon this project. It's been a true pleasure.

Lastly, thank you to my loyal readers who have continued to support me through difficult times. Your enthusiasm for my work has been a real light in the darkness.

About the Author

Laura Purcell is a former bookseller living in Colchester with her husband and pet guinea pigs. She is the author of seven novels, among them *The Silent Companions*, which was a Radio 2 and Zoe Ball ITV Book Club pick and *The Shape of Darkness*, winner of the inaugural Fingerprint Award for Historical Crime Book of the Year. Her short story 'The Chillingham Chair' was included in *The Haunting Season* anthology, which was an instant *Sunday Times* bestseller. She also wrote *Roanoke Falls*, a dramatic podcast for Realm, working with John Carpenter and Sandy King Carpenter.